MORE THAN MY HOMETOWN

CLAIRE HASTINGS

Cover Design by Y'all That Graphic
Cover Photo by CJC Photography
Edited by the Happily Editing Anns

https://www.clairehastingsauthor.com/

1

EWAN

How does that eighties song go? It's a perfect day for a white wedding? Something like that.

And today is the absolutely perfect day for Dolly McLain's wedding. Which I suppose is also my older brother Hux's wedding. Although is any wedding ever about the groom? Not one I've ever been to.

This one isn't the exception either. This is Dolly's wedding. Her real wedding. The perfect, happily-ever-after, ride off into the sunset wedding that she deserves. It's a year later than the one that didn't happen, but this is it. This time it's for real.

This time it's to Hux.

How it should have been to begin with. Something we all know, but are keeping our mouths shut about, because there are just some things that don't need to be said out loud. Especially on one's wedding day.

"About damn time you wifed her up," Anton, brother number three in the lineup says, smacking Hux on the back.

Okay, maybe Anton is saying things out loud.

Once the instigator, always the instigator...

Hux raises a single eyebrow, glaring back at him in the mirror of the small room my five brothers and I are shoved in while we wait for the guests to arrive at the church. Everything goes still, none of us moving, with only the hum from the vent in the background as we wait for Hux's reaction. It's a line we've all heard a hundred times come out of Anton's mouth trying to get a rise out of Hux, who as the middle of seven kids is about as stereotypical as they come—stubborn, nonconforming, and complicated—but he's also steady and unflappable.

Something Anton loves to try and mess with.

"It is, isn't it?" Hux laughs.

Tension dissipates instantly, all six of us bursting into laughter.

"You owe me fifty bucks, by the way," Milo, brother number two, says to Hux, cracking open a Southern Brothers Party Mode and handing it to him.

Hux takes the bottle, his expression turning curious, asking the same silent question the rest of us are. Milo doesn't answer him right away, simply continues to play bartender—a role he knows well as owner and operator of Southern Brothers Brewing with his best friend Brandt Rawlins—handing us each a bottle from the cooler he snuck into the church.

"Care to explain?" Gus, our oldest brother, finally prompts after a long moment of silence.

"I bet Brandt when we opened Southern Brothers who would be the first to get married, and it wasn't Hux." Milo shrugs, plopping down into one of the folding chairs set up in a semi-circle. Revered Terry clearly didn't put a lot of effort into making sure we were going to be comfortable as we waited.

"He guessed Hux and Dolly?" Anton questions, not bothering to hide his skepticism. Which is totally fair, since it's not like they were a couple back then.

Milo shakes his head. "Naw, he guessed Ewan and Mai—"

He stops himself before he says her name, but it doesn't matter. I still hear it. My brain still automatically finishes it.

Maisey...

"But since I didn't guess Hux, I gotta pay up."

I swallow hard, shifting my weight, trying to pretend like his almost slip of the tongue doesn't affect me. Like I'm not thinking about her. Like I haven't been pretending not to think about her all week. Wondering if she'll show at the last minute—be a surprise guest at her cousin's wedding.

Especially since I'm technically here with someone else.

Even if that someone else is just a friend.

To be fair, that's all Maisey was too. Sort of. Because there isn't a word for what she and I were—this weird in-between of more than friends but not exactly *more than friends*. We were each other's person in every way, but never crossed that line of physical intimacy that comes with that second part. Not for lack of want to on my part, but for lack of guts to try.

I've wondered damn near every day for more years than I can count if I should have tried.

Emily Barrowcliff, though, is one hundred percent friend, without any thought of crossing that line. From either of us. Although, these last six months, it's been a lot of fun to let our small town of Hickory Hills think otherwise. If for no other reason than it's meant no one has asked either one of us embarrassingly personal or prodding questions in places like the grocery store.

"I don't see how that's Hux's problem," I say, joining in so that no one accuses me of being too quiet.

Problem with being the family introvert is that after a while if you don't contribute, they force you to. Which only makes it worse.

"Because he's the reason I have to pay up," Milo responds, a silent *duh* at the end of his sentence.

"Still doesn't make sense." I shake my head, letting it go, since I know there won't be any logic to it.

"Love doesn't always make sense, baby bro," Jace, the brother one up from me coos, as if he knows anything about it. Which he does not. He's as single as I am.

In fact, of the seven of us, Jace and I—numbers five and six respectively—are the last two single Hayes kids standing. One by one our siblings have paired off, starting with our younger sister, Willa, with her now husband, Nash, which led to Milo falling for his fiancée, Brenna. Then Gus met his fiancée, Margeaux. Hux and Dolly—well, their story was decades in the making. Most recently, Anton even managed to find his match in Sawyer, proving there really is a lid for every pot.

"Like you have any room to talk, Jace," Gus quips. "Those books you litter the coffee table with don't make you an expert on anything."

"Don't act like you haven't picked up a tip or two from them, August," Milo teases, leaning back against the folding table, his trademark smirk plastered in place.

Gus rolls his eyes, his own trademark scowl fighting back. He has a point though—just because Jace is the family wild card who isn't shy about his non-guilty pleasure of reading romance novels doesn't make him an expert on love.

"'Specially since Ewan has a date to this event, and you don't." Hux points his beer bottle at Jace.

"What's your point?" Jace shrugs.

"That later tonight, after spending the evening hanging out and dancing with a beautiful woman, he has the chance at going home to something other than his right hand," Anton explains.

"It's only Em."

My response is immediate, reflexive. Almost too much so. Because the second I say it, I almost feel guilty.

And my brothers are right there to call me on it.

"You say that, but you two sure have been spending a lot of time together lately..." Gus says, no doubt fishing for something.

I don't take the bait though. I'm not a trout.

"Gus..." Milo warns.

Thanks, Milo...

"What?" Gus claps back. "Tell me I'm wrong."

He's not wrong. I'm still not taking the bait though.

"It's Hux's wedding. We should be focused on him," I say, deflecting again.

I've gotten good at deflecting. Comes from years of practice as not only the youngest brother and the family introvert, but also from years around the boardroom table with them. Because they aren't just my brothers; we're also the executive arm of Hayes Industries, the Fortune 500 company that our family has owned and operated out of our rural Georgia town since the 1800s. What started off as two blacksmiths making guns turned into crops and now is a major corporation, employing the majority of Hickory Hills, covering industries including guns and ammo, a paper mill, agriculture, a brewery, personal safety, and my bait and tackle shop. Our father, Auggie, is currently at the helm, although Gus is now executive vice president, so we're all not-so-secretly expecting a retirement announcement out of the old man any day now.

My money is on shortly after the first pregnancy announcement from one of the three couples getting married this year. The second our parents are going to be *grand*parents, that is going to become their full-time focus.

Hux shrugs, glancing at his watch. "I still got twenty minutes until I'm allowed upstairs. Besides, I don't think it would be the worst thing in the world for my bride to have one of her best friends and cousin end up with my brother. Just sayin'.'"

Just sayin'...right...

I heave out a sigh, throwing my head back. Apparently we are going to have to go over this again. Despite my having discussed this—at length—with both Hux and Milo before.

Not to mention, Em isn't the only one that description fits...

"It's not like that." I take a long swig of my beer, letting the crisp taste flow over my tastebuds. "Look, I've told y'all— Em is great. We all know this. She and I have a lot of fun together, and yes, we've been spending a lot of time together since Willa's wedding last summer, but it's just not like that."

Don't get me wrong. Emily is a beautiful woman. With her family's trademark blonde hair, blue eyes, and a fun smile, someday she is going to make someone very happy. That someone simply isn't me.

"Could it be though?" Anton asks, his normal button-pushing tone missing.

I look at him, waiting for there to be a follow-up question. One that is designed to get under my skin. Except nothing follows. Just a silence, with five pairs of eyes waiting on my answer. Eyes that I know love and support me, and have my back no matter what. Despite all the shit they might be giving me in this moment.

I swallow hard, looking between each one of my brothers. Our differences are staggering, even with all of us in matching tuxes. Still, deep down, they understand.

"No." I shake my head. "I know on paper it makes sense, since she's the town recreation coordinator and she likes all the same outdoorsy shit I do, which is great, because how often do you find someone who isn't weirded out by that? But...but no. She's not..."

She's not Maisey.

A fact that I'm reminded of every time I look at her. Those sparkling blue eyes that Emily, Dolly, and Maisey all inherited from Mrs. Phillips, the town matriarch and the actual matriarch of their family.

A hush falls over the room, a damper put on the whole mood. Leave it to me to kill the entire thing. I should have kept my mouth shut. That would have been the better route to take. Usually is. I have a track record for opening my mouth and ruining everything.

After all, that's exactly what happened with Maisey.

You'd think I'd have learned by now. Guess not.

Sucking in a deep breath, I lift my arm to take another swig of my beer, but am cut off by Hux damn near tackling me and wrapping his arms around me in a bear hug. Easily the biggest of us, his lumberjack-esque frame is nothing to mess with and sends me stumbling back a steps, trying to catch my balance again as I knock over a couple of chairs. At least we didn't do any damage. Reverend Terry would have our asses.

"Right woman is out there," Hux whispers, low enough so only I can hear, patting my back.

"Not really worried about it," I choke out, trying to breathe, his arms still tightly embracing me. Making it even more awkward, my arm—beer still in hand—is caught between us. "Would like my arm back though."

Hux chuckles, letting go and stepping back just enough to look me in the eye. The wave of emotion that washes over his face makes my heart squeeze, and I can tell that he knows exactly what I'm feeling. The ache that comes with knowing the one you want is one you can't have. For Hux, it was because she was with someone else. For me, she's simply the one who got away.

The one who more than ten years later, is who I see when I close my eyes. The one whose voice I hear when it's just me out on the water or up in a hunting stand. Whose touch I think about—no, crave—when I'm all alone at night.

None of that matters now though. Because she's not here. She's somewhere far, far away, living her dream. Just like I'm living mine. Sort of.

"Hi hi!" my sister's voice calls out as the door flies open.

Willa steps into the room, her sky-blue bridesmaid dress almost the same color as her eyes, looking at us like she expected to find a pack of hyenas. Smiling, she coos, her expression softening as tears fill her eyes.

"You boys really do clean up nice," she says. "Almost makes one forget what a group of hellions you are."

A former Miss Georgia—just like our mama—on the outside, our baby sister is the picture of grace. To those of us who know her, though, she's also the walking, talking definition of spitfire, and will cut you like a razorblade, walking away before you even realize you're bleeding.

"You want to be the pot or the kettle there, Wills?" Anton quips.

"I'm an angel. I don't know what you're referring to." She smiles so sweetly, you'd almost believe her too. If you didn't grow up with her.

"Ha!" Milo scoffs. "Funny, I seem to remember you causing plenty of trouble when you were sneaking around with—"

"Shush!" she cuts him off with a snap of her fingers, and I stifle my laughter. Of all of us, Milo is the one she's closest to, so he can get away with saying a lot. "Enough about me. It's time to get Hux married."

"That line didn't work for me," I mutter.

"That was fifteen minutes ago," Hux says. "I'm allowed upstairs now."

"You know, if you get too nervous, I'm happy to kiss the bride for you," Jace quips, getting in one last jab.

"That won't be happening," Hux declares, the rest of us laughing at Jace.

Hux barrels past us, not caring who or what might be in his way, determined to get this show on the road. Can't blame him there—today has been a long time coming and he is ready for that forever to start. Out of the corner of my eye, I see Anton fist-bump Jace, the two of them clearly up to something. Should have known Jace didn't come up with that one on his own.

Willa shakes her head, laughing as she turns to go, the remainder of us following her up the stairs to the lobby of Hickory Hills Baptist. The soft hum of the guests already seated fills the air, heightening the buzz of the moment. If you weren't feeling the electricity already, you are now.

"Ready for this?" Emily asks, lining up next to me.

"Just like we practiced. No tripping down the aisle. Got it."

"We got this."

"We do."

2

MAISEY

I HAVE BEEN a lot of places in the last ten years. Austria, Turkey, Vietnam, Thailand, Spain, Italy, Portugal, Peru, Nicaragua—that last one being a major highlight—but there is really only one place I want to be right now. A place I never in a million years thought I'd miss so much.

Hickory Hills, Georgia.

Of all the map dots, in all the world, it's this one. A town of a few thousand people, forty minutes from the interstate. How's that for ironic?

Yet, it's somehow the only place I want to be. The place my heart has been longing for. Craving. Turns out Dorothy was on to something with that whole *there's no place like home* thing.

A home that hasn't changed one bit.

Slamming the door of my rental car behind me, I straighten out my sundress, taking a moment to let my surroundings settle around me. The shared parking lot between Hickory Hills Baptist Church and the Hickory Hills Town Library is full of cars and trucks that I don't recognize immediately, yet still look so familiar that I bet I could guess who they all belong to.

Both the church and the library look exactly the same as they did when I left, although there's an addition to the library that looks fairly new. So maybe some things do change.

I smile to myself, slinking across the parking lot to head inside. I'm halfway up the wide stone steps that lead to the front doors, and a small wave of panic hits me. On the other side of these doors is my past. Maybe my future too. But definitely my past.

One thing is for sure—being back in Hickory Hills is not a simple thing. It's been a long, long time since I set foot across the town line. Since I packed up what I could in a rucksack and hightailed it off on a mission to see the world.

But if there was anything that was going to bring me back here, it was my cousin Dolly's wedding. Well, that and the other thing. But outwardly, Dolly's wedding.

Which is happening just inside this church. The one I need to walk inside. I simply need to remember to breathe.

That's it. Breathing. Breathing is good.

Breathing is what I tell my patients to do all the time. Inhale deeply, and then let it all out, slowly, until there is nothing left in your lungs. Then repeat.

Alright, here goes.

"Maisey Margaret Phillips!"

Oh, for fuck's sake...

I'm not a full two steps inside the church and I am already being triple named. By quite possibly the worst person in the world too. This is probably God smiting me for not coming back to visit my mama for who knows how many Christmases and Easters, and I'm not saying I'm perfect, but *for the love*, do I really deserve this?

"Aunt Hattie," I greet, putting on my very best Southern

manners and turning on my heel to change direction and head toward her.

As one of my father's older sisters, I know that Hattie Burch is family and therefore I will treat her with respect. That said, she is also something else. A sharp-tongued busybody, she has been the go-to for town gossip for years and has no problem inserting herself into the lives of others, telling them exactly how they should be living it. Even from afar she's tried to interfere with my life, emailing me articles and websites she finds about safety risks in different countries and advising why it "would not be wise to visit."

"What are you doing here?" she asks, her question coming out more like an accusation rather than actually being happy to see me.

Good to see you too, Aunt Hattie...

"I was invited?"

She huffs, air puffing out of her nostrils like a dragon. "But you RSVP'd no."

"My schedule changed. The network of hospitals I was working in down in Nicaragua didn't renew their contract with my agency, so—"

"So you were fired?"

I close my eyes, wondering if I count to ten whether it will stop me from strangling the old bat.

"That's not how being a traveling nurse works, Aunt Hattie. Especially on the international level. The hospitals didn't renew the contract with the agency, so that contract ended. I'm still employed with the agency, just in between contracts."

"Dress it up however you want, young lady. You lost your job."

Well, this has been a very uplifting and life-affirming few minutes. Time to go find my parents. At least they'll be happy to see me.

"Does the bride know you're coming? It's rude to show up to a wedding unannounced."

I bite the inside of my cheek, upping my patience count to twenty.

"Nope, it's a surprise," I say. My aunt opens her mouth to respond, but I keep talking, not letting her get there. "She told me when I sent my regrets a couple of months ago that if anything changed, I was welcome to come, even if it was last minute, so I know she'll be okay with me being here."

There, that should put that matter to bed.

The doors open again, and we both pause as Judge Robinson and his wife walk in. I expect them to stop and chat—no doubt making a comment about how long it's been since they've seen me—but they simply give us a nod and keep moving toward the sanctuary. Damn, the respite would have been nice. Heck, that might have even been the chance at the escape I needed.

"So you lost your job and slink back to town unannounced, just to show up at a wedding unaccounted for?" Pursing her lips, she gives me the most judgmental once-over I've ever received. Contestants at the Westminster Dog Show are scrutinized less. "I know you have this whole free spirit thing going, but manners are still a thing, Maisey."

"Dolly's wedding is a pretty big deal and—"

"You weren't here for the last one," she cuts me off.

You know, I'm starting to think that counting to one hundred isn't even going to be enough at this point.

"True, but this is the real one," I say, forcing a smile. "No one actually wanted to see her marry Jeff. Dolly and Hux, though? That's different. Plus, Grandma Amelia's hundredth birthday is next month, and there is really no missing that."

Take that, Aunt Hattie. *Two* damn good reasons for me to be back. Spread those around town.

Let's not lie here; that's what she's really after—the inside knowledge so that when word gets out, she's the one everyone calls and asks. A master class in gossipmongering.

I'm not letting her in on the real reason I'm here. The secret that I'm keeping.

That I'm here to collect.

To make good on a deal I made twenty years ago. A pact sealed with blood—okay, ketchup, because even thirteen-year-old Maisey was concerned about blood-borne pathogens—between two people who were so intertwined they couldn't imagine their lives without each other. Or well, two kids who were innocent enough to not be able to picture past their sixteenth birthdays and the idea of twenty years in the future—and ever being that "old"—was an impossibility.

The deal was simple. Classic. A tale as old as time. If we're not married in twenty years—by our thirty-fourth birthdays—we marry each other.

I turn thirty-four next month, while his is later this summer.

As fate would have it, I'm single. So is he.

If that's not the universe telling us something, I don't know what is.

Especially after the abrupt end to my contract and the expiration of my work visa with it. Two things that are crucial for an international traveling nurse.

"Mother will be happy to see you."

Oh my stars, Hattie Burch just said something nice. Okay, she said something factual. But it was said without her normal tone, so I'll take it. Seriously, I don't know how Dolly and Emily do this every day.

"Speaking of mothers, I should go find mine. If you'll excuse me…"

With a nod, I'm off, my patience and manners all used up. I hear the creak of the doors as I move, leading me to believe she's about to find someone else to sink her teeth into.

Entering the sanctuary, it takes me a second to locate my mother, an internal groan releasing when I spot her strawberry blonde bob. She's all the way up front, and I can feel each new set of eyes land on me as I make my way to her.

Ahhh, small towns.

"Hey there, darlin', you made it on time," Mama greets, scooting into the pew to make room for me. "I was starting to get worried."

"Weekend traffic through Macon hasn't changed," I lament. "Where's Daddy?"

"He's escorting your grandmother down the aisle. Originally it was going to be Landon Noble, since he's best man, but after she slipped last month at the Southern Brothers St. Paddy's party, Landon told your daddy he thought it would be a better idea if he escorted her, thinking she might be more at ease, and therefore steady on her feet, with him."

I smile, my heart squeezing at my father's second-in-command at the fire department caring enough for my family that he would think of such a thing. Landon has been the assistant fire chief for what feels like forever, and when my father finally retires, will step into the role as the head of the fire department with ease.

"That's so sweet."

"Landon grew up good," Mama comments, giving me a little nudge, and a not-so-subtle eyebrow waggle. "He's still very shy and quiet, but he's as steady and sweet as they come."

Got it, Mama...

I nod, letting her commentary die. As sure as I am that Landon is all those things, he's not the one who I see when I close my eyes. The one who makes my heart skip a beat if I come across a patient with the same name. He who I've measured all others against.

Spoiler alert—they've all come up short.

Music fills the air, changing the subject for me, and everyone turns to face the aisle. Awws and coos ring out as my father, dressed in his full Class A's, escorts his almost one-hundred-year-old mother down the aisle. Emotions swell up in me, forming a lump in my throat as I watch her slowly make her way, holding on to her son like he's Prince Charming. For someone her age, she's still so spry, but I can still see why Landon thought it would be better to have Daddy do this. I make a mental note to give him an extra squeeze when I see him later.

"Maisey!" she coos, sliding into our pew. "No one told me you were coming!"

"Mama, you're supposed to sit in the front row," Daddy tells her.

"I'll sit where I please, Jeremiah."

I suppress a giggle, loving that she still has all her sass.

"Surprise!" I whisper, as Auggie and Belle Hayes walk by, taking their seats. "It was a last-minute thing."

"Oh, Dolly is going to be tickled to see you."

I hope she's not the only one...

"And just wait until you see those Hayes boys all dressed up. I know that's not what they mean by if looks could kill, but, be still my heart."

"Mama!" my father scolds, and there's no holding in my laughter this time. Fuck, I cannot wait to be an old lady and say whatever I want.

"What? Am I not allowed to appreciate what fine, contributing members of society those young men have become?"

My father rolls his eyes, turning his attention back to the processional, a soft shift in melody making way for Hux's sister, Willa, and her husband, Nash, looking as gorgeous and graceful as I remember her from high school. Turning to me, my grandmother gives me a conspiratorial wink, making me right at home.

One by one, the Hayes brothers make their way down the aisle, looking like grown-up versions of the guys I remember. Each one of them different and distinct, but there never being any doubt when you lined up all seven of the Hayes kids that they were siblings.

Same as there wasn't any doubt that they would take over the Hayes empire, keeping that Fortune 500 company that was founded by their ancestor during the Civil War—the same one that employs most of our small town—going strong.

"That's Sawyer, Anton's girlfriend," my mother whispers, pointing to the pretty brunette on his arm. "They met last summer. She's also an agriculture expert."

"And the pretty redhead with Gus," Grandma adds. "That's Margeaux. She spells it funny because she's from Louisiana, but she is sharp, that one. A lawyer."

"And of course you know Brenna," Mama throws out there.

"Kinda," I say. "She was still a kid when I left."

"She isn't one anymore. And Milo Hayes took notice," Grandma comments.

"Mama!" Daddy scolds.

"They are engaged, Jeremiah. It is not a secret."

"Em and Dolly caught me all up on that whole thing," I tell her. "Including exactly how Brandt discovered their secret."

I waggle my eyebrows, letting her know that I'm in on the juicy part of the story. Grandma's eyes go wide. Oh, apparently that's tea she doesn't have.

"You will have to tell me that story later."

"Oh, look, here's Em!" Mama says.

I twist, my heart rate speeding up. Not only at the idea of

seeing my friend and cousin in her bridesmaid dress, but because we're quickly running out of Hayes brothers. Three have already walked down the aisle, and one is the groom, leaving two. Only one of which I care about.

Ewan Hayes.

I blink, and there he is. Same as his brothers, he's an older version of himself—the same ruggedly handsome blond-haired, blue-eyed boy who preferred to be out in nature than confined to a classroom. Staring at him now though, there is something different about him. Something off. Ewan has always been mysterious in his own way—preferring to keep to himself and only speaking when he really has something to say—but this goes beyond that. It's like something is missing.

My heart stops, my breath catching as they pass us, wondering if he saw me. If his body is going to betray him the same way mine is right now, skin heating up and brain starting to short-circuit because all he can think about is what it will be like to have our arms around each other again. To be Ewan and Maisey again. To find out what forever feels like.

If he even wants to be Ewan and Maisey again. Things didn't exactly end all sunshiny between us. No, not end. We didn't *end*. We simply followed our independent dreams for a while. That's all.

But we have a pact. Sealed in ketchup.

Pausing briefly at the top of the aisle, Ewan turns toward us and winks. My insides leap, stunned beyond belief at that move. A wink. *A wink.*

That is until I see Emily return the gesture, and I realize he was not looking over at me at all. He was winking at her.

Ewan was winking at Emily.

"Aren't they cute?" Mama whispers.

"Ewan and Em?" I choke out.

"They've been…*hanging out…*" Grandma adds.

Hanging out? Em's been hanging out *with Ewan…holy shit…*

"That's her word for it at least. I don't know if that's code for something."

"Mama!"

My father's reaction fades into the distance as the room starts to spin. Everything I thought I knew mere seconds ago crashes down around me. This is not how this was supposed to go. At all.

Ewan Hayes might not be single after all.

So much for our ketchup pact.

3

EWAN

IT IS a damn good thing for Huxley Adams Hayes that today is the happiest day of his life. Or else, he might have ended up a dead man.

Actually, he still might.

There is still a very good chance he does not live to see his honeymoon. Because he dead-ass stood there, looked me in the eye mere hours ago after hugging me like I was dying, and told me he "understood" and the "right woman is out there." But didn't have the balls to give me a heads-up that *she* would be here.

And since I'm the brother that owns the hunting gear store, he should probably worry.

A store that *she* named.

Fuck me...

Squeals fill the tent, wafting through the spring air, drawing the attention of everyone in attendance. The women responsible for the high-pitched audible attack don't seem the least bit bothered, however, all five of them too busy jumping up and down in a group hug, caught up in their own excitement of being reunited. My heart squeezes, the sight evoking so many emotions all at once. Including a whole bunch I'm not sure I have names for.

More than anything, it's the reminder to breathe at the sight of the blue-eyed blonde at the center of the hug huddle. Something I may or may not be failing at right now.

A heavy hand lands on my shoulder, and I flinch, the weight of it catching me off guard.

"Of all the gin joints, in all the towns, in all the world…" Milo mutters.

"…and she walks into mine. Ours," I correct. "She walks back into ours."

It's just as much her hometown as it is mine…

My eyes are still trained on Maisey—I couldn't look away if you paid me—as the girls finally separate. The versions of Alice Evans, Rose Adler, Emily, Dolly, and Maisey gathered on the parquet dance floor look the same as they did when we were teenagers, the same mile-wide smiles on their faces and mischievous glints in their eyes. The ones that come when a girl squad is together and joins their powers together like *Captain Planet and the Planeteers.*

From our spot nestled next to the bar, we have the perfect view of the whole tent. The event of the season, most of Hickory Hills is in attendance, spread out across the tables, finishing up their meals and heading out to the dance floor to party the night away. Most of the major moments of the evening—first dance, speeches, cake cutting—have already concluded, so from here on out, it's pure party time.

Or if you're the family introvert, sit back and observe.

"You talk to her yet?" he asks, not even trying to pretend to be nonchalant about it.

"And say what?" *All the things I should have said ten years ago?*

"I can think of a couple things."

I can think of more than a couple. Problem is, they all

should have been said a long damn time ago. And since I didn't say them then, I don't get to say them now.

"Can't avoid her forever," he continues.

"I'm not going to avoid her for forever. Just for tonight." *And then tomorrow. And however long she's in town for after that...*

"Ewan," Hux says, coming up behind me.

I whip around, glaring at him. Immediately, he stands his ground, raising his arms. I'm a big guy, but Hux is easily the strongest of the family. That's what happens when you're the family lumberjack—running the lumber and paper division of the family business. Push comes to shove, I can hold my own against him, especially if I'm pissed enough, but I'd never win. We both know it.

"A heads-up would have been nice," I seethe through gritted teeth.

"I didn't know, I swear," Hux tells me. "Honest to God. If I knew, I would have told you. Promise."

I tighten my fist, wanting so bad to believe him. To know that my brother has my back.

Another squeal rips through the air, stealing my attention. I look over my shoulder, waves of golden hair reflecting in the dim lights catching my eye immediately, and I know exactly who that sound came from. That knowledge solidifies something else in me—a truth that this whole town knows soul deep and is celebrating today. The love of Hux and Dolly.

And Hux is standing next to me right now, worried about *my* feelings, with his brand-new bride across the room. And there is only one way that would happen.

Maisey's appearance truly is a surprise.

I nod, unballing my fist and exhaling. Hard. Because I'm still having to think about how to breathe. Breathing—the thing that is supposed to be the most natural function on this earth. But no, not with Maisey Phillips within a hundred feet of me. All that does is make me forget everything except the most horrible words I've ever uttered in my entire life.

This town is my life—with or without you in it...

Regret settles over me, as if it's not my ever-present shadow, dampening everything around me. The heavy beat of the music matches my pulse, speeding up as my mind whirs with what to do next. As much as I want to slip out and go home, there's no way. It would be noticed if one of the groomsmen went missing. Not to mention, we have a big send-off planned.

"Ewan," Hux says, knocking me out of my headspace.

I look at him, the realization of my silence hitting me.

"Yeah, yeah." I nod. I turn toward the bar and raise my hand to signal the bartender, who thankfully understands my unspoken request and hands me another beer. I'm not usually a big drinker, but tonight might need to be the exception. "Question then, I guess is, why…"

"To see you, silly!"

Laughter pairs with the slight lilt on the feminine voice cutting me off. Narrowing my eyes, I turn, pretending to glare at my partner in crime for the evening, Emily, who is beaming at me like she's a small child who just learned where someone is hiding candy.

Reaching out, she takes my beer from my hand, taking a sip, her knowing smirk growing as she waggles her eyebrows and hands it back to me.

"Emily Minerva Barrowcliff, it's a sin to lie," I playfully chastise.

"Did you just triple name me?" she scoffs, hand flying to her chest in mock horror. "And I am not lyin'."

I don't say anything, letting my facial expression be all the response required as I take a drink.

"Just because you don't believe me, doesn't make it a lie."

Milo snickers. "She has a point."

Not a good one...

I glare at him, raising an eyebrow. He's supposed to be on my side.

"Don't you have a fiancée somewhere?" I ask him, hoping he'll get the message that he has somewhere better to be. Hell, for that matter, so does Hux. Spinning around, I start to give him the same lip, but find he's already gone. Presumably to find his bride.

"Listen to the girl," Milo suggests, slapping me on the shoulder. "Might do you some good."

"I always liked him," Emily comments, taking my beer again as we watch Milo walk away. "So, what do you say? Shall we grow a pair and go talk to the pretty girl?"

Classy, sassy, and totally smart-assy—that's Emily. That's what makes her so much fun to hang out with. But that doesn't change my answer.

"No."

"What? Ewan Porter Hayes!"

My eyes go wide. Did she...

"You are not the only one who can triple name," she sasses.

Well, damn...I underestimated this one. I knew the sass was strong with the women in this family—there is no way a single family produces our town matriarch, Mrs. Phillips, who in her late nineties is still slinging one-liners, Mrs. Burch, the town gossip, plus Dolly, Emily, and Maisey and not have a strong line of sass. But still. I had no idea Emily even knew my middle name.

What I do know is that she won't drop this. So I'm going to need a better idea to distract her. Something to get her mind off of the idea of me talking to Maisey. Thankfully, the wedding gods—and the DJ—have my back. The music shifts, the heavy dance beat fading into a soft melody, slowing everything down.

"How about a dance, Em?"

I hold my hand out, smiling like I mean it. And I do. She's my date, and my friend, and I've been genuinely looking forward to us spending this evening together. We had a lot of fun together at Willa's wedding last summer, and my plan was for us to have just as much tonight.

Placing her hand in mine, she returns my smile, letting me drag her out onto the floor. Seconds later, my arms are around her, and we're moving in time with the music, the whole conversation forgotten. Or so I think.

"Seriously," Em whispers, her tone a lot softer this time. "Why are you being such a fraidy-cat?"

"Because."

"Because why?" she pushes.

"You know why."

She doesn't. Not really. No one does.

No one except Maisey.

I've never fully admitted to anyone that I pushed her away. Or worse—that I'm the reason she hasn't come back to town since she packed up after college. Something that I know has left many members of this community heart-broken—myself included.

"Because you were a dumb boy who let the girl he was secretly in love with leave town without admitting his feelings for her because he was too chickenshit to open up and put his heart on the line? And you've been kicking yourself ever since because you should have just told her that you not only loved her then but that you still love her now?"

My mouth drops open, as if it completely unhinges, and I stare at her, in total awe. There's a little more to it than that —okay, a lot more—but fuck me, she nailed it. I've never felt so called out in my life. And I have five older brothers and a spitfire younger sister.

I pull Emily closer, sucking in a deep breath, trying to find the right way to respond.

"How'd you…?"

"It's written *alllll* over you, buddy. Always has been, since we were kids. Same way as Hux's devotion to Dolly was. You Hayes boys aren't as hard to read as you think you are."

Right. Good to know.

"Which is how I know you're all messy inside right now, aren't you?"

"That's one word for it," I grumble, looking over her head, taking in the other couples on the dance floor.

Every one of my brothers is out here, holding their women tight. Even Jace found a partner in Michelle, the eight-year-old daughter of one of Dolly's cousins. And then there are my parents, nuzzled together like they're the newlyweds and not going on forty-plus years of marriage. All while I'm holding a girl who I only have platonic feelings for. A girl who is currently calling me out about my feelings about another one.

Yeah, messy is a good word for it.

"Ewan, listen to me," Em says, looking up at me. Her blue eyes shine, reminding me of Maisey's, sending a pang through me. "As your friend, I promise you, she is not here for this wedding. Well, not *just* here for this wedding. She is here for *you*. Talk to her."

If only it were that easy. If it were, I'd have called her—years ago. Hell, I'd have picked up the phone at any point over the last decade. Not to mention, where's she been? It's not like I was ignoring all her calls. Of course, after what I said, I wouldn't have called me either.

Still, why now? After all this time, after everything I said, why now?

"It's not that simple, Em."

Emily scrunches her face. "Maybe. Maybe not. But, we won't know until you try…"

The song starts to fade, and she starts to pull back, but she holds on to my gaze, letting me know she's not going anywhere. That this conversation isn't over.

"And say what exactly?" I challenge, just to be difficult.

"*Hi* is usually a good opener."

I stop, a chill running down my spine. The whole world stops, everything around ceasing to exist except the voice that I only hear in my dreams. I'm afraid to move. Afraid that if I do, I'll discover that this isn't real. Or worse, it is, and it'll somehow end worse than it did before.

"H-h-hi," I choke out. *Great, that was smooth…*

"Hi, Ewan," Maisey says, and fuck, if my name on her lips doesn't sound like the most comforting thing in the world. Like falling into bed after a long day.

"Maisey."

"This one was a special request," the DJ says, cutting through the music as the tune changes. With a flick of his wrist, we go from traditional ballad to unmistakable opening of George Strait's "Check Yes or No."

Making my heart plummet.

"Well, if this isn't kismet…" Emily says, that evil twinkle returning to her eye. If I didn't know better, I'd think she planned this. Actually, I don't know better. She very well may have. "I'll leave y'all to it."

Giving me a wink, Emily quickly exits the dance floor, leaving Maisey and me standing there like two awkward poles sticking straight up in a stadium blocking the view of an innocent ticketholder. Heat rushes to my face, and I swear, if I could find a way to burrow into the ground right here, I think I would.

"Right, well, so, ummmm," Maisey sputters over George

as he croons about Emmylou in her pink dress writing a note in the third grade.

At least she's feeling as weird about this as I am. That at least lets me know that maybe she wasn't in on this. Or if she was, it backfired.

"Maisey," I hold out my hand, muscle memory taking over.

Wordlessly, she takes it, sending me straight back to when we were us. The connection is still there, the both of us instantly knowing exactly what to do, what beat to start on, losing ourselves in the music. In the dance. Because this was our song.

It had started innocently enough at an all-ages event at The Giddy Up, the local honky-tonk teaching line dances one Sunday afternoon. We'd spent hours practicing the cowboy cha-cha until we'd perfected it, wearing out this song, until it was so engrained in us that there was no way it could ever belong to anyone else. That we could never not dance to it. Just like now.

Holding her again like this—spinning her around, her body against mine, our fingers intertwined—for the life of me, I can't figure out how I survived without her.

The song ends, and we slow, the bubble we've been in for the last three minutes bursting. Out of the corner of my eye I see and feel the eyes that are on us. Judging by the way Maisey stiffens in my arms, she does too.

Leading us off the dance floor, I sidestep an older couple trying to give us some space. The last thing I want right now is to be the center of attention.

Maisey grabs my hand, stopping me. I look down at it, then up at her, my heart slamming into my rib cage. Breathe, I need to breathe...

"Ewan, I..." she starts, rocking backward and biting down

on her lip in a way that makes me wonder what that lip tastes like.

"I should find my brothers." My voice warbles, cracking like a pubescent boy. "We've got a big send-off prepared. I should make sure we're ready."

"I was hoping we could catch up."

Catch up. Maisey wants to catch up. With me.

Heat washes over me, the cool breeze flowing through the tent doing nothing to counter it, my mind going blank. I should say something. Anything. Except I can't because I don't know what to say. Still.

I love you. I've always loved you. Never stopped loving you, and it broke my heart when you left...

"Ewan, we'll be thirty-four this year and—"

I yank my hand away. Thirty-four. Thirty-four.

That's why she's here.

Our pact.

4

MAISEY

Booby Trap.

The massive wood-burned sign stares back at me, damn proud of itself, if I do say so myself, and I can't help but smile. It's one thing to know that someone went and did something, but it's another thing to actually see it with your own eyes.

And I'll be, Ewan Hayes really did take Knox County Bait and Tackle and rename it to The Booby Trap. Fuck, I would have loved to have seen the looks on the old-timers' faces when he did that. My Aunt Hattie must have had a fit.

I kill the ignition, the hum of my rental car's engine quieting, as I reach for my phone, rereading my text thread with Emily for the 9413th time to verify that Ewan still likes his burgers the same way he did before.

> Burger order is still medium with cheddar, horseradish, tomato, and onion, right?

EMILY

> that's what he ordered last week, so unless he's changed his mind since then

> and you're sure there's nothing between y'all? I'm not stepping on toes? Because he acted kinda weird when I cut in...

I'm sure.

weird how? Y'all were adorable together on that dance floor.

> When I told him I wanted to catch up he got squirrelly and basically did an about-face

ha, Mais, if anyone knows better, it should be you. You can't just ambush Ewan like that. You have to ease him into talking.

Ha.

That's the thing—maybe Emily and others have to ease Ewan into talking, but I never did. That was always the beauty of who we were. I was the one person on this earth who could ambush him. There was no "hello" or "what's up" to start a conversation with us. Because everything was a continuation of one great big conversation that went in a million different directions and could tangent and pivot at any moment. With me doing most of the talking.

No part of me expected that to have changed. I figured we'd pick up exactly where we left off when I moved away. Guess not.

Or well, not yet.

Food solves everything though.

Gathering the to-go containers, I pile out of the car and climb the wooden steps onto the front porch of the old bait and tackle shop. Originally built in the 1940s as a hunting cabin, Bryon Jennings bought it in the sixties, converting it into Knox County Bait and Tackle. The store always did well —with Silver Lake right in town and the Flint River not far, fishing has always been a big part of the community.

"Alright, here goes," I mutter to myself, flinging the door open.

A bell overhead tinkles, announcing my arrival, and Dennis Williams looks up from the lure he's tying, cocking his head to the side, as if he isn't sure whether he should greet me or usher me back out the door. I smile politely, not sure if he'll remember me—this was his retirement gig when we were in high school, and he certainly hasn't gotten any younger.

"He's around the corner, doin' inventory in the archery section of the addition, Miss Maisey," Dennis says, nodding his head toward a door in the back right corner of the store.

"Addition?"

Dennis nods. "Yup. Take a look-see. Think you'll like it."

I wander farther inside, my eyes scanning over the store. It looks different—fresher—than it did when it was Knox County Bait and Tackle. Whatever changes Ewan has made have certainly breathed fresh air into the place. Walking through here, though, feels oddly…familiar. Like I've been here. Which, I have, but I haven't. Not in this layout. Still, I know it.

Turning at the arrow that points me in the direction of the hunting section, I step into a large, open room with bright lights and open shelving. That's when it hits me.

I know this layout.

Because I designed it.

This is exactly what I drew out on a set of napkins that night in Miami. The Hayes rifles front and center—because this store is owned by a Hayes after all—with the safety gear on the opposite wall. Archery has its own section in the back, and I would bet my life had I followed the stairs in the original part of the lodge, it would have taken me to an entire camping and "wilderness enjoyment" display.

My insides clench, my head spinning in one direction as

my thoughts whir in another, giddy little butterflies taking flight in my chest. Ewan followed our plan. There's a chance that maybe—just maybe—he's still open to this. To us.

That he could still choose me.

Despite what we said.

"Maisey."

The deep rumble of Ewan's voice knocks me from my trance, pulling me back into the moment. At least until my eyes land on him. If I thought he looked good all dressed up in his tux, then I simply wasn't prepared for everyday Ewan. Dark jeans and tee with The Booby Trap logo—a simple font with bobbers for O's—that fits him like a glove, clinging to his muscular frame, and a matching ballcap, making him look every inch the outdoorsman he is. It's nothing fancy—in fact if I were to guess, those jeans probably haven't been washed in a month—yet it's more than enough to stop me dead in my tracks and remind me of everything I've been missing.

Making me question why I left in the first place. What on earth possessed me to think there was anything outside of this town. Outside of him.

"Hi," I squeak. "I-I brought lunch."

Ewan stares at me, eyes flicking down to the Dolly's bag in my hand then back up to me, but doesn't respond. At least not verbally. His blue eyes are as expressive as ever, letting me in on exactly how he's feeling and all the doubt that is flowing through him.

Meaning I will need to kickstart the conversation. Some things never change.

"I grabbed us burgers, but I went with chips instead of fries since I figured those travel better. I had Nico throw some in right before I left too, so they're fresh."

"Back for thirty-six hours and already have this town wrapped back around your little finger." Ewan laughs, shaking his head and turning back to the box of arrows at his feet.

"Hey!" I put the to-go bag on the ground and march over to him, ready to defend myself. Until I see the trademark Hayes smirk on his face, my indignation lifting as I realize he's teasing me. Doesn't mean he's getting off that easy. "Not my fault I'm loved and adored by all. They missed me."

"Keep telling yourself that."

"I will." I cross my arms, and the move shifts my boobs up, catching Ewan's eye. Just as quickly, he looks away and I shift again, dropping my arms. That wasn't what I was trying to do, and I don't want him to think I'm throwing myself at him. "More than that, when I mentioned to Dolly on Saturday that I was going to stay in town awhile, she asked if I'd be interested in helping at the diner this week while she's away, so I was already there."

Ewan stands up straight, nearly knocking over a display of protective eyewear. At his full height, he towers over me by a good six or seven inches, my small stature never more on display than when we're next to each other.

"You're not headed back to…" he trails off, like he's trying to think of what country I was in.

"Nicaragua. And no." I swallow hard. "That contract ended. So, I'm here for a bit. Which works well, with the wedding and Grandma's big birthday, and other things…"

"Other things," he repeats. "You mean our pact."

"Yeah." I rock back on my heels. "The ketchup pact."

"The ketchup pact?"

I giggle, unable to help myself. "That's what I call it in my head. Since we swore our oath with ketchup, instead of blood."

"Even then you were a contradiction. There was no containing your spirit, but still concerned about first aid safety."

Neither of us speaks, his comment hanging in the air like a slowly deflating balloon, wafting in the awkward silence. I know he meant it as a compliment. But that doesn't help me form a response. And the longer we go, the bigger the silence grows, the more damage I fear it's going to do.

So I blurt out the first thing I can think of.

"Dolly also volunteered up her old apartment, which was super sweet of her, and works out perfect, because it means I'm not back with Mama and Daddy. Plus—"

"Why are you really back, Maisey?"

"What?"

I stumble, his question catching me so off guard I physically react, sending me in the direction of those arrows. I catch myself, thankfully before I make a mess of both myself and the store. This would not be the place to have an accident.

"Why, Mais?"

"We're about to be thirty-four, and we're single, so…" I suck in a breath. "I mean, you are single, right? I mean, Mama and Grandma were all titter-y about it, but Em said you two were just friends and—"

"We are."

His face is solemn, solid, and other than crossing his arms, he hasn't moved a muscle. The teasing smirk is gone, but all that doubt is still there in those eyes. Shit, I should have insisted he eat first. This would have been better over food.

"Are you saying you weren't serious about that pact?" I ask, my heart starting to race.

I'm not sure I want the answer. Because I was. Always have been. Deep down, I always thought he was too. If he wasn't—or worse, he changed his mind—I'm not sure that's an answer I can handle.

"I was when we were thirteen. But those are things you say and don't actually collect on."

My resolve cracks. "We swore it in ketchup."

"Mais," he sighs, stepping in closer to me. "Tell me what's going on. The truth. It might've been years since we've seen each other, but I can still read you, and you're not telling me something. I can see it all over your face."

Emotion rises in my throat, settling right at the base, threatening to choke me. At least it's not tears. I've already shed more of those than I can count recently, and don't think I can bear to shed anymore.

If there is anyone on this earth I could cry to, it's Ewan. He's my person. Or, he was. The one, single being on this planet who would understand. That I could fall apart to in this way. That I could share all my inner thoughts and feelings to without judgment.

I want to tell him so badly. I want to bare my soul and break down and be nothing but a puddle. But I can't. Something is still holding me back. Maybe it's the not knowing if he's all in too; I don't know. Or maybe it's simply having learned that I can't be that person anymore. Either way, some secrets aren't meant for sharing.

"I told you." I clear my throat, regaining my composure. "My current contract was canceled, so since I was in between contracts and with everything going on here, and us on the eve of the birthday we agreed on, it all seemed like kismet."

Ewan steps back, closing his eyes, his lips pressing into a hard, thin line. And my heart rips in half.

I know that look.

That isn't anger. It's much worse. It's hurt. Pain. A straight shot to the heart.

Fuck...

"Gotcha..."

His voice is barely above a whisper, so low and soft I

wouldn't have heard it if I wasn't listening for it. Nonetheless, it might as well have been the loudest thing I've ever heard.

"So, I'm just your backup plan? Your dream didn't work out, and you happened to have this pact that we conveniently made with a household condiment as kids in your back pocket, so…here you are?"

Ouch…

Ewan Hayes has always been a man of few words. He chooses each one carefully, waiting for just the right moment to deliver them, and when he does, boom. Just like now.

Each one is a double-edged sword, dripping with both torment and venom. Making sure that I know how much he's hurting, and inflicting it right back.

"Ewan, you are not a backup plan."

You never were…

Tears prick the corner of my eyes, panic rising in me as I try to find a way to tell him everything I've wanted to since that moment after college. The one where I stupidly looked at him and told him that if he didn't want to go with me, I'd go alone. And then did.

The moment I took a risk and picked wrong and have been paying for ever since.

How do you tell someone that walking away from them is the biggest mistake you've ever made?

"I gotta go," Ewan says, nodding and pushing past me.

"What?"

I spin on my heel, moving so fast I make myself dizzy for a second. I look down at the to-go bag, then back up at his backside as he walks toward the door.

"I thought we were having lunch?"

"I have Munch," he calls over his shoulder.

"You have what?"

He stops at the door, sighing heavily. He flexes his hands around the doorjamb, turning to me, his eyes so full of hurt.

"Munch." He swallows hard, as if he's trying to stop himself from saying something. "I'm sure Dennis would like the burger. He'll eat pretty much anything you put in front of him."

Another nod, and he's gone, leaving me standing in the middle of the room, alone.

So much for kismet.

5

EWAN

I really wanted that burger.

Almost as much as I want *her*.

Which is a big problem. Not a new problem. But a *big* one, nonetheless.

I climb the stairs at Hayes Industries headquarters two at a time, the craving for Dolly's horseradish growing stronger with each heavy thud of my boots on the tread. To the point it almost rivals my curiosity about the taste of Maisey's lips. Almost.

I bet it wouldn't overpower it though.

Because something tells me there isn't anything on this earth as sweet or addicting as Maisey Phillips's kiss.

The last thing I need to be thinking about right now is kissing her. Or ever. That ship has sailed. Ketchup pact or not. We were kids when we agreed to that. Kids who didn't know better. That was long before all the things we said to each other—things that can't be unsaid—and all those miles we put between us.

Before I picked Hickory Hills over her.

An unmistakable smell hits my nostrils the second I

round the corner for the executive conference room, distracting me from my thoughts. Given its potency, I'm a little surprised I didn't smell it sooner, that unique and prominent aroma indicating one thing and one thing only.

Fried catfish with Miss Harriett's homemade garlic tartar sauce is on the menu.

Miss Harriett, the Hayes Industries catering manager, has been in charge of the kitchen for forever. And I do mean forever. As in longer than any of my siblings and I have been alive. She is, without a doubt, one of the best cooks in Hickory Hills.

And once a week, she spoils us at Munch—short for Monday Lunch—the weekly lunch meeting where the heads of each department at Hayes get together to discuss the inner workings of the company. And by heads of each department, I mean my siblings and me. After all, the seven of us are the ones who keep this ship on course.

Our areas of expertise are as distinct as we are. Milo, a secret chemistry nerd, runs Southern Brothers Brewing with his best friend, Brandt, as well as the taphouse bar they opened a couple of years ago here in town, Pour Decisions. Hux, lumberjack and environmentalist, oversees the paper-mill and lumber division, while Jace leads personal safety, his passions for self-defense and "safety first" catching a lot of people off guard. There's a reason we call him the family wild card. Anton has always been passionate about one thing —okay, three—the precious three Ps. Peaches, peanuts, and pecans. Handing over the agriculture arm to him was a no-brainer. Willa oversees our charitable giving department, regularly reminding all of us that it's our responsibility to support the community that keeps us going. Leaving Gus as executive vice president, responsible for more than I can fathom, while still trying to manage the original branch of guns and ammo, since they still haven't identified someone to backfill his role after he was promoted.

Then there's me—owner, operator, sole proprietor of The Booby Trap. Ask my siblings and they'll call it a bait and tackle shop. But it's more than that now. It's a hunting, camping, and fishing dream store, locally owned and operated, staffed with people who actually hunt, camp, and fish, ready and willing to help you find what you need. Take that, big box brands.

My stomach grumbles audibly as I turn into the conference room, making its opinion known that if we pass over the catfish the way we did the burger, riots will likely ensue. The noise is louder than I think, catching the attention of Gus, Milo, and Anton, all of whom are already sitting at the long conference table, plates stacked high with food, shoveling it like it's their last meal.

"Is your stomach telling you to eat or auditioning for a horror movie?" Anton quips. As instigator of the family, he lives to push our buttons, and never misses a chance to poke at us. "That was your stomach, right? You're not hiding a wild bear or some other beast in there?"

I roll my eyes, focusing on filling my plate. If those three are already here, I don't have to hold back on my portions. Hux is already on his honeymoon so won't be in attendance, and with fried catfish on the menu, Willa will be skipping the meeting. How she knows when this is served I'll never know, since Miss Harriett refuses to divulge the menu beforehand, but she always knows and refuses to attend. Not because she doesn't like the meal—she does, as we all do—but she doesn't want to spend the rest of the day smelling of fish and garlic.

High-maintenance little sister means more for me...

My stomach growls again, betraying me, and all three of my brothers laugh. I flip them the bird over my shoulder, earning more of a laugh, their lack of sympathy not a surprise.

"Should we be worried that your stomach is more vocal than you are?" Gus asks as I sit.

I shake my head, letting them know I don't want to talk about it, hoping they take the hint. There's a fifty-fifty shot they'll respect it. Depends on what else they've got going on.

"So, Sawyer caught the bouquet..." Gus says.

Thank fuck...

"Sawyer didn't *catch* anything," Anton corrects him. "Dolly handed it to her."

"Still..." Milo comments.

"Still nothing," Anton chuffs. "Look, I'm not saying it's not happening. And I'm not saying she's not 'next.' But, Dolly couldn't just throw the damn thing and let one of those little girls catch it? She had to walk it right up to Sawyer and make a thing of it?"

"Pressure's on, dude..." Milo jokes.

Their conversation fades into the background, their voices melding together into something that resembles Charlie Brown's teacher. I should pay attention. Should know what happened at the rest of the wedding after my dance with Maisey. Truthfully, the rest of the evening is a blur, coming into focus only surrounding moments where I saw Maisey, my heart stopping and then kickstarting back to life each time.

Half listening to my brothers now, I don't even remember the bouquet toss, or Dolly handing it to Sawyer instead of tossing it. I don't have a clue where I was at that point. Wait, no—I do. I was standing next to my father, watching as Maisey lined up with the other single women, thinking to myself that if I had told her how I felt years ago, she wouldn't have to be lining up to fight over a bundle of flowers.

Ewan, we'll be thirty-four this year...we swore it in ketchup...

Her sweet voice fills my head, splitting my heart in two. Emily wasn't wrong; she's here for me. Just not for any of the reasons I want her to be. Or even because she *wants* to be.

No, I'm a secondary option. The backup plan. Where you go when life didn't turn out like you thought.

When you're suddenly in your thirties, not married, and your biological clock is ticking, you turn to the man that you could always count on. Because you swore it in ketchup.

Fuuuuuuuuck...!

Searing pain rips through my chest, like someone took a blacksmith's fire iron and stabbed me with it. I drop my fork, the food in my mouth turning sour, and I force myself to swallow. The start of tears burn the corner of my eyes and I snap them shut, refusing to lose it here.

If I can get through this meeting, then I can get back to the store and lose myself in inventory for the rest of the day. I can cry all I want when I'm alone counting arrows and bullets. Have my own personal pity party among the fishing lures. Come to terms with being her backup plan in my own way, on my own time.

But that is after I get through Munch.

"Ewan."

It's Gus's voice that cuts through the fog. Still, it takes a minute for it to register and another to collect myself enough to open my eyes and face them. Four sets of concerned eyes stare back at me, Jace having joined the group, each one of them as silent and still as a tomb.

The urge to spill my guts conflicts with the even stronger desire to hide. To turn inward and never share another thing about myself ever again.

"What's the bigger mess right now, your head or your heart?" Gus asks.

It's the same kind of question he'd ask at any given point during one of these meetings of any one of us, helping us try to strategize or figure out how to attack a problem we're facing in our department. Only this time, instead of having his game face on, his tone being all business, there's a softness to him that I haven't seen in years. Since I was a little kid with a broken arm, and he was nothing more than my big brother looking out for me. Not the boss, or an executive on the rise. Just the oldest of seven, looking out for the rest of us.

"I...I..." Shaking my head, I try to clear the noise, but it doesn't work. "I don't know."

I push my plate forward, the sight of my lunch making my stomach lurch. Shit, no one tell Miss Harriett that was my reaction—she'd be so offended and I don't know that I could ever live with myself if I knew that I offended her.

"So, are the rumors true?" Jace asks. "She's back? Like staying in town back?"

I nod, throwing in a shrug for good measure. Because, I'm not entirely sure I'm the authority on this. Maybe in this room I am. But overall, probably not. Although, depending on what source is feeding the Hickory Hills rumor mill, they might have substantially more information. The bits and pieces passed along to me were a bit lacking. Even if they did come straight from the horse's mouth.

"Why now?" Milo asks. "Can't just be the wedding."

I shake my head, sucking in the deepest breath I can manage, stretching my diaphragm to the max. If I'm going to drop this bomb, I'm going to need all the oxygen I can get.

"She wants to collect on our marriage pact."

Silence.

I expect shouts, a mix of swears and hollers, all of my brothers' voices melding together as they fight to be heard over each other, clamoring to express themselves in shock and awe. Instead, there's nothing. Crickets. Punctuated by the hum of the vent and ping of Anton dropping his fork on the table.

That's unexpected.

"How legally binding is this…pact?" Gus asks cautiously.

Okay, there's the overserious, grumpy fucker we love.

"We can consult Margeaux on the legal implications of Heinz and their 57 varieties, but I'm pretty sure not at all."

"What?"

"We were kids, Gus," I snark. "Mandie and Jason Pike had just gotten engaged and that was all this town could talk about. I'd built a campfire in the backyard and we were roasting hot dogs, and she was rambling on and on—in the way that only Maisey can, you know? Holding an entire fucking conversation with herself while you just sit there?—worrying about what happens if we grow up and no one wants to marry us. If we never meet our soulmate. So we made a pact. If in twenty years, we're both still single, we'd marry each other. And we sealed it in ketchup."

"Ketchup?" Anton questions, lifting an eyebrow.

"Cutting ourselves and sharing blood was gross to teenage Maisey. She was a nurse even then."

He nods, accepting the answer.

"So, she does want to marry you." Milo smirks, leaning back in his chair and resting his hands behind his head.

"No, she doesn't," I snap. The words taste sour in my mouth, bile rising in my throat. "I'm her backup plan."

"You don't—" Jace starts.

"Know that?" I cut him off, standing up abruptly, my chair rolling behind me so quickly it slams into the wall. "I do."

"Ewan," Gus warns.

"What? I do."

I start to pace, the anger rising in me again. At least this time I can let it out.

"Her contract was canceled. That's why she came back. Only after her dream didn't work out did she come back!"

"But she did come back," Anton points out. "If she didn't want you, she wouldn't have done that. She wouldn't be trying to collect."

I stop and stare at him. When he puts it like that, he makes it sound so simple. Like there's a chance. But there isn't. Not after what I said. There's no way.

Shaking my head, I swallow hard, fighting off the next round of tears. I have never felt this out of control in my life.

"Why do I feel like there is still something you aren't telling us?" Gus asks.

Because there is...

I turn and glare at him. When did he get so good at this? This has to be Margeaux's influence, because Gus has never been able to read people like this. That was always Milo's superpower.

"He's leaving out the fight they had before she left," Milo says, his voice calm and even, like he's narrating a story.

And there it is.

"It wasn't a fight," I correct him.

It wasn't. There was no arguing on either of our parts. Zero yelling. Lots of tears. Plenty of pleading. Begging—so much begging. But no raised voices.

"Then what was it?" Jace asks.

I shrug, not knowing how to answer.

Milo pushes to his feet and crosses his arms, his face going blank. He waits, eyes trained on me, but I don't budge. I can't say it.

"That was when he broke both their hearts, because when given the choice of seeing the world with the girl he loved, he chose Hayes and Hickory Hills over her."

Milo's words sting, almost as much as the collective gasps

from the other three. Still not as much as the memory of Maisey's tears.

"This town is my life—with or without you in it..." I murmur, stumbling backward. "That's what I told her."

My back hits the wall, the thud making the wall shake. Pain radiates down my spine, and I know I'm going to regret it later, but right now, I don't care. I'm too emotional to move.

"You're a dumbass, baby brother," Anton declares across the table.

Thanks?

"But, some good news," he adds. "You're getting a second chance. She came back."

"Like I said, she *does* want to marry you." Milo parks himself beside me, patting my knee. "No woman is showing back up after you said that unless she *wants* you. Condiment packet or not."

"No." I shake my head. "Second chances aren't real. They are things that happen in Jace's books."

Jace perks up, for half a second pretending like he's offended. His guilty pleasure for romance novels is a well-known fact, although Jace will flat out tell you he finds zero guilt in the pleasure he takes in reading them.

"Ummm, what do you call Dustin and Kenzie?" Jace asks.

I scoff. Using the town's most famous couple—country mega star Dustin Wild and his hometown sweetheart turned wife Kenzie Noble—as an example isn't fair. Because their story is something that inspires not only romance novels, but country songs.

"Rock stars get second chances, not real people."

"Beg to differ, sir," Gus chimes in.

Fuck, fate gave him and Margeaux a second chance too. Well, kind of. They were more missed connection. But still, it took a second go for them as well. Shit.

"Ewan," Anton says, standing up and leaning over the table. "Answer me this. Do you love her?"

Seriously? Is he seriously fucking asking me that? I'm sitting on the damn floor of our conference room halfway to a breakdown and he's asking me that?

"Yes."

"And you want a future with her? You want to cash in on this agreement?"

"I don't want to be her backup—"

"Forget about that part," he stops me. "Do you want a future with her?"

His eyes hold mine, and I can tell he's serious. Something that Anton often isn't. But I also know that when it comes to almost losing the life you want with the person you want it with, he learned a hard lesson last summer. So if there is someone I should be listening to, it might be him.

"Yes."

"Then you need to tell her. You need to be honest with her. About all of it. Hold nothing back."

"He's right," Milo says. "Fess up about why you chose to stay after graduation, and how you've felt ever since. About what you want now."

"And be ready to listen to whatever she has to say in return," Gus adds.

I nod, taking in their advice. I trust these three with my life, and I know how solid their relationships are. The only person better to give advice would be our father.

"And then kiss the fuck out of her," Jace tosses out. "Actually, lead with that. A hot, wet, sloppy kiss."

"Well now," Auggie drawls, walking into the room. He pauses a couple of steps in, eyes dancing around the room, taking in the scene. "That's some advice. I was about to apologize for being late, but should I be worried about what I missed? Ewan?"

He looks directly at me, concern taking over his features. I can only imagine what this looks like to walk in on—me scrunched up against the wall on the floor, Milo down here with me, Gus leaning on the table directly across from us, with Anton and Jace on the other side, everyone's attention on me. Looking to each one of my older brothers, I take in their silent answers, clearing my throat to respond.

"Just some brother shit." There, that covers it.

Our father nods, his version of the Hayes smirk appearing. "I do like it when y'all can handle it amongst yourselves. So, shall we?"

Turning to the catering table, he fixes himself a plate as the rest of us correct ourselves. Milo and I help each other off the floor, exchanging one last hug before we sit.

"Pour Decisions confessional is always open," he jokes, referring to his brewery's taproom. "Party Mode, or Sob Story, is always cold. Depending on the occasion."

"Depending on how all this goes down, I might just have to take you up on that."

"You got this."

I'm glad someone thinks so.

6

MAISEY

THE SOUND of the rain tapers off, somehow leaving me feeling raw and exposed, despite being curled up comfortably on the couch, a selection of comfort foods spread across the coffee table.

Because when the boy you secretly gave your heart away to a long time ago breaks it for a second time, only one type of metabolic havoc-wreaking caloric crap won't do. Nope. This requires both salty and sweet. Multiple types of chocolate. And a pie.

Because pies before guys. Always.

Pretty sure Hollie Berry taught me that one.

Shifting my legs out from underneath me, I turn the volume down on the TV, the cast of *Bones* no longer having to compete with the weather outside to be heard, and grab another handful of Chex mix. Really, what I need to do is get up off the couch and at least stretch. My body isn't used to this much down time—going from twelve-hour shifts on my feet to couch potato is not ideal. But here we are.

I glance at my phone, not sure what I expect it to do. The inanimate object isn't exactly going to sprout legs and suddenly perform "Singin' in the Rain." I suppose I could text Emily back and answer her question about how it went at The Booby Trap, telling her no, despite her awkwardly worded question, Ewan did not "take me right there in the camping section" and there was no "epic make-out session."

Except then I would have to tell her how it really went. And that I thought I couldn't hurt any more than I did when I tried to give him my heart the first time and he didn't want it. Turns out, the glued-together pieces of your heart being ripped back apart by the same person, once again telling you that they don't want you, hurts more.

A lot more.

Stupid me for thinking that our pact meant something. That *I* meant something.

Ugggggh...

Throwing my head back on the couch, I try to clear my mind. To think of something—anything—other than replaying our conversation in The Booby Trap earlier today. But the only scene on tap seem to be *the* conversation. The one that lives rent free in my head, permanently on playback, in a weird technicolor nightmare, making everything more vivid and intense. Like watching *The Wizard of Oz* for the first time and going from black and white to color, the shock hits me, blinding me, even though I know exactly what's coming.

"Come with me," I'd said, so full of hope and excitement. The butterflies thrumming through my veins had been working overtime as I'd summoned the courage to lay it all out there.

"Where?" Ewan's laugh was easy, light, as if he'd thought I was simply being hypothetical.

A week after college graduation, the world was at our feet. There was only one thing I wanted though. Him. Same as I always had, but never had the guts to say out loud. I was pretty sure he felt the same, so the only thing left was for one of us to say it. To pull the actual trigger on forever. And Lord knows, Ewan Hayes put the *silent* in strong and silent type, so he would not be the one doing it.

It was up to me.

"I got a job offer," I told him, climbing into his lap.

We were sitting on the couch in his parents' house, Magnolia Manor, in the middle of the afternoon, but I didn't care. If I was going to do this, I was doing it. I also knew that if anyone were to walk in, they wouldn't care. We'd been so close for so long, it wouldn't have registered. And if it had, then any commentary would have been in the *about damn time* camp.

Straddling him, I wrapped my arm around his neck, making myself comfortable. His hands found my hips as if on autopilot, and the thought of kissing him took over. But that would come after I got this all out.

"To be a traveling nurse," I continued, holding his gaze with mine. "It's our chance to see the world. To experience more than Hickory Hills. Go on all sorts of adventures."

The confused look I got caught me off guard. It was a look that told me that I would have made more sense if I had spoken in ancient Russian.

"You want more than Hickory Hills?"

It was my turn to be taken aback. He knew this. I'd talked about all the places I wanted to go, the things I wanted to see and do, for as long as I could remember. It was the whole inspiration behind applying to work with this international program.

"There's more to life than our hometown, Ewan. You've got to know that," I laughed.

"No."

No?

"No? No what?" I asked, sitting back. "No, you don't think

there's more than Hickory Hills or no, you won't come with?"

Ewan looked at me like he was examining me. Trying to figure out the right answer to an exam or if he should clip the red wire or blue wire to stop a bomb from going off.

"Why do you want to go?"

"Because I want more than this!" I throw my arms out wide, gesturing to everything surrounding us. Hickory Hills, Georgia, small-town life in general, all of it. "I want to go on adventures. And I want you there with me."

"Why?"

Wh...what? How can he ask that?

"Because I want you, Ewan."

He was stock-still underneath me, no part of him moving even a millimeter. If it weren't for the fact that I could feel his exhale, I'd worry he was dead.

"Not if you want me to leave, you don't."

My heart stopped. My stomach plummeted and the entire room spun, but the most important part was that my heart stopped.

"Excuse you?"

Shifting underneath me, Ewan picked me up and placed me on the cushion next to him before standing up. The look on his face was placid and plain, his eyes full of hurt, making me want to reach out and comfort him. Except he was causing the same pain in return.

"I can't leave here. My life is here. I have obligations to my family. To Hayes."

"Can't or won't?" I challenged, my heart starting to shatter.

"Does it matter?"

"It does. It matters to me, Ewan. If you don't want me, if you don't want a life together—"

"So, you're going? No matter what my answer?" The hurt in his voice sliced through me like a knife through butter.

I nodded. "That's my plan. But I want you to come with me. I want us to be together."

There, I said it.

"Then you should go."

He turned away from me, leaving the pieces of my heart skittering across the floor like broken glass.

"What about you? What about our chance at—" I choked out.

"This town is my life, Maisey—with or without you in it."

This town is my life, Maisey—with or without you in it...

Fuck, how those words haunt me. No, that's not true. It's not those words that haunt me. It's my lack of response to them.

It's knowing that instead of following him out to the garage —where he always went to start tinkering with something as a way to get space from his family—and forcing the conversation, I sat there. I didn't go after him. I didn't tell him half the things I had planned on. Including those three not so little words.

I can't even begin to imagine how different my life would look if I'd done that. If I'd marched right out there and screamed at the top of my lungs, "I love you, Ewan Porter Hayes! And I know you love me too!" But I didn't. Instead I slunk back home, accepted the job, and packed my bags.

A week later I rolled down his driveway, told him I was headed to Turkey, and hugged him goodbye.

And because of that, I'm sitting here now, dunking Pringles in Nutella.

The pitter-patter of the rain picks up again, ever so slightly, but it's enough to knock me out of my headspace. Enough to make me realize that tears running down my cheeks are real and current, not solely part of my memory.

Maybe I do need to text Emily back. Or even call her. Have her come over. Tell her to bring Alice and Rose while she's at it, and then I can word vomit this all out, getting it out of my system to people who will not only understand, but maybe have some advice.

Pushing up off the couch, I groan, my body not happy with my lack of movement for the last few hours. That doesn't stop me from scooping up a bite of the pie though, letting the chocolatey flavor settle on my tongue as I stretch.

I tap open my texts, noticing that I have a second from Emily that I missed along the way. This one just as smart-assy as the first.

EMILY

> Checking to see how the lunch bombing went! 😉

> Did he take you right there in the camping section, knocking everything over and making a mess in a seriously epic make-out session?

> Since I haven't heard from you, I'm going to assume that epic make-out session turned into a no pants dance and y'all have scarred poor Dennis for life! Lol

> But seriously, LMK how it all went, and if you actually got him to talk

I scoff, rolling my eyes at my cousin. She is the only person I know who can manage to use the term *no pants dance* well into our thirties. Sighing, I try to figure out what to say, my thumbs moving across the screen slowly, typing and retyping as I carefully choose my words.

I'm all but ready to hit send when a heavy knock on the door startles me. I drop my phone, the device hitting the carpet with a heavy thud. Looking over at the door, I wonder why Emily didn't just call. Her follow-up texts didn't come in that long ago, so I can't believe she's that anxious to know what went down that an in-person visit was required.

Unless it's not her.

No, has to be. She's the only one who knows where I'm staying. Other than my parents. And they are definitely not doing a drive-by.

The heavy knock starts up again, this time more rapidly. Fine, fine.

"I'm coming!" I holler, marching over to the door. "Keep your pants on, Em—"

I throw the door open and stop. Because staring back at me, backlit from the single street lamp, rain-soaked, and breathing heavy, isn't my cousin.

It's Ewan.

7

MAISEY

Ewan...

My breath catches, my heart right there in my throat, making it impossible to swallow. I try to inhale, my entire chest constricting, reminding me of all the oxygen he stole straight out of the atmosphere.

He looks better than anyone has any business looking in a gray T-shirt turned almost charcoal thanks to the rain.

There's a million things I want to say. That I want to ask. Starting with how he knew where to find me. But the words don't come. I can't make them go. I can only squeak out two little syllables.

"Ewan."

He takes half a step toward me, closing the already small distance between us, stealing what's left of my ability to think.

"I lied."

W-wh-what?!

"I love you. I've always loved you. Always."

Always...always. My mind reels, that simple, six-letter

word sending my world into a tailspin. Never mind the three not so little words that were paired with it.

Always.

Who does he think he is, dropping that word like that?

"You, Maisey…you were my life. Not this town. *You,*" he says, his voice warbling slightly. "I not only would have sworn it in blood, but I would have married you right then and there had Judge Robinson and our parents let us get away with such a thing at thirteen."

I reel back, the blow of his words hitting me like a wrecking ball. They're everything I've wanted to hear for so long—the words I've secretly fantasized about—but they don't seem real. I bite down on the inside of my lip, testing to make sure I'm not dreaming. Sure enough, I feel the sharpness of my teeth, letting me know that I'm not in some junk food-induced coma on the couch.

This is real.

"The only thing I ever wanted was for you to see me as more than a best friend. To cross that line. There were so many times I almost told you, and I chickened out every time, so afraid that you didn't see me that way. That you viewed us as a younger version of Hux and Dolly—the perfect platonic pair."

Ewan continues, the words rushing from him like water over Niagara Falls. As if him not getting it all out in a single breath might kill him.

"I had this whole plan in my head, that we were going to come back here after graduation, and I was going to convince Old Man Jennings to sell the shop so that I could make it part of Hayes, and take that plan you'd drawn up on that napkin when we were in Florida and put it into action. That once we were back here, in Hickory Hills, and I was living up to my family name, you could see me as someone who was worthy of you."

Worthy of him? My heart slams against my chest, the ability to breathe becoming harder and harder the more he continues. He really thought that? He thought he didn't deserve me? No, this isn't right.

I look up at him, not sure what I'm going to find, but still shocked by what I see.

Tears.

Ewan's blue eyes are glassy and there is no mistaking the tremble in his bottom lip. Raindrops run down his face, but do little to disguise the pain once the dam breaks. Turns out, tears and raindrops look nothing alike.

"I know you used to talk about seeing the world all the time, but I never thought you'd actually leave. And that day that you asked me to go with you, I should have said yes. I know that. And not a day has gone by that I don't regret my answer. That I don't regret missing out on the adventures that we could have had. Because I was too deep in thinking that I had to stay here, be a *Hayes*, instead of..." He trails off, swallowing hard. Pressing his eyes shut, he inhales hard and deep, like he's pushing down every emotion he's ever felt. I want to reach out, to grab him and tell him it'll be okay, but I'm paralyzed in place. "All I know is I missed ten years of being your best friend. Ten years of loving you from far away instead of up close. And I don't want to miss the next ten. Backup plan or not, I want a future with you, Maisey."

You do?

I stand here, stunned, my body as frozen as a block of marble. I should react—say something, anything—but can't. My vocal cords are betraying me. It's like a wad of cotton has been shoved far down my throat, preventing anything else from moving past it.

"Say something, Maisey," Ewan says, his voice cracking. "Even if it's just telling me to get the hell off your step."

I try. I really do. But I can't; I'm too shocked.

Ewan Hayes loves me.

Another long moment of silence passes, my insides doing a conga line, while my outsides fail to react in any sort of matching form. The rain picks up again, the sound of it echoing off every surface. Ewan's face falls, his eyes fluttering shut as he sighs, his whole body deflating.

He nods curtly, flicking his gaze back up to me. "It's been good to see you, Mais."

Turning slowly, he dips his head, as if that's somehow going to save him from the rain, then heads down the small flight of stairs. I watch him, my pulse thundering, heart calling out to him like a ship in the night, trying to bring him back.

Maisey Margaret Phillips...don't be a dumbass...

I can hear my grandmother's voice loud and clear in my head. Although, to be fair, Grandma probably wouldn't use the word dumbass. She'd tell me to stop being *dumber than a bag of hammers* or some other gentle Southern insult. But either way, she'd have no problem tearing me up one side and down the other over this.

That boy did not just stand here pourin' his heart out for you to not do the same, young lady...

No...no, he did not.

Without another thought, I take off running. The rain is cold, my bare feet scrunching from the shock as my toes hit the puddles. But I can't let him get away. Not again.

Good thing he didn't get far.

"Ewan Porter Hayes!" I scream into the rain. "You're an idiot!"

Ewan spins around, his hands tucked into his pockets, fractals of light from the streetlamp shining through the rain behind him. He opens his mouth to respond—maybe to argue—but I don't let him.

"I love you. I always have. You have never been my backup plan. Ever. You were my primary plan. At least until you told me you didn't want me."

I swallow hard. Reaching down to find the same courage he did to tell me all those things. And I do.

I find the small box I've kept hidden inside me of all the things I've wanted to say. Wanted to scream at him. And I unleash it. Right here, in the middle of the pouring rain, in the back alley between the main strip of stores downtown, the old historic house that has been converted into apartments.

"How could you possibly believe that I didn't love you? How?" I throw my arms out wide, not bothering to fight the tears that push through. "That was the whole reason I made the ketchup pact to begin with. Because I thought the only chance I would ever have at being your girl was to be *your* backup plan. And that day I asked you to come with me? That was me handing you my heart, you dumbass! That's why I told you I wanted us to be together!"

I suck in a breath, getting ready to unleash the next round. To continue to let him have it. To put him in his place.

But Ewan has another idea.

He closes the gap between us in three massive strides, his gait purposeful and determined. I don't have time to breathe, much less think, before his hands are cradling my head, fingers weaving through my hair, and his lips are pressed to mine. He captures my mouth in a hard, punishing kiss, and everything stops.

All out stops.

Instantly, I see stars, the gentle power of his lips and the taste of his tongue overpowering me in a way that I can't describe. Every inch of me starts to tingle, this indescribable feeling flowing through me like lava, from the top of my head straight to the tip of my toes. Nothing else matters, nor will it ever matter again. Because right now, all there is, is this.

The safety and peace of Ewan Hayes's kiss.

I grip on to him tighter, trying to make this last. I've waited so long for this, resigned myself to never knowing what this would be like, and I know that no matter when it ends, it will be over too soon. But then he deepens it, yanking me in closer, his tongue swiping against mine, and I'm done for.

Nothing else will ever live up to this.

Slowly—hesitantly—Ewan pulls back, his lips lingering against mine for a beat, sending another shock wave through me. I attempt to catch my breath, something that is easier said than done, not sure that I can stand on my own two feet.

Rocking backward, I try, my knees wobbling, but Ewan is right there, catching me as I stumble from his knee-weakening kiss. I hold on tight, wrapping my fingers around his thick forearms, feeling the blood rush through my veins with each beat of my heart.

"Probably should have done that a long time ago," Ewan whispers, resting his forehead against mine.

I chuckle, for the first time in forever feeling like I have my best friend back. Damn, it feels *good*.

"Timing was never your thing," I joke, hoping I can still do that.

He scoff-laughs, and even without looking, I can feel the smile spreading across his face. The Ewan smile—the shy, sheepish grin that still gives me butterflies.

"That's why I had you."

I nod, shivering, although I'm not sure if it's his openness and sincerity or the spring rain that is causing my reaction. Ewan doesn't seem to think twice though, scooping me up like a groom carries a bride, scurrying across the pavement and back up the stairs. The small overhang at my front door doesn't do much, barely covering one of us, but it's better than the parking lot.

"So, what now?" I ask, uncertainty creeping in.

There's a part of me that would still marry him tomorrow if he asked. Head straight to the courthouse, stand in front of Judge Robinson, and promise to love him until death do us part. But there's another who wants answers. Who is still hurt.

"I don't know, Mais," he admits, placing his hands on my hips. I shudder out a sigh, wanting to fall into him. "I know we both have so much left unsaid, and have a lot to catch up on, but...I..."

I nod. Because I know. He doesn't have to say it out loud. Even after all this time apart, we're still connected enough for me to know what he's thinking and feeling. Which means I know the whole mess that is inside his head right now. Because it's the same one inside mine.

"Ewan, I..."

"Y'wanna go fishin'?"

Huh...what?!

I blink, hard, trying to make sure I heard him properly. That he just asked me what I think he just asked me.

"Wh-what?" I stutter, staring back at him blankly.

"Y'wanna go fishin'?" he repeats, as casually as ever.

As if he didn't just turn my entire world on its axis with a single kiss, now he's asking if I want to go fishing.

And yeah, I do.

Fuck, yes, I want to go fishing with Ewan Hayes.

Because what I wouldn't have given all these years to be asked that question. To have Ewan look at me, with that sheepish grin, and ask me if I want to go fishing, the same way he would have asked me when we were younger. Like this is any other day.

Smiling, I look up at him, feeling like I'm on top of the world. Like for the first time in a decade, I'm myself again.

"More than you know."

8

EWAN

I THINK Maisey forgot that going fishing means being up before the sun.

Giving her credit where it's due, she's up and at 'em when I knock on her door at o'dark-thirty. She just doesn't look very happy with me about it. Add that to the unchanged column—Maisey is still not a morning person.

"There's coffee, right?" she grumbles, climbing up into my truck.

Is there coffee? Of course there's coffee...I'm not a monster...

I lean over her, reaching for the center console and grabbing the to-go cup I prepared special for her. My arm brushes against her breasts, and my insides tense, suddenly on high alert as we make contact, wanting more. Wondering what is going through her mind right now, and if this brief, barely there touch is messing with her as much as it is me. It's taking everything in me to think of something other than that kiss. The damn good kiss.

And how I want to do it again.

"Hazelnut creamer and two sugars," I say, handing her the cup. Panic briefly washes over me, my brain suddenly second-guessing if this is still how she takes her morning caffeine jolt. Right behind it is the realization that all the things I think I know about her, I'm going to have to learn all over again.

But then she smiles.

Instantly, heat spreads through me, that smile just as magical now as it was when we were kids. Even more powerful than it has been in my dreams these last ten years. It about knocks me on my ass, but then Maisey slips her hands around mine, holding both it and the cup, grounding me to her.

"Please tell me you didn't go out and buy hazelnut creamer just so you could make me coffee?"

"No, I already had it." Heat rushes up the back of my neck, giving me away. "I still use it."

I pull back from her, still fighting the urge to kiss her, and close her door. I'm around the truck and climbing behind the wheel in no time, greeted by that same disarming smile.

"Still?" she prods. A cute little yawn escapes, prompting her to take a sip.

"Picked up the habit from you." I shrug, as if it's nothing. "When you left, there was a mostly full thing in the fridge, and I wasn't about to waste it. Found I missed it when I tried to switch back."

It was how I imagined you tasted...

Turns out, I was wrong.

Her kiss tastes nothing like the sweetened creamer she loves so much. It's better. Sweeter. Fuller. A whole lot more satisfying.

"Still a man of mystery, Ewan Hayes," she coos, taking another sip.

I shake my head—I am anything but. Truth be told, I'm pretty damn simple when it all comes down to it. I'll take her thinking that though.

We make the rest of the short drive over to Silver Lake in silence, the early morning darkness feeling like a blanket surrounding us. Nothing about it awkward, just two people still in the process of waking up, listening to the radio as the gravel crunches under the tires.

Twenty minutes later, we're in the water, nothing but the early morning quiet surrounding us. The *Hooked on a Reeling* gently moves along with the waves, the soft, easy movement threatening to lull me back to sleep.

"Do we really have to use live bait?" Maisey scrunches her nose, not bothering to hide her borderline disgust. "It's just so…"

Raising an eyebrow, I wait for her to finish. The night-crawler precariously held in between her thumb and fore-finger wriggles like the metaphorical worm on a hook—errr, well, almost on a hook in this case—as if it knows its moments are numbered.

"Yucky," she finishes, her blue eyes pleading with me to give her an out.

I chuckle, unable to hold back. The woman is a trauma nurse and sees all sorts of God knows what when it comes to blood and guts, broken bones, and other injuries. But putting a worm on a barbed piece of metal is what pushes her over the edge.

"Do I need to bait your hook?"

It's a simple question. Two possible answers—yes or no. Maybe a please thrown in there. But the sly smile and the fiery flash in Maisey's eyes betray her thought process. And it's anything but simple.

"Even after all these years, that still sounds dirty," she giggles, the sound echoing out over the open water, vibrating through the air and settling right in my chest.

"Pretty sure only you can make that dirty, Maisey."

Although right about now I'd like to make her dirty. Find

out what those soft little moans she made last night when I kissed her turn into as I make my way down her body. As I explore other parts of her. Discover if the rest of her tastes as good as her mouth.

No—stop. I need to stop.

We'll get there. I know we will. But I'm not going to rush it. I'm not going to make this about something it's not. This is about forever. I'm going to act accordingly.

Taking the nightcrawler from her pinched grip, I slide it onto the hook, piercing the barb through the little pinkish brown blob. Maisey recoils, her features still scrunched, but her eyes never leave my hands.

"Dirty or otherwise, I'm happy to do it."

"I know…" she whispers, leaning forward and winking conspiratorially. "And I'll let you."

Fuuuuuuck me…so much for keeping this aboveboard…

I need to think of something else to talk about. Something that isn't going to get me in trouble thinking about all the things I want to do to her. Something that will get us on the track we're supposed to be on.

Only, I don't know what track that is.

I know exactly what I would have done in high school with best friend Maisey. The one I had a crush on, but didn't have the balls to do anything about. But that's not who is sitting here with me now.

This Maisey is something else entirely. Just as beautiful—maybe even more so. But this Maisey knows my feelings. This Maisey ran out into the pouring rain to tell me she feels the same.

And suddenly, I don't know what to do with that.

"I can hear you thinking," she teases, nudging me with her shoulder.

"Oh yeah? And what am I thinking?"

"That I already tangled my line and you don't know what you're going to do with me?"

Holding up her rod, she smiles sheepishly. Sure enough, there's a small tangle in the translucent filament. Nothing that she couldn't work out herself, but it gives me a good excuse to busy my hands, distracting me from my thoughts.

"What am I going to do with you?" I mutter teasingly, as I take the rod from her. "Can't take you anywhere."

"Oh, you can take me anywhere," she quips, hands flying over her mouth almost instantly.

We both freeze, the prettiest shade of pink creeping up her cheeks in the dim light of the boat. My dick twitches, the semi I was already sporting from brushing up against her earlier now a full-blown erection, my imagination trying to fight for top billing with a list of ideas.

"That's not what I meant. I mean, it's what I meant, but..." She stops herself, yanking the rod out of my hand.

"Careful how you handle my rod there. Don't want to be too rough."

Eyes going wide, Maisey gasps, right before bursting into laughter. It's enough to send us both into hysterics, breaking the weird tension between us. At least some of it.

Plopping down onto the bench seat, Maisey rests her reel in the holder, still laughing.

"So, you bought Knox County Bait and Tackle and named it after a strip club," she prompts, changing the subject. "Tell me, who lost their shit first, Aunt Hattie, Mrs. Chamberlain, or Reverend Terry's wife?"

I park myself next to her, adjust her reel so that it's positioned properly to actually have a chance at catching something, then tighten mine so it doesn't cross with hers in the water.

"Actually, Miss Belle," I answer, waiting for her surprise.

Maisey sits up straight, my response catching her as off

guard as I expected. Nodding, I give her a minute to process that one.

Mama wasn't on the trip down to south Florida with Maisey, Hux, Dolly, and me where we encountered the establishment—complete with a building that had these two spherical shapes with nubs on the domes—but she's heard the story. She'd laughed initially, going along with the clever idea, shaking her head every time I brought it up but never truly believing I'd go through with it. Until the purchase went through and I started to work on the branding.

"It wasn't so much that she disliked the name," I continue. "She one hundred percent agreed with you that The Booby Trap was a better name for a hunting and fishing store, but she also knew how certain people in town would react, and she was not havin' it. Auggie had to talk her down."

"Miss Belle mad is a sight."

I nod. Yes, yes she is. A former beauty queen, my mama is a true Southern belle and is not to be messed with. She can curse you out, up one side and down the other, all while still smiling, leaving you unsure if you were even insulted. However, when she is mad, you will know it. That woman can stop traffic with a single look.

"I know Hayes Industries is still privately owned, but is there a board? Did the name have to be approved?" Maisey asks.

"The board would be seven of us—well, eight if you include Auggie, but he rarely votes these days. And the board would have to approve if the store was a part of the company."

"The Booby Trap isn't part of Hayes?"

"It is in the sense that I own it, and I'm a Hayes, and I have a legal interest in Hayes Industries. But on paper, Hayes Industries has no ownership over the store. I didn't use Hayes money to purchase it."

Maisey licks her lips, a subconscious move as she scoots in closer. Confusion is written all over her face, and I know I have a lot more questions to answer. This was not where I saw this morning heading, but maybe we need to get all this out now.

"Why?"

The single-word question slams into me like a wrecking ball. Closing my eyes, I exhale, pushing all the air from my lungs as far as I can. Here goes.

"Needed to prove that I could? I knew that Hayes money was available to me; that's how Milo got the seed money for Southern Brothers. But I wanted to be able to live up to the family name on my own. Build something. By that point, all my brothers had their businesses figured out and were deep in them. Willa had just won Miss Georgia. I felt like I had something to prove. So I took out a loan, bought the store, and got busy following this business plan drawn out on a napkin."

She smiles, the pink returning to her cheeks. She's so fucking cute I can't stand it. The urge to haul her into me rises in my chest, my hands aching to hold her. To know what her body feels like nestled into mine, curled up together as we watch the sun rise.

"And Auggie was okay with that?"

"My business, my decision. It was a risk, but we talked through the whole thing and he supported me if that's the route I wanted to go, and I decided it was. Gus tried to argue that meant I wasn't part of the executive board for a hot minute, but Auggie overruled him there too."

Maisey chuckles, the little sounds paired with the shake of her head saying that she's not at all surprised by that part of the story.

"Enough about me. What's your favorite place you've

been?" I ask, genuinely curious and fighting back the urge to do something stupid.

Maisey sighs, a dopey smile taking over. "That's like asking someone's favorite child. They're all special in their own way."

I scoff. I know that is exactly what Miss Belle would say if she was asked if she had a favorite child—that each one of the seven of us was unique and she loved each one of us evenly, for exactly who we are. And overall, I don't doubt that's true. But I also know that on any given day, at any given moment, exactly how we rank depends on any number of factors, including how much of a pain in the ass we were each being.

"But…"

"Nicaragua."

"Why?"

Sighing, she rests against the back of the boat, and I think I fall for her a little more. Watching her like this makes me hate myself even more for missing the last decade of having her by my side.

"It was the first time I was in a more leadership role, which was a fun new challenge. Plus, I really liked the community I was in. It was a smaller city, so still urban, but not so large that it was overwhelming. The whole vibe of it was just so…on point."

"You were there awhile, right?"

Please don't let that sound stalkerish…

"Eighteen months. Which was the longest I'd been posted anywhere. Usually my assignments last nine to twelve, sometimes as short as six months."

I nod, wanting to find the balance of not interrupting, but wanting to ask her something to keep her talking. The sweet melody of her voice fills my veins like a drug.

"Nicaragua was just so…different. Europe was so much

fun, and it's still a dream to get back to Iceland. But being in Central America was a completely different experience."

"I'll trust you on that. And wait, Iceland? As in the rival team from the Mighty Ducks?"

Giggling, Maisey nods. "Pretty sure that's not what they want to be known for, but yes. We hopped over for a couple of days when I was in Austria to see the northern lights and it was the most beautiful place I've ever seen. I instantly fell in love and put it at the top of my request list. I've been holding out hope for years that a contract would become available there, but nothing ever has. You'd love it."

"Why?"

"It's very outdoor oriented. All sorts of different hiking and camping things going on, including multi-day treks with volcanoes and waterfalls and whatnot. And they have these sites where you can rent these little glass igloos to sleep in to see the northern lights—I think that would be so cool."

Maisey lights up, starting to rival the northern lights, as she continues to talk about the far-off island country. I file away each tidbit she mentions, nodding along as I make my mental notes, not sure if I'll ever need them later. Maybe not, but who knows, there could be a test at some point. Then again, just getting to listen to her ramble like this is more than enough. It's everything I've missed summed up in one little action.

"And the blue lagoon, which is the geothermal hot spring, like an hour-ish or so outside of Reykjavík. It's amazing."

"So, it's a great big public hot tub?"

I'm not sure what about that sounds amazing.

"A geothermal hot spring," she corrects. "It's one of the wonders of the world. Even you have to admit that's cool."

Okay, yes, that's cool. I'll give her that. And I'm sure it's an incredible experience. Everything she rattled off sounded great actually—even better if she'd be with me. Then again, so are the woods just outside town where cell service is spotty and there isn't another person for miles.

Maisey stretches, the hem of her tee riding up, showing off the soft skin of her tummy. It's tan—perfectly sun-kissed—making my mouth water. The boat rocks gently beneath us, the early morning sun starting to peek up over the horizon.

"Still no desire to travel, huh?"

I shrug. "I get out."

"Fishing and hunting trips don't count." She giggles, playfully shoving me with her bare foot. I hadn't even noticed that she'd slipped her flip-flops off, her oversized joggers doing a good job of hiding her legs.

"I also go camping."

"Ohhh, sorry. I forgot about camping…" she teases.

"I did get a passport a while back," I admit.

"You did?"

There's no hiding the shock in her voice. Or the question. The one that I'm not really sure I want to answer.

"You said the other day your contract was up, so, no more Nicaragua?"

I hate myself for asking the question. It feels like I'm asking for all the wrong reasons. Like I'm trying to change the subject. Like I'm prying. Like I don't trust her and her intentions. When really, what I want is to know more about her. Her life. How this whole traveling nurse thing works.

She shakes her head, the regret and disappointment clear. Looking at me, she swallows hard. "The cancellation of the contract came out of nowhere. Usually I know my end date —and in this case, I had another six months until I was scheduled to leave. The overall, big contract that my company had with the Ministry of Health wasn't up for renewal or anything either, but there were some changes, and politics…" Her voice wavers, eyes fluttering closed as she fights back unchecked emotion. "For reasons I'm not privy to, they decided that using a service such as ours wasn't the way to go, so they terminated it. I'd been there for eighteen months and had really become a part of the team at the hospital and involved in the community. And then basically overnight, my job and work visa were terminated."

Maisey's eyes meet mine, the little bit of light from the rising sun catching in the sheen from her unshed tears. My heart squeezes, wanting nothing more than to erase her pain.

"I'm sorry."

"It's not your fault," she replies, a wry laugh escaping. "Unless you're in cahoots with the Nicaraguan Ministry of Health."

"I am not."

A slight tug on my pole steals my attention for a split second, making me think we're going to see some action. A quick glance over tells me it's a false alarm, and I can turn my attention back to where I really want it—fully focused on the blonde beauty sitting next to me.

"Then there is nothing for you to be sorry about."

"Well, that's not true, and we both know it," I admit.

"You're not alone in that, Ewan." She sighs, voice heavy with an emotion I can't name. Turning to look out over the water, she mumbles something to herself before continuing. "I won't lie. I held on to this secret hope in the back of my head for a while that you'd come chasing after me. Just show up randomly on my doorstep or in the ER that I was working in and sweep me off my feet. But, how were you supposed to know?"

Maisey sniffles, turning back to face me, a single tear running down her cheek.

"I cut you off." Her voice breaks ever so slightly. "It never occurred to me that you were hurting too. But that's why I never came back, because I was dying inside and knew that it would kill me to see you not hurting, and I didn't want to see you being all incredible when all I wanted was to break."

My heart shatters. In the back of my head, I can hear the actual ping of the first crack, the spiderwebbing immediately following as all the pieces fall, scattering like glass.

"That's why I have my passport."

"Wh-what?"

I reach over, cupping her face in my hand and wiping away her tear. "Damn thing might actually be expired now for all I know, but that's why I got it. Because I was going to follow you."

I swipe away another tear—this time on her other cheek—letting my statement sink in.

"Right after you left, I second-guessed everything. I applied for the loan and the passport on the same day, told myself whichever came through first, that was the universe's way of telling me what to do. Milo told me I was stupid, but I was so in my head about all of it, and what did he know? He was still single." Maisey chokes out a laugh, the sound beautiful even though it's strained. "Loan came through first, so I stayed, followed the plan I had put together. I figured you'd be back at Christmas, or after a year's assignment, and we could talk it out again. That you'd have worked it all out of your system. But then, you never came back. And I never heard from you. Just snippets from Dolly or your mama about how much you loved what you were doing. About how your dream was coming true. That's when I realized that I couldn't get in the way of that."

"You wouldn't have been in the way, Ewan. If I'd known..." She shakes her head, sniffling again. "We can coulda, shoulda, woulda all day. But for two people who were so close, we really sucked at communicating, huh?"

"Apparently only about the important shit."

Sputtering out a laugh, Maisey shifts, knocking the poles

as she moves. My hand juts out to stabilize them, cut off by Maisey climbing into my lap. The move is easy, succinct, and natural. My pulse starts to race as my soul eases, having my girl right where she belongs.

Maisey feels it too, the way she relaxes into me a sign that she needs this just as much. Burying her head into my neck, her breath tickles my skin with each exhale, moving in time with the waves beneath us. I drag my hand up and down her back, running my fingers along her spine, enjoying the feel of this way more than I probably should.

"New pact," she says, pulling back. Resituating in my lap, she locks her gaze with mine. "No more secrets. We use our words. All of them."

"I don't know that you want all my secrets, Mais," I joke.

"I do. I want all of them, Ewan."

"So you wanna know about how back in middle school when Jace and I finally didn't have to share a room anymore, Miss Belle found the dirty magazine I had stashed under my mattress while shuffling all our stuff around? Which led to her making Auggie take me on a drive so we could talk about it, and I don't know what I was more thankful for, that my dad was not as judgmental as I expected him to be—maybe because this was his sixth time to have such a conversation— or that I hadn't actually taped my crush's picture over the faces of one of the, errr, models like I had thought about. Because the conversation probably wouldn't have gone over quite as smoothly had they seen your face taped onto one of those women."

"Ewan!"

"You said all my secrets. Pretty sure I never told you that one."

For damn good reason too...

Maisey shakes her head, her smile still brighter than the sun at this hour, making my insides feel funny. Pretty sure admitting that truth to the beautiful woman in your lap isn't supposed to make her giggle, but mine doesn't seem fazed by it.

"As embarrassing and weird and yet, somehow oddly flattering, as that story is, I mean big ones. New ones."

I knew what she meant. I also couldn't help but take the opportunity that was right in front of me to tease her. To bring back a little bit of what made us, us. Ewan and Maisey. Her wild and free spirit and my quiet, introverted one.

"Deal," I tell her. "Do we need ketchup? Because the closest thing I've got on the boat is bait paste."

"No," she answers, shifting in my lap so that her core drags across my crotch. I bite back a groan, digging my fingers into her hips. "I'm not quite as afraid of bodily fluids as I used to be."

My dick twitches again, understanding every inch of her double meaning. For all my self-reminders to behave all morning, if there was ever a moment to seal with a kiss, this is it.

Running my hands up Maisey's body, I weave my fingers into her beautiful blonde hair, cradling her head. She lets out a sigh as I draw her in close, my pulse kicking up a notch. Our lips are a whisper away from each other, and I hear it.

The snap of the line.

Maisey and I both freeze, as if we're not sure. There's no mistaking it, though, as the rod closest to me rattles in the cup, flexing as the line pulls.

I'm on my feet in a flash, grabbing the pole and handing it to her.

"Ewan, I didn't know how to do this then, and I certainly don't know how to do this now," she tells me. "This part has never been what coming fishing with you was about."

"It is now. We're in this together."

I wrap myself around her, steadying the rod in her hands.

Whatever is on the other ends tugs again, so I guide Maisey's hand to the reel, and start to turn.

"That's it, nice and easy," I whisper directly into her ear. "Nice and easy, and then tug…"

We yank backward, the two of us working against both the fish and the water. Maisey squeaks, so I lighten my grip, whispering in her ear again. Shuddering against me, she nods, following my instructions, leaving me to wonder for a split second if that's how she likes it.

Fish, Ewan, fish…

Turning my attention back to the water, we tug harder, reeling in faster, winning the battle.

"Net!"

Maisey ducks out from under my arms, grabbing the fishing net from behind us and holding it out over the water. I give the rod one last good heave, yanking it back as hard and fast as I can, drawing the bass out with it. Maisey is right there with the net, catching the sucker to help bring him into the boat.

"Ummm, he's kinda little, isn't he?"

There is no missing the judgment in her voice, nor is there any missing the opportunity to walk straight through that door.

"Thought it wasn't about how big you are, but what you do with it that matters," I quip.

Maisey blushes, mumbling something that sounds a lot like "I wouldn't know," but she turns away from me as she says it so I can't quite tell. Despite our new pact from a moment ago, I don't want to push. Not here. Because if what I heard is correct, that's an entirely different conversation—for the both of us.

"Yes, he's smaller than average," I answer seriously, going into fishing guide mode. Giving our catch the once-over, he looks to be about ten inches, in good health, and that we're his first hook. "Which means he's still a little guy. Probably only about a year old."

"We're not going to keep him, right?"

"No, catch and release, baby." I hold out the bass, offering it out to her. "Want to drop him back in?"

"I am not touching the fish."

I laugh, slipping him back in the water, once again remembering who I am talking to. Blood, guts, and triage is perfectly fine, but no touching live fish.

The sun climbs over the horizon, the bright light a harsh reminder that we have a real life to get back to. Turning to Maisey, I pull her into me, holding her close as I tuck a piece of hair behind her ear.

"This morning didn't go how I thought it would," I say.

"Is that good or bad?"

"Good. I promise." I press my lips to her forehead. "Be mine, Maisey."

Giggling, she looks up at me, eyes glassy with tears.

"I can't imagine being anything else."

9

MAISEY

THIS IS NORMAL. Totally, totally normal. At least that's what I'm trying to tell myself. That and I don't need to stress eat about it.

It's been more than a week since we went fishing. Since Ewan asked me to be his. Since he almost kissed me on the boat. Which means it's been a little more than a week since he kissed me in the rain.

That seriously epic, straight out of the movies kiss.

And he hasn't kissed me since.

Which is totally normal, right?

We're taking it slow. We're figuring out what this is and who we are to each other again. Which is to be expected. It's what we talked about.

I stab my fork into my piece of pie, harder than I should, the tines vibrating from hitting the plate underneath. The clink catches not only me but also Dolly and Emily off guard, both of their heads snapping up to look at me across the table at Oh, My Lard!—our friend Alice's bakery. But I ignore them, too lost in my own thoughts to explain.

Because how do I explain how easily Ewan and I slipped

back into being *Ewan and Maisey*—all our old habits and idiosyncrasies coming so naturally. We're us again. And it feels good.

Actually, I take that back. It feels better than good. Feels better than it ever did before. Better than I could have ever imagined. Other than the fact that he hasn't kissed me again, which is making me a little...unsure.

I stab my pie again, this time scooping up the large bite and swallowing it without chewing.

"And just what did the chocolate Heath bar do to you?" Alice chides, cocking her hip to the side as she wanders over.

She looks me up and down, giving me the once-over, like she's considering whether or not she can trust me with the rest of my snack. To be fair, that's an honest question.

"Nothing," I mumble, shoving more in my mouth.

See, not eating my feelings at all.

There's no need to. We're not teenagers. We're adults, who are building a relationship with a solid foundation. One that doesn't require that we jump into bed with each other.

Only I *want* to jump into bed with him.

The bell over the front door tinkles, an older couple I don't recognize walking in. Alice gives me another look to tell me that she doesn't believe me before turning to go take their order.

"Now that the cabinets are installed, and the trim is done, the Scarboroughs say that it shouldn't be much longer. They think we should be able to start moving in within the next two weeks," Dolly says, clearly mid-update.

I shake my head, trying to clear the cobwebs of my thoughts and pay attention to what my friend and cousin is saying.

"It'll be so nice to finally be in our little white house!"

"I bet Gus will be glad to have you out too," Emily jokes.

Dolly laughs. "Oh yeah. He and Margeaux put Jace on countdown. Once they're married this fall, he's out."

"I've got ten bucks that says he drags his feet in finding a place so that he doesn't have to move out," Em chuckles.

"I told him my apartment was all his—'course that was before someone showed back up. Then again, that someone might be all moved into the second floor of the bank by this fall…"

Dolly's playful and teasing tone barely registers over my thoughts, everything still sounding so far away. Like they're underwater even though they're barely three feet across the table.

All moved into the second floor of the bank…ha! That's a thought. While I've spent plenty of time over at Ewan's new place—a beautiful apartment that is the entire second floor of the old Middle Georgia Bank and Trust building, bought and renovated by the Hayes family when that branch was closed after a merger—I'm a long, long way from moving in. Hell, I'm a long way from spending the night. The furthest I've gotten is some cuddles on the couch while ordering in a pizza and watching a movie. Like a very respectable pair of high school freshmen.

"What'd I miss?" Rose Adler asks brightly as she slides into the seat next to me. No, not Adler—Adams. She got married over Christmas. To the guy she got snowed in with. Only Rose…

"We're taking bets on how long until Maisey moves into the bank," Em replies, not skipping a beat.

What? No, we're not…

"Like actual bets? Money bets?" Rose clarifies. "If so, I've got twenty on the Fourth of July."

Excuse you?!

Dolly must see the panic on my face, because she reaches across the table, taking my hand. "We're kidding, Mais."

Her voice is calm and even, but does little to assuage my internal panic. My worry that Ewan's *be mine* wasn't the ask that I thought it was.

"How long was it until Hux kissed you?"

I blurt out the question like a cat hacking up a hairball. The need to know burns inside me as if it's going to eat me alive. Because somehow a little insight into the brain of one Hayes brother might shed some light into another.

Granted, of all the Hayes brothers, Hux and Ewan aren't the most alike. Then again, they aren't the most unalike either. Come to think of it, all six of them are pretty unique. So my logic might be flawed here.

"Kissed me? Or *kissed* me?" The waggle of her eyebrows doesn't leave a whole lot up for interpretation as to her meaning for her second question.

"Regular, everyday, you're my girlfriend, kissed you." I toss in a little shrug of my right shoulder, trying to play it off.

It doesn't work.

Anxiety rises up in me again, and I know that my friends see right through me. Because there is no way that it's not written all over my face—Maisey is a lovesick wreck.

Stabbing at my pie again—this time breaking off a piece of the crust—I shovel it in like it's my job. At the rate I'm going, a second piece is going to be needed. Stat.

"Things moving slower than you'd like?" Rose asks.

Sighing, I slouch back in my seat, trying to separate myself from my pie. Eating my feelings is a seriously bad habit—a vice that I've always had and have leaned into more and more since I've been away and haven't had the best support system around me—and I need to stop. This is Hickory Hills. These are my girls. Those who listen and don't judge.

"I dunno. I just…"

I just what? Want to discover if the taste of Ewan's lips

solves all of life's unanswered questions? If the feel of his hands on my body fills the gaps and cracks that I feel deep in my soul? If being with him—in that way—will be what's been missing this whole time?

Actually, yes. That is what I'm wondering.

"We're Ewan and Maisey again, and it's great. Better than great. We got it all out there and slipped back into being us again so easy. But you know what *Ewan and Maisey* never did?"

"Kissed?" Em offers up.

I point to her, signaling that she hit the answer square on the nose. "Kissed. And we've had all these little moments since that would have been perfect. Ones where I think he's going to, because it's like he starts to lean in and then he stops or something happens and we get interrupted by a fish or something and—"

"You got interrupted by a fish?" Alice asks, reappearing.

I nod, unable to help my smile thinking about the little guy and that perfect morning spent out on Silver Lake. That was our only catch of the day, the sun rising shortly after and warming everything up. But that didn't matter. It was the first step in being us again. The first step in patching up one of those cracks inside me.

"That's the most Ewan thing I've ever heard," Em says with a laugh.

"*You* could kiss *him*, you know," Dolly sasses. "It's no longer 1956, so you don't have to wait for him to make the move."

I stare back at my cousin, part of me wanting to smack the know-it-all, shit-eating grin right off her face, another part wanting to smack myself for not telling myself the same thing. Because I'm pretty sure that's the advice I gave her about asking out a guy in college.

Actually, I know it is. And the growing smirk she's wearing confirms it.

"And then, once you've put him in his place—or well, kissed him into place—you can drag him back to the bank and get what I know you really want," she continues, giving me a knowing wink.

I swallow hard, my insides clenching at the thought of Ewan's hands on me. On the two of us tumbling into his apartment, mouths fused together, not watching where we're going, knocking things over as we try to make it to the bedroom, a flurry of limbs trying to undress each other. Fuuuuuck…that's exactly what I want.

Dolly leans forward, lowering her voice, her smile turning borderline evil. "And Mais, when you get what you want, don't be quiet about it. Because I promise you, Ewan is dying to give Willa some payback."

Errrr…what?!

"Oh, you just know Ewan's got a secret dirty side to him," Rose mutters, biting her lips, her own salacious grin appearing. "It's always the quiet ones."

"Know from experience there, Rose?" Alice quips, smacking her shoulder with the back of her hand.

"Sure do."

The rest of the group laughs, but I barely register the humor, my mind still stuck on Dolly's instructions. Don't be quiet about what? And why is Ewan dying to give Willa payback? Payback for what? What is it that my friends know that I don't?

"Expand and explain," I say. "Payback for what?"

Shaking her head and laughing, Dolly sits back. "Go kiss your man."

"You're just going to hold this information hostage?"

She wouldn't. Would she?

I glare at her across the table, the temptation to reach for the pie again growing by the second. Although this time it's to throw at her. Because she would. She definitely would.

Worse, she is.

"C'mon, tell me."

"When you woman up, I will."

Uggggh....

As an only child, I never had to fight for the attention of my parents. However, with cousins like Dolly and Emily, plus their siblings, I certainly had all the push and pull that came with siblings. Even now though, I wouldn't trade it.

Looking down at my phone, I note the time, doing the math in my head. "It's already four fifteen. He's helping Chet Farlow chaperone the seventh-grade environmental science camping trip until Saturday. They are rolling out at four thirty."

"Then you better get moving," Rose challenges.

"And what? Roll into the middle school parking lot, march on up to him, climb him like a tree, and plant one on him? In front of a group of thirteen-year-olds? And their parents?"

"I'd recommend skipping the climbing him like a tree part," Emily comments. "Maybe ask if you can borrow him for a second, slip between the cars, tell him how much you're going to miss him, and then plant one on him. But, yes."

"Maybe throw in a *there's more of this when you get back*," Rose adds, waggling her eyebrows.

"You have to be kidding." I glance around the table, all four of them staring back at me expectantly. They are not kidding.

"Welcome home, Maisey," Dolly taunts.

Well...shit...

My insides tighten, the scene Emily described playing out in my mind, much like the one of us tumbling through his apartment did moments ago. Although this time, it's not just longing that it comes with. It's more. It's pure desire. Pure excitement.

A bubble bursts inside me, releasing a feeling I can't name. It's comforting, invigorating, and energizing, making me feel like I could burst into giggles and take over the world all at the same time. I haven't felt like this since…I don't even know when. A long damn time. It's the feeling of being at home mixed with the thrill of a first love and the wonder of what will come next.

Only one way to find out.

Picking up my fork, I shove the last bite of pie into my mouth as I push back from the table, not bothering to say goodbye to my friends. I'm on a mission now. A very important mission.

Ewan and I promised that this time we would communicate. We would tell each other things. I meant that promise. That means telling him how I'm feeling and what I want. It means taking matters into my owns hands if necessary.

Or my own lips, as it may be.

I'm out the door of Oh, My Lard! and down the street before I can think. I'm all muscle memory and autopilot as I make my way toward the middle school, simultaneously amped up and worried that I missed them. My worry is tamped down by my brain trying to make a game plan—attempting to work out exactly what I'm going to say when I get there. When I see him.

Pulling into the parking lot, my heart leaps as I see the caravan of charter buses lined up on the far side of the lot, groups of students and parents still milling about.

Oh, thank goodness…

I throw the car into park and launch myself out of it, running across the pavement toward where Ewan is standing talking to Chet and some of the other chaperones.

"Ewan!"

He spins around, eyes going wide, breaking away from the group and rushing over to meet me.

"Maisey."

He bends down to greet me, scooping me up in his arms and holding on tight as my feet leave the ground. I bury my face in his neck, inhaling the deep, musky scent, letting myself get lost in him. His lips press lightly against the curve of my neck, a chill rippling down my spine, and I know that I can't hold back any longer.

"I'm so glad I caught you."

"I didn't realize I needed to be caught," he jokes, setting me back down.

"You did," I pant, taking half a step back, but not letting go of him.

"And what are you going to do with me now that you caught me?"

There's a teasing lilt to his voice, as if he's issuing me a challenge. One that I'm not only accepting, but am going to demolish.

"I'm going to kiss you."

Fire flashes in Ewan's eyes, and that's all the signal I need.

Tightening my grip around his neck, I push to my toes, yanking him into me and pressing my mouth to his. Instantly, everything hushes, except for the sound of my pulse rushing through my veins. Ewan's lips are soft and strong, letting me run the show, even though he's more than capable of taking over at any point. It's an intoxicating feeling, knowing that I'm in control. One I can't get enough of.

Or maybe that's Ewan I can't get enough of. The taste of him. The feel of him against me like this. Of him holding me this tightly, in public, declaring that he's mine.

I try to deepen the kiss, seeking his tongue with mine, but I can't get the right angle. Whimpering, I try again, pushing up more on my toes, my lack of height proving to be an issue.

Ewan smiles, the curve of his lips as he continues to kiss me tickling mine, his hands moving into my hair. Leaning down, he adjusts our angle, giving me the leverage I was looking for and taking this to a whole new level.

One that I will never recover from.

Off in the distance, a whistle blows, startling me. I pull back, the real world sneaking in, reminding me where we are. Who we're around. And that we might want to behave.

"Fuuuuck, Maisey…"

1 0

EWAN

I INHALE AS DEEPLY as my lungs will let me, then try and push it a little more, still holding on to Maisey for all that she's worth. Which is my entire life—and then some. I need to get my wits about me—and calm my raging dick—because the last thing I need before leading a hundred seventh graders into the woods for three days is a raging hard-on.

Maisey seems to have other ideas though.

Wiggling in my arms, she rubs her perfect self right up against that hard-on. Fuck me. She is not fighting fair. At this rate, I'm going to be hard for this entire fucking trip.

I let out a groan, my eyes fluttering shut, saying a little prayer that there aren't a hundred plus sets of eyeballs on us.

"Are you trying to kill me?" I yank her into me, thrusting my hips forward, making sure she feels that bulge and just what she's doing to me. "Because you do know that I have to go help teach kids about the joys of nature."

She giggles, sending another zing down my spine. Seriously, she fights dirty without even trying. So unfair.

"I was just making sure you had a reason to come home on Saturday is all."

The comment is light, flirty, and I can tell it's meant to elicit a certain reaction. But there's more to it. There's something underneath that tone that tells me this wasn't just some flirty nothing.

Locking my eyes with her, I hold her gaze for a beat, making sure she knows that she has my full and complete attention. That she has all of me. Despite the chaos surging in this parking lot.

"I already had every reason to come home. What would make you think otherwise?"

That pretty shade of pink tinges across her cheeks, Maisey's eyes flicking away for a second.

"Because you hadn't kissed me since that night in the rain. Even though you asked me to be yours, you haven't made another move. So, I wanted to make sure you knew that you can. That you should. Unless you're rethinking things."

In true Maisey form, her resolve never falters. Her voice is steady, calm, and even. The brief flicker in her blue eyes gives her away, however. The one you'd never catch unless you knew to look. And after all these years, I know to look.

"I'm not rethinking anything, beautiful," I reassure her, pressing my lips softly to her forehead. "I will admit to holding back though. Because I've been afraid if I kissed you again, I wouldn't stop. I almost didn't stop that night. Fuck, even stopping now, when I know we have a massive underage audience, damn near killed me."

Maisey lets out a single chuckle, her cheeks tingeing an even deeper pink.

"More than anything, I don't want you to think that I don't respect you. That this is about something other than being your man, your partner. It was a ketchup pact, not a condom pact."

Throwing her head back, Maisey lets out a loud roar of laughter. It rolls through her whole body, the infectious sound working its way into me, until I can't hold it in either. I didn't mean for it to be that funny.

Sucking in a breath to control herself, she looks up at me. "Ewan, I am not opposed to you respectfully disrespecting me."

Well then…

Unable to hold back my smirk, the corner of my mouth tilts in response. Because if that's what my girl wants, then it is game on. Instantly, my pulse kicks up a couple of notches, my brain flooded with all sorts of naughty thoughts—the kinds of things I've only fantasized about over the years. Things that now have the potential to be a reality.

"Mais—"

I'm cut off by a scream. A high-pitched, ear-splitting scream. The kind that makes your blood run cold and you feel down deep in your bones, echoing through them as if some kind of weird muscle memory.

That sound is more than enough to cool my ardor, sending the hairs on the back of my neck straight up. It also sends Maisey into high alert.

She's out of my arms faster than Superman's speeding bullet, her trauma nurse spidey senses clearly tingling, every alarm bell in her head sounding at full blast. Head whipping around, she zeros in on the source of horror as another scream rings out.

I watch as a group of kids gather round, Maisey sprinting across the lot like she's trying out for the Olympics. Following as fast as I can—not nearly as quick as her—I fight my way through the group trying to give her enough room to do whatever it is she's going to need to do.

Then I see who it is.

Little Kendall Farlow, Chet's daughter, is on the ground wailing, big fat tears streaming down her cheeks as she clutches her arm. My insides tighten, the shrieking toddler an overwhelming sight.

"Hey there," Maisey coos, kneeling down beside her. "Hi, I'm Maisey. Can you tell me your name?"

Kendall screams again, rolling away from Maisey, which lands her on the side of her hurt arm. When that results in more pain, she lets out another ear-piercing sound and rocks back into the same position.

"It hurts, I know," Maisey continues. "But I'm a nurse, and I'm here to help. But I need to know your name first."

"It's Kendall," I say, trying to help.

Maisey turns around, giving me a look that says *thank you* and *not helpful* all at the same time. "Ewan, will you help push everyone back? Give Kendall and me some room to breathe?"

Her voice is still that same steady, calm, and even as it was earlier, but this time, there's an *I mean business* tone to it. She's in nurse mode. I do as she says, moving everyone back, telling them there's nothing to see, and making them move over to where the buses are. We should be leaving soon anyway.

Or well, maybe not now that Chet's kid is hurt.

"Your name is Kendall?" Maisey asks, the sweetness back in her voice as she returns to the toddler. Chet and his wife, Kate, both push past me, running over to be next to their daughter. "That's a pretty name. Can you tell me where it hurts, Kendall?"

Stepping away for a moment, I dial the local emergency number, dispatching our paramedic team. I trust that if this truly needed a full-on 911 call, Maisey would have hollered that instruction at me, so our local team should be able to do the trick.

Then I make one more call. Because there is someone else who is going to want to see this.

Turning back to the scene, I find little Kendall sitting in

Kate's lap, her cheeks still bright red and eyes still puffy, but her tears dried up for now. Maisey is kneeling down in front of her, a toddler arm carefully balanced in her hand, examining it the best she can. All while gently and calmly reassuring Kendall.

I'm mesmerized by the sight. By the way she took charge, without hesitation or question. Just ran across the parking lot, started barking orders, and went into boss mode. All while comforting her patient. This might just be the most impressive thing I've ever seen.

I can't imagine what she'd be like if there'd been actual bloodshed.

Somewhere in the background I hear the sirens, but they barely register. I'm too taken by watching my girl in action. Watching how she's completely owning the moment.

"So, why did you need us?" Landon Noble, assistant fire chief and lead paramedic asks, laughing as he sidles up to me. "Seems like Maisey has this completely under control."

"Because Maisey doesn't have her medic bag!" she calls over her shoulder, semi-sarcastically referring to herself in third person. "Which makes it kinda hard to fashion a splint and sling."

"That's fair," Landon responds, stepping in and handing her his.

I hang back, laughing at her response and that she is taking absolutely zero prisoners here. Had you asked me ten minutes ago, I would have told you that I didn't think I could love Maisey Phillips any more than I already did. But watching her like this is proving me wrong. Because I am falling for her even harder now.

"So...her local certs current?" Landon whispers, leaning into me.

I look at him, blinking hard. I actually have no idea.

"They are," a deep, booming voice says from behind us.

It's not loud enough for anyone but Landon and me to hear, but there's no mistaking it. Especially since it belongs to the other person I called. Spinning around, I nod at Fire Chief Phillips, Maisey's dad, taking in his proud smile as he watches his daughter.

"It's part of what is required for the company that she contracts with," he continues. "She has to maintain accreditations in at least one state in her home country. So she is one hundred percent legal to practice as a nurse paramedic in the state of Georgia."

Damn, that's good to know.

"Does that have any bearing on…" I trail off, gesturing to what's happening in front of us. My mouth goes dry, worry creeping up that this could have gone wrong if she hadn't been licensed.

"Oh no," Landon says. "Her jumping in to help until we got here, regardless of any kind of medical training, is covered under the Good Samaritan law. It's more that I'm short an EMT. Having a fully licensed nurse paramedic at the ready almost seems too good to be true. Think she'd be willing to help out while she's here?"

"You'd have to ask her," I tell him. "I don't speak for her."

"No, but I bet you could convince her to say yes," Chief Phillips chimes in.

Errrr…

I swallow hard, not sure what her father is implying. Nor am I sure I want to know. He and I have always gotten along, but then again, that was before my status changed with his daughter. Fuck, I don't even know if he knows that my status has changed with his daughter. I might need to address that.

"Chief, I—"

"I should head out before she sees me," he says, cutting me off. "Ewan, we should do lunch next week."

Oh, he knows…

"Yes, sir."

He turns on his heel with a nod, disappearing as quickly as he appeared.

"Okay, hard to really know anything without X-rays, so a trip to Tifton is in your immediate future," Maisey says, pushing to her feet. Kate rises with her, holding Kendall on her hip. "Judging by what I can feel, I have no doubt something is broken. It's just a matter of what and how broken."

"Just what we need," Kate sighs.

"Could be worse. At least it's not her face," Maisey jokes.

"Very true."

"Give me a few minutes to find a replacement chaperone and—" Chet starts.

"Nope," Kate cuts him off. "You go. This is the highlight of your year, taking these kids out on this thing. We'll be fine. It's only a couple of days."

"I'll go with you to the hospital, if that'll help," Maisey offers.

"See? We're all good. Get the kids in the buses and into the woods," Kate instructs.

Chet looks to me and shrugs. "You heard the woman."

"I sure did."

We gather everyone up again, starting a new round of goodbyes with parents. This time it's faster, at least a little bit, since most of the bags are already loaded.

Wandering over to Maisey, I gather her in my arms, trying to sneak in one more kiss before we take off.

"That was the most impressive thing I've ever witnessed," I tell her, capturing her lips with mine. "Serious fucking turn-on."

"If that does it for you, you should see me when someone needs stitches."

"Don't tease me; I just got my dick calmed down."

Maisey giggles, kissing me thoroughly, and I'm hard all over again. So much for that.

"We're back Saturday. See you then?"

"Without question."

I lean in, kissing her one more time. It's risky, all the kids around, but I don't care. The floodgates have been opened and there's no going back. She's an addiction—a habit I don't want to break.

"Ewan!"

Now, that's a voice I wasn't expecting.

Maisey and I step back, turning in unison to face my mother.

Where did she come from?!

"Mama…"

I know that I am a fully grown man and I have done nothing wrong—okay, *almost* nothing wrong—but I still can't help but feel like a little kid who was caught with his hand in the cookie jar and is about to get that hand slapped.

"Don't y'all have the environmental science trip?"

"We got a bit delayed because Kendall Farlow took a tumble," I say.

"Oh, I hope she's okay."

"She is," Maisey adds. "Likely a broken elbow, but overall, not world ending. Speaking of, I should probably head to Tifton. Kate's already left and I told her I'd meet her at the ER."

Right. Well, now this is awkward. Because I one hundred percent want to kiss her goodbye—for the fourth time this afternoon—but my mother is standing *right here*. Sure, my parents are the least prudish people on this earth, never shying away from a little PDA themselves, happily being the model for a healthy marriage not only for my siblings and me but for all of Hickory Hills. But that doesn't mean I want to kiss the woman I'm newly…*with*…in front of her just yet.

Fuck.

Maisey, however, apparently doesn't think twice. Pressing up onto her toes, she presses a quick kiss to my lips.

"See you Saturday."

"Oh good, then you'll be home for Sunday dinner," Miss Belle says. Then, not skipping a beat, she adds, "Ewan, why hasn't Maisey made an appearance at Sunday dinner yet?"

Nicely placed guilt trip, Mama...

"She will on Sunday. Promise."

"Perfect! Maisey, I'll give you a call and we can do lunch while he's out camping."

"Sounds good," Maisey says. "But I should go—don't want to leave Kate waiting."

I grab her hand and steal another kiss before she turns and runs to her car. Miss Belle gives me a knowing look that I choose to ignore, opting to go with a simple, respectful nod to excuse myself to my assigned bus.

Ten minutes later, we're finally on the road, the wild teenage chatter surrounding me fading into the background as I think about the events of this afternoon. About how amazing that kiss was. How amazing Maisey was. And just how much I want to make sure I do everything I can to make sure she stays in Hickory Hills.

Pulling out my phone, I notice the little text icon, wondering how I missed it.

MAISEY

Sunday dinner? As a girlfriend?

I chuckle, quickly tapping out a response. Because there's only one thing to say to that.

Welcome to the family, baby

11

MAISEY

"I can't show up empty-handed to Sunday dinner!"

The wave of panic grows as I pace around Ewan's kitchen, opening and closing the cabinets in search of something I can throw together. But it's Old Mother Hubbard's cupboard up in here. I know he was out of town for a good portion of this week, but damn.

I maybe should have realized this last night. But I was too caught up in listening to Ewan's stories from the trip to focus on anything else. To the point where I fell asleep on the couch and had to be carried to bed.

"Except, you can?" Ewan replies sleepily, stretching as he pads into the kitchen from the bathroom. "The rest of us do."

I huff out an exaggerated sigh, whipping around to bring him into my meltdown, needing him to understand the thought process that has me up and going a million miles an hour this morning, but the sight of him stops me dead in my tracks. He didn't bother to put on a shirt, showing off his bare chest, the smattering of light hair across his pecs almost shimmering in the overhead kitchen lights, while his pajama pants hang low on his hips, more of that light blonde hair trailing south. My mouth goes dry, the ability to think completely disappearing from my skillset. I know I slept next to this magnificence last night, but seeing it on display like this first thing in the morning is something else entirely.

Stepping into me, Ewan places his hands on my hips, kissing me softly, letting it linger, like this is our every Sunday morning. A lazy morning of sleeping in after staying up too late the night before doing God knows what and then hanging out in our pajamas until it's time to head to Magnolia Manor. A girl could get used to this.

"Maybe *you* do," I tell him, easing back from the kiss. He runs his hands up my sides, dipping them under my tank top, the calluses on his hands rough against my skin, sending a shiver through me. Or maybe that's just Ewan's touch in general. "But this is my first one as…as…"

I trail off. I said the word the other day in a text, but saying it out loud feels different. Heavier. Official.

"My girlfriend?" Ewan finishes for me, his version of the infamous Hayes smirk taking over.

"Yeah, that."

I pull away, starting my whirlwind search over again. There's got to be something in this kitchen that I can whip up. Even if it's basic. Actually, it's going to have to be basic based on what I'm seeing. That and it's already—

Oh shit, it's noon. How the hell did we sleep until noon?

Oh, that's right, we were up until the wee hours with Ewan entertaining me with stories from spending three days in the woods with seventh graders.

Still, we have to be there at his parents' in a couple of hours, and neither of us have showered. I should have taken care of this earlier in the week. Should have thought of this sooner. This is what I get for never having actually been someone's girlfriend—my etiquette game is severely lacking.

The women in my family would be horribly disappointed if they were to ever find out.

"Maisey," Ewan says, his voice deep and rugged, yet soothing in a way that makes my body react instantly. "The wheels in your head are moving way too fast. What's with the freak-out?"

"I'm not freaking out," I defend, not bothering to look at him.

Instead, I continue to dig. I pull what I can from the pantry, turning and placing it all out on the large marble countertop of the island that separates the kitchen from the living room. A jar of peanut butter, powdered sugar, graham crackers, and a bag of chocolate chips—that's about all I've got to work with. But, it's enough. Peanut butter bars it is.

"Yes, you are."

Coming up behind me, Ewan wraps himself around me, burying his face in my neck, nipping at the skin. I moan, leaning back into him, giving in to his warmth and the feel of him as his hands roam around my front, up under the hem of my tank. One hand remains still, fingers toying with the top of my sleep shorts, holding me against him while the other heads north, straight for my breast.

Heat flushes through me, anticipation taking over as a callused hand cups my breast, the tip of his fingers circling my nipple. I let out an involuntary moan, ready for more. Fingertips continue to circle, my nipple pebbling under his touch. I arch my back, trying to silently direct him to where I want him.

Then he stops.

"Talk to me, baby."

I shudder out a sigh, resting my head against his bare chest, letting the safety of his arms surround me for a moment longer. A warm and comforting bubble that I never want to leave.

I spin around to face him, leaning against the counter. "I had lunch with the Hayes women on Friday."

"You did?"

I nod. "Miss Belle was not kidding when she said we were gonna do lunch while you were away. I thought she meant the two of us, but then I got to Dolly's and found a table for seven."

"You were ambushed."

"I sure was. But it was…" I stare into his beautiful blue eyes, letting myself hold on to them, wishing I could go swimming in that perfect shade. "It was so much fun. They are the most impressive group of women. And each one of them seems like the perfect counterpart to your brothers. I mean, I knew Hux and Dolly were a great pair; we've always known that. But..like, Margeaux? She might just be the smartest woman I have ever met. Did you know that she has an MBA *and* a law degree?"

Ewan nods, smiling. He leans in, tightening his hands on my hips. "If you only knew how close Gus came to missing out on her. Might be the only woman on this planet willing to put up with his grumpy ass."

"I knew Brenna had taken over as town pharmacist for Mr. Hovland, but I didn't realize she'd bought the whole business from him. She's twenty-seven and a business owner! In my mind she's still that little tween girl who got all moony-eyed whenever Milo came around."

"She still gets moony-eyed over Milo. Only now he gets moony-eyed in return, and it's nauseating. I suggest giving them a wide berth."

"And Sawyer?" I continue to ramble, ignoring Ewan's quip about his second oldest brother. "Also scary smart. And quick on her feet. I bet she gives Anton a run for his money."

"That she does. You'll get to see it in action this afternoon. It's more than worth the price of admission, I promise."

"That price being not showing up empty-handed," I reiterate, the nerves resurfacing. "It's rude."

"The price is you, being you."

Strong fingers dig into my hips, Ewan's mouth capturing mine in a hot, hard kiss. It's the kind of kiss that fantasies are made of—all fervor and passion, erasing your mind and making you want more. My limbs move independently from me, toes pushing me up closer to him, while my hands desperately try to hold on to his biceps. The graze of his teeth along my bottom lip sends me reeling, another involuntary moan escaping as I try even harder to close the already imperceptible distance between us.

"Somehow, I don't think it's my sisters-in-law that have you all worked up," he whispers, kissing along my jaw toward my ear. "Or Sunday dinner."

"No, right now that would be you."

"Is that so?" he growls, slipping a hand down the backside of my shorts and palming my ass. "Because I'm pretty sure what I'm doing is calming you down."

I open my mouth to argue. To tell him no, this is absolutely getting me worked up—and wet—and if he's not careful, this conversation is going to take a turn, but the graze of his teeth on my earlobe stops me. His strong hands knead my flesh, and I am putty in his hands. I'm ready to confess all my sins, including exactly what has me in a tizzy this morning.

Because Ewan's right. It's more than simple manners and etiquette for showing up to Sunday dinner.

It's the shift I felt this week. The unknown thing inside me that woke up one morning and didn't feel quite as much like the outsider anymore. And that baby step I took to maybe making Hickory Hills home again. To putting my roots back into the ground.

"I-I want this," I stutter.

Moving his hand from my ass around to my front, Ewan

slips it between my legs, running a single finger through my wetness. I shiver, the feel of him there so overwhelming I can barely breathe. And all he did was take a single swipe. Didn't even get close to my clit.

Holy shit...

"That's very clear, baby," he whispers, nipping at my neck.

"No, not this," I pant, my thoughts trying to catch up. "I mean, yes, this. But, also, the big this. Ketchup pact this."

Ewan grins—a cheesy, overexcited child on Christmas morning grin—fire flashing in his eyes. His hand moves again, swiping me once more, again avoiding my clit, but still managing to send a rip of pleasure through me. Then, it's gone.

Hand quickly removed from my shorts, Ewan is holding on to my hips and lifting me up onto the counter in the blink of an eye. I squeak, the movement catching me by surprise. More than that, the new, darker shade of his eyes drives me wild.

"Landon has an opening on his emergency response team, and asked if I'd be interested in filling in for however long I'm in town. I told him yes."

The words tumble out of me, like dice out of the cup while playing Yahtzee. I keep my answer simple, same as I did with Landon. I'm not ready to say the real words out loud yet, even to Ewan. They're big and scary and if something changes, I don't know that either of us can go through that hurt again. But right now, I know what both my head and my heart are telling me.

I'm not leaving here any time soon...

"Good girl," Ewan growls, his eyes going even darker, his grip tightening on my hips as he yanks me forward.

My body betrays me. Lust rips down my spine, those two words evoking a very different meaning in this moment.

Doing exactly what he wanted them to do, making me instantly wet.

"Y-y-you don't seem surprised," I choke out, as teeth graze along my collarbone, halting my thoughts in place.

Ewan reaches for the hem of my tank, lifting it over my head, the cool air hitting my skin making me shiver. Or maybe that's him and the way he's looking at me. Like I'm the last cupcake at the picnic and he hasn't eaten in a week.

"Landon asked if your credentials were still active in Georgia while we watched you work your magic with Kendall. I told him he needed to talk to you."

Dipping his head to my breast, he takes my nipple into his mouth, running his tongue along the taut peak.

"Ohhhhhh…"

The strangled sound is out of me so fast, I don't know if it's in response to what he said or what he's doing, but at this point it doesn't matter. I am all his.

"Watching you like that…how you didn't hesitate, taking charge, barking orders at everyone around you, but then were so soft and sweet and gentle with Kendall…fuuuuck, Maisey, it was the sexiest thing I've ever seen…" Ewan's hands glide up my thighs, his mouth still laving at my breasts, and it's all I can do to concentrate on what he's saying. "I was already having a hard enough time holding back. But after watching you like that, I spent half that camping trip thinking about all the dirty things I wanted to do to you when I got back."

"I told you, you have my permission to be disrespectful."

A deep rumble erupts from Ewan's chest, vibrating through me as he lets my nipple go with a pop. A quick yank and he pulls down my shorts, capturing my surprise with a hot, hard kiss. One that has me all but begging for more.

"Oh, we'll get to that, baby," Ewan whispers into our kiss.

"But right now, I want one thing, and one thing only. To show you exactly how much I want you."

I don't have time to think—I barely have time to breathe—before Ewan drops to his knees, pulling my shorts down the rest of the way. Pushing my knees apart, he settles in between them, kissing his way up my thighs, alternating sides, his fresh morning stubble scratchy against my skin.

"You have no idea how badly I've been craving a taste of this pussy."

My insides clench with anticipation and desire. No one has ever said anything so deliciously dirty to me, leaving me feeling so wanted and so beautiful at the same time. I want to respond, but am not sure I can find the words, my mind filled with nothing but the sound of my heartbeat thrumming through my veins.

"Then what are you waiting for?"

Ewan smirks, looking up at me, his eyes locking on mine. They're dark, hooded, and filled with a deep intensity, almost as if I had issued him a challenge. A personal one that he has no intention of backing down from.

Eyes still holding mine, not wavering for a second, Ewan grasps ahold of my thighs and runs his tongue the length of me, flicking my clit as he finishes. And then he does it again.

"Fuuuuuck!"

A new, blinding pleasure tears through me, like a hot knife through butter, consuming me. I throw my head back and try to grab on to the countertop, but can't find anything to hold on to. Ewan doesn't stop though, continuing the same motion, then following it up by circling up one side or down the other, keeping me on the edge each time he changes his rhythm.

"You like that, baby?" he asks, doing it again. It's all I can do to moan out a yes, incoherent as it may be. "What if I do this?"

He switches it up, circling my clit with his tongue, stealing my breath for a second.

"Gah!"

"Mmmmm-hmmmmm…"

He chuckles, sending vibrations through me, and I'm done.

I'm nothing but a puddle of moans and purrs as he licks, sucks, and nibbles at me, each new movement, each new flick of his tongue, an adventure all on its own. Each turning me on more and more, keeping me on the very edge. Like that coin game at the old-school arcades with the bar that keeps pushing and pushing, but nothing ever falling.

That's what I feel like right now.

Right there on the edge, but never tumbling.

Every one of my nerve endings is standing up, ready to fire at will. But Ewan somehow knows how to play my body perfectly, keeping me right there.

"You are so fucking sweet, Maisey," he murmurs, moving his thumb to my clit and slowly circling it, drawing out the teasing even more.

"Ewan…" I plead.

I can't take much more. Every inch of me feels like it's on fire and is about to explode. I need to know how I get to—

Ewan slides two fingers inside me, his tongue zeroing in on my clit at the same time. My vision goes hazy and I slam my eyes shut, my voice disappearing as I try to scream. I move—or at least I think I do—the feel of Ewan inside me too much and not enough at the same time, his fingertips brushing along a spot that makes me go dizzy. He does it again, tapping that same spot, and I see stars.

"Fuck!"

White-hot pleasure shreds through me. I detonate, pure euphoria taking over, and I swear that I leave my body for second, Ewan keeps working my body over, not leaving me for a single second.

I have no idea how long it takes me to return, my head still fuzzy and my heart beating faster than should be possible, as I slowly open my eyes. Kissing his way back down my thighs, Ewan pushes back up to his feet, peppering even more kisses along my bare tummy and along my chest before sitting me up and kissing me properly.

Wrapping my arms around his neck, I savor him, tasting myself on his lips. In my new blissed out state, I'm falling even harder for this man than ever before. Not because of what he just did to me—although that won't be held against him—but for all the things he said before. For how he sees me for me, respecting my choice of profession, and is here for it. Considering this is someone who knows almost all my secrets, that's saying something.

"Ewan," I murmur, burying my head in his shoulder.

Pulling me into him, he wraps his arms around me in a bear hug, his warmth enveloping me.

"Yeah, baby?"

"I still can't show up empty-handed. Not the first time." I pull back, fighting a smile as I look at him. "My mama and Grandma would never let me hear the end of it."

Ewan chuckles, kissing me softly. "Understood. Let's go shower and then we can swing by Wright's on the way over. Sound good?"

"Are we conserving water?" I ask, trying to be cute.

"Oh, there will be none of that," Ewan goes serious. "I have plans for you in the shower too."

"Oh?"

Ewan winks, lifting me off the counter and walking toward the bathroom.

"Yup."

12

EWAN

Okay, I lied.

This definitely feels different from Sunday dinner before. Even with Maisey. But...why? We've done this. Lots. This shouldn't feel weird. She's Maisey. My person. The one who has always belonged in the chair next to me at that table.

"Told you..." she whispers in a sing-song tone, looking up at me through her side-eye.

Her ability to read my mind is only half comforting in this moment, since it does little to ease this weirdness. At least I know we're in it together. The way it should be.

I side-eye her back, pausing on the top stair of my parents' front porch long enough to steal a kiss under the umbrella I'm holding. She told me all right. And I'm man enough to not argue about it.

Taking her hand, I don't bother to knock, letting ourselves in like we own the place. A low hum of voices wafts through the air, the welcome vibrations surrounding us like a warm hug, letting us know that all is right. Something inside me clicks, settling the unease that has started to rise, the muscles in my back releasing as I exhale.

"Why, Maisey, you are practically glowing!" my father announces, sauntering down the stairs. "Y'all must have had quite the morning."

And we're back to things being weird...

The plastic container of store-bought brownies crunches under Maisey's grip, her fingers reflexively tightening as her face flushes. Auggie doesn't seem to notice the weirdness in the air thanks to him unknowingly calling us out though, continuing his jaunt to cross the room in as few strides as possible, wrapping my girl in a dad-like bear hug, clearly thinking nothing about his comment.

"It's so good to have you home, darlin'."

It's good to have her home...

I sigh, watching Maisey relax into his embrace, returning the squeeze, my own insides doing the same thing, enjoying the moment. Because this is how it's supposed to be. Or at least how I always thought it was. In high school I wouldn't have thought twice about walking into this house with Maisey, my parents giving her a hug. Now, I'm savoring the moment.

Still, can't let the old man have all the fun.

"That's enough, Dad," I say, nudging him gently with my shoulder. "You're making it weird."

"I'm doing no such thing," he defends. "Can't a man hug his favorite girl?"

"Mama's in the kitchen," I retort, not skipping a beat.

Maisey giggles and quickly covers her mouth, trying to hide her allegiance. My insides squeeze again, that beautiful sound going straight to my groin, making me have to fight the urge to kiss her. If I start that again, I know I won't stop.

"Well now, Maisey, I think someone is jealous..." Auggie tsks.

Another giggle escapes as she lets go, moving from my father to me and wrapping her arms around me. Wordlessly, she rests her head against my chest and there's no fighting my smile at this point. Or my automatic reaction of pulling her in closer and pressing my lips to the top of her head.

This is right where she belongs.

"He missed you," Auggie whispers, winking at Maisey.

"Dad."

I groan, unable to hold it back. Not that his statement is untrue, but does he really need to rat me out like that? He could at least pretend to be on my side. Then again, it's no secret to men in this family that Auggie likes his daughters-in-love—as he's recently taken to calling them—more than he does his actual sons.

"I think I missed him more."

Fuck, yes...

The front door opens, stealing our attention—or better yet, taking the attention off us—as Milo and Brenna walk into the house.

"Are those brownies?" Milo asks, taking the container from her.

"Yeah," Maisey admits sheepishly, the tinge in her cheeks deepening. "I felt like it would be rude to show up empty-handed. I planned on making something, but..."

She trails off, and I can see the words get caught in her throat. But what?

But Ewan spread me out on the kitchen counter and made me his meal instead? Licked me like he was searching for the center of the Tootsie Pop? All until I saw stars and screamed his name? Never mind what we got up to in the shower afterward.

Damn right she's glowing...

I tell my brothers a lot, but that might be a bridge too far.

"Whatever the reason, I'll eat them." Milo shrugs, busting open the container and heading to the kitchen.

"Milo!" Brenna scolds.

"Someone's got to before Dolly sees."

"Before Dolly sees what?" comes a voice from the kitchen. Dolly's voice to be specific.

My sister-in-law's bright, bubbly, blonde head pops around the corner, her eyes going wide in an instant. Like a homing pigeon, she narrows in on the store-bought goods, their artificial goodness sending out radio waves alerting her to their presence.

"Are you really eating that in my home?"

"No," Milo mumbles with a mouthful of brownie.

"I don't remember anyone dying and making you matriarch. Or you taking over this house," Jace hollers from the couch on the other side of the great room that blends into the kitchen. We make our way toward the group, cautiously joining the fray. "Wouldn't that be Margeaux anyway, once she marries Gus?"

"When it comes to food, I relinquish that power to Dolly," Margeaux comments from over toward the stove.

"See," Dolly claps back.

"I'm not touching that," I mutter, loud enough for only Maisey to hear as we join the group.

Gus, Hux, and Jace are seated on the couch and love seat, not paying attention to the baseball game they have turned on the TV, while Miss Belle and Margeaux move about the kitchen working on something. Dolly, looking like she just stepped out of a cooking magazine in her jeans, blouse, and frilly blue seersucker apron, smiles at us as she walks back to join them, nodding at Sawyer sitting at the counter, Anton standing behind her, holding up her end of the bargain of staying out of the way.

Shaking my head, I let go of Maisey, giving her hand a squeeze as I nod to the fridge, silently asking if she wants a drink. She nods, taking a seat next to Sawyer, and it's like something inside me clicks. My insides swell, suddenly feeling very full as I take it all in. Everything about the scene feels exactly as it should be. Despite the gross, wet, rainy weather outside—or maybe because of it—everything in here is warm, sunshiny, and light.

This is what I want. I just hope it's truly what Maisey wants as well.

"Milo," Miss Belle says, looking up at my second oldest brother.

He stops, brownie midway to his mouth, still not bothering to look guilty. Dolly chuffs, shaking her head. Maisey hold up her hands in surrender, ready to take the blame. But Miss Belle cuts her off.

"Are you helping support someone new?"

"Huh?" he mumbles, mouth full.

"Your shirt. That's not one of your brands. Is that a friend's place? Someone local? I haven't heard you mention them."

I turn to look at Milo's shirt, taking a moment to fully read the logo over his heart. When he walked in, I didn't think twice about it—simply assumed it was a Southern Brothers shirt and that was that. But now that I look at it— the perfect cerulean color of the shirt, with the massive circular logo, a large, overflowing barrel of apples in the center, with the words Cummins Cider around it—that isn't a Southern Brothers brand. In fact, I've never heard of Cummins Cider.

Cummins Cider.

Come inside her.

O..M...F...G

I choke on my laugh, trying to stop myself, immediately turning to the fridge so my mama doesn't see. Milo has always been the sassy brother and loves his punny, borderline inappropriate shirts. But that one...wow. He's brave to wear that one in this house.

"No, Mama, it's..."

"Cummins Cider," Miss Belle says. "Cumm—"

She stops short, the smile on her face slamming on its brakes faster than a car who just passed a cop while going sixty in a thirty.

"Milo Jasper Hayes!"

"Oh, triple named!" Anton exclaims from across the room.

"It's funny!" Milo defends. "Brenna bought it for me."

Miss Belle turns to Brenna, wide-eyed at first, like she can't believe that this beautiful young woman would ever do such a thing. Then, a split second later, she softens, knowing exactly who her child is, and that he found his perfect match in said brunette.

"For the love of all things, you two…" She sighs. "Just do not wear it any place that someone will see."

Milo shrugs, as if he may or may not heed our mother's warning.

"Cummins Cider. They related to Dickens Cider?" Jace asks, pushing up off the couch and walking over to the fridge.

I grab a couple of Cokes, handing him one, then cross the kitchen to join Maisey. Without thinking, my smart-ass response bubbles up.

"All part of the same pub crawl."

"Oh!" Milo exclaims, giving me a high five. We laugh, the two of us already able to feel our mother's eyes rolling behind us, tired of our shenanigans.

"A pub crawl you've never been on," Anton quips.

Shots fired.

I freeze, a sharp chill shooting down my back at my older brother's clapback. As the instigator of the family, Anton's always been right there to push everyone's buttons and have some kind of comment about something. Very little is off-limits when it comes to what he won't tease us about, but in the months since he met Sawyer, he's toned it down quite a bit. Part of me likes to think it's because he's grown up some, or maybe it's that he learned his lesson after losing the bet that his stupid mouth got him into in the first place.

Then he does something like this.

A hush falls over the room, no one seeming to know how to react to that comment. No, that's not true—they're all waiting on me. So I do the only thing I can think of.

I flip him the bird. With both hands.

It's a cliché response, but it's all I got right now. The rest of me is too busy trying to tamp down an insecurity I didn't realize I had. Something that hadn't even occurred to me to be worried about. Until now.

I swallow hard, maintaining my outward composure so that no one has any idea that internally I'm a little freaked out. That a perfectly normal, brotherly insult would send me reeling.

I look to Maisey, our eyes locking, and that's when I see it —her question.

Shit.

Despite what my brother's comeback implies, I'm not totally inexperienced. My list of experiences and partners is just short. Really, really short. And there's nothing wrong with that.

Unless the woman you love has been all over the world and potentially has had all sorts of international lovers who probably know a myriad of incredible sex tricks you don't.

Maybe I didn't blow her mind as much as I thought this morning...

"You're not really my type," he replies, pulling me back into the moment.

"Knock it off. What'd he do to you?" Sawyer smacks him with the back of her hand, before giving Maisey a nod.

I smile, liking that those two have already formed a bond.

Rounding the counter, I hand Maisey her Coke, the insecure voice in my head still whispering away. My sexual history was never going to be a secret from her—I don't plan to have any secrets when it comes to Maisey—but it had never occurred to me until this moment that I might not live up to her expectations.

I turn to go join my brothers on the couch, but Maisey grabs my wrist, stopping me. Her brow furrows, those beautiful blue eyes going a shade deeper, as her mouth turns downward, her silent question as loud as can be. I shake my head, trying to just as silently communicate back to her that it's nothing, but she's not having it.

Tightening her grip on my wrist, she pulls me into her. "What did Anton mean?"

"Nothing." I shake my head again. "He's being Anton. That hasn't changed either. Still an instigating shit."

She doesn't believe me—not fully—but lets it go anyway, understanding that if she's going to get me to talk about it, this isn't the place. Letting go, she presses her lips together and nods.

My chest tightens, all the happy, sunshiny feelings from earlier slipping into the background. Really, I shouldn't let this get to me. It was a stupid, offhand comment. Anton has made a thousand over the years. I'm sure he's probably forgotten he's made it by now. Hell, it was this kind of comment that forced him into the bet with Hux, and subsequently the rest of us, resulting in him asking out Sawyer. He came out of that one smelling like roses—eventually—but only after he stepped in it. A couple of times.

There is no reason I should let him get to me now.

"So, The Booby Trap," Gus says, as I plop down on the couch.

Errr...what?!

I look at him quizzically, wondering if I missed part of a

conversation that he's circling back to. Knowing Gus, I might have. All business, all the time, he's probably been talking shop while the rest of us were laughing at the T-shirt.

"What about it?"

"You're still the sole owner."

I continue to stare at him. Stating facts about my own business to me is not having a conversation. Especially facts that I'm proud of. My share of the family money I was gifted at graduation was used for renovation and expansion. And my loan? I was able to pay it off in a fraction of the loan term, so I now own the store outright, and business is booming. All this also means it doesn't fully fall under the Hayes Industries umbrella, a fact that drives Gus absolutely insane.

"I think we really need to seriously discuss bringing it into the fold and making it an official part of the company."

And there it is…

"Things are fine as they are," I insist.

I take a long swig of my soda, trying to focus on the game. I look over at Hux, who is watching his new wife intently, a shit-eating grin on his face. Won't be getting any backup from him—got it.

"You need to think long term, Ewan. About what happens when…" He gestures with his hand, like I should follow his thought process. Only, I don't.

"When what?"

"When Maisey leaves again."

His words hit me like a bullet. If my footing hadn't started to feel a little wobbly thanks to Anton's stupid comment, this would be more than enough to do it. As it is, this knocks me on my ass. Good thing I'm already sitting.

When Maisey leaves again...

Not *if,* but *when.* Like it's a foregone conclusion. Something that will happen.

My stomach churns, the room spinning as I work to find some kind of response. In my lack of one, Gus continues.

"If you go with, who's going to run the store? Is it going to be protected? If it's under Hayes, then you've got us to make sure that—"

"Really, dude?" Hux cuts in. Okay, maybe I do have support from him.

"All I'm saying is, we should have a plan for when Maisey leaves again."

I reach down deep, ready to pull out a response. One to tell him to just knock it off. That we are not having this discussion. Especially not at Sunday dinner. But then from behind me comes a voice that cuts through me like the sharpest razor blade there is. One that does all my dirty work for me.

"Sorry, boys. Can't get rid of me that easy."

13

MAISEY

As much as I wish there was a record scratch or time came crashing to a stop with my comment, it doesn't. I mean, it was good, but it wasn't that good.

Still, it was enough to leave Gus dumbstruck. Not something you see every day.

"I thought Ewan said you're back in town because your contract was canceled," he rebuts, as if that's some kind of argument.

"It was."

Ewan looks at me from over the back of the couch and I smile, reaching down and squeezing his shoulder. Something is eating at him—has been since Anton made that pub crawl remark—and while I know he'll tell me when he's ready, I want him to know I'm here. And we aren't going to be playing the "let's gang up on the baby brother" game today. Baby brother brought backup.

"So, you'll eventually accept another, at which point—"

"Gus!" Margeaux calls from the kitchen. It's a mix of loving and chastising at the same time, in a way only a partner can pull off.

Holding up his hands in surrender, Gus throws himself back onto the couch. I can't help but feel a small sense of victory.

"Fine, fine, we don't have to talk about it now. Just promise me that before you accept anything and you two take off to parts unknown, we will have a discussion and make a plan. Okay?"

My victory fades at his words, quickly replaced by something else. *You two...*

My heart leaps, pulse skittering through my veins, making my head feel dizzy for a second. His concern wasn't about me leaving Hickory Hills or Ewan. About breaking his heart all over again. It really is all about the business, because he thinks my leaving means Ewan leaves too.

The two of us. Together.

Tears prick at the corners of my eyes, trying to force their way out. I swallow hard, fighting to keep them back, and rush over to where Gus is sitting, throwing my arms around his neck.

It takes him a second, but he hugs me back, whispering, "I'm not a monster."

"No," I laugh. "Just a big brother."

"The way you say that actually makes it sound worse," he grumbles.

"Only some days. Not today though." I squeeze him again before letting go, not wanting to make this too weird.

"Boys!" Willa exclaims, announcing her presence as the front door slams behind her. "Your assistance is required outside."

"All of us?" Hux asks.

"Yup, Nash needs your help unloading the truck."

"It's raining," Jace comments.

"You are not the Wicked Witch of the West; you will not

melt, princess," Anton snarks, shoving the second youngest brother as he heads for the door without question.

"Depending on which canon you subscribe to, Elphaba didn't actually melt, you know."

Wait...what?!

Dumbfounded, I look to Ewan as he stands to head outside, trying to make sense of what I just heard. Jace has always kept us on our toes, but that comment was straight out of left field.

"Jace reads romance novels, and likes to brag about it," he tells me, squeezing my hip gently as he turns to go.

I start to reach for him, sensing a distance in him—a wall that he's thrown up—and starting to worry that it's more than just Anton's comment. That somehow mixing me into family time isn't working.

"Either way," Willa continues, clearly annoyed her brothers aren't following her orders. "There are dahlias, soil, and all sorts of other stuff that need out of the truck. And if you get a move on, y'all can have it in the shed before it starts raining again."

I watch them go, wishing I knew what was going through his head. Taking a seat at the counter between Sawyer and Brenna, I let out a long exhale, trying not to think about it. Because if I know anything about Ewan, this is who he is— introverted and intensely private. Playing everything close to the vest is his specialty, carefully choosing who he lets in.

I am once again the lucky one he's chosen.

"We've actually had the perfect amount of rain this spring," Sawyer says, pulling my attention back to the conversation. "I mean it when I say it has been the *perfect* spring. Everything about this has been optimal, textbook even, leaving us with the exact right numbers across the board. Temperature, weather, moisture levels, all of it. It's been really exciting."

"I'm just glad there is someone else out there who finds it as exciting as Anton does," Miss Belle coos.

"Because the rest of us are sick of hearing about it," Willa adds on.

"But am I going to get peaches?" Dolly asks, looking over at Sawyer like a little girl who just asked Santa for a pony.

Beaming from ear to ear, Sawyer nods. "If this continues, you won't be able to move for all the peaches. We'll be giving them away or inventing new things to do with them."

"Can 'em," I tell her. "We can them when we have an over-abundance. It's a whole thing."

"We all end up in Aunt Paula's basement—that's Maisey's mama," Dolly explains, her eyes going wide with excitement. "For a canning party. It's messy as fuck, but so much fun."

"And where you will be caught up on all the town's gossip, courtesy of Hattie Burch," Willa adds, grabbing a drink.

I groan, the thought of Aunt Hattie jabbering on like she has all the answers to the questions we never asked ruining the idea of a canning party before we even start. We've successfully avoided her since the wedding, but I know that won't be the case for long. Especially once she gets wind of Ewan and me being back together. Or my agreeing to work with Landon.

"She came into the drug store the other day, telling me all about you patching up Kendall Farlow when she took a tumble in the middle school parking lot," Brenna comments, nudging me.

"How does she even know that? She wasn't there."

I don't know why I question this. Hickory Hills is a small town, and things get around. And Aunt Hattie has a way of making sure she is at the center of it all.

"You think something happened in this town and Hattie Burch doesn't know about it?" Miss Belle gives me the softest side-eye that ever existed, spreading veggies out onto a plate on the island. "Maisey, I know you have been gone, but you should know better than that."

Miss Belle has a point. I do know better.

"I'm surprised she isn't blowing up your phone over you and Ewan. It's not like you two have been *quiet* about it," Dolly says, her emphasis on the word quiet clearly code for something I'm not picking up.

As is the waggle of her eyebrows.

I look to Sawyer and Brenna, hoping maybe they under-stand what is trying to be communicated, but neither of them seem to have even caught on to the code. Not helpful.

"She's probably saving it for in person," Margeaux adds. "Waiting until she can corner you in the produce section or something."

"She didn't..." I say, my disbelief barely scratching the surface. Because let's face it, she did.

Margeaux turns around to face the group, a massive smile on her face. "To be fair, she wasn't questioning me about Gus, because we were still a secret at the time, so she was trying to play matchmaker and set me up with Jake Wright. As I picked up bell peppers."

"Is there a better time?" Brenna jokes.

I sigh, shaking my head, my insides feeling as light as champagne. It's the same feeling I had the other day at lunch with these women, all of us instantly clicking, even though we're vastly different individuals. Everything about this moment feels exactly as it should be.

Like family.

Just like when I was a teenager and came over for dinner, the warmth manages to surround you in a way that you know you'll never forget. At the heart of it all is a simple meal, although it's a lot more of a production now—with a lot more women in attendance—but the feel is the same. The love is still there. The laughter still flows. It's still Dolly flitting around the kitchen making us all try different recipes she's come up with—only now she has a partner in crime in Margeaux. Looking to my left and right at Sawyer and Brenna, I bet I've got partners in crime with them too if I want them.

"If she didn't learn her lesson after Noel told her off, then she never will," Willa remarks.

Err...come again?!

"Wait, Noel Keller told her off?" I choke out my question, whipping my head over to Willa for confirmation, not sure those are words I ever thought I'd say. She nods, smirking, her pride for her husband's twin brother shining through.

"Oh, yes." Miss Belle smiles, her own version of the devious Hayes smirk making an appearance. "I know it may seem like things are the same, but you missed some stuff while you were gone."

No kidding...

"Well, I don't plan on missing anything else for a while. I didn't tell y'all on Friday because it wasn't officially official, but I agreed to fill in as an EMT with the fire department."

"So...you're staying?" Brenna asks hesitantly.

I nod, nerves swirling in my tummy. This announcement feels like a rehearsal for letting the rest of Hickory Hills know. For preparing myself for the reactions of everyone I know to have comments about this news.

"There's still a lot to figure out, but...yeah." I shrug, trying to keep it nonchalant, even though I'm feeling anything but inside. "It's time for my next chapter, and that chapter is here."

With Ewan...

A chorus of squeals and yays bounces off the kitchen walls, filling me to the brim. Like I can finally exhale and stop waiting for someone to ask why I left all those years ago.

"Your parents must be thrilled," Miss Belle coos.

"Yeah, Mama, *no one* was thinking about Chief Phillips's reaction," Willa snarks. "Ewan's, on the other hand…"

I press my lips together, trying to hold in my reaction. Miss Belle rolls her eyes, ignoring her daughter's comment.

"Was Ewan over the moon when you told him?" Dolly asks. "Did y'all celebrate? *Loudly?*"

Her emphasis is there again, and this time Margeaux catches it and gives her a look, but it still doesn't make any more sense.

"He's—" I catch myself, stopping midsentence. Dolly's taunt from the bakery earlier this week slides into my brain, lighting up like a marquee on a dark night.

Because I promise you, Ewan is dying to give Willa some payback.

I gasp, pointing at my cousin. "You owe me an explanation!"

Dolly throws her head back, a loud, boisterous guffaw bursting out of her. Her expression turns mischievous as she looks to Willa and then me, like she can't wait to spill the tea.

"I missed something," Sawyer comments.

"I think we all did," Brenna replies.

Dolly shrugs, still playing it coy. "I'll give you a hint. It's why you moved out of the loft." She points to Brenna, before turning to Margeaux, her smile growing wider. "And you are very excited Hux and I are all but moved out."

"Ohhhhh." Brenna giggles, leaning over to look at Sawyer. "Be happy Anton lived alone."

Sawyer shakes her head. "True, but I lived *here* when I first came to town, so…"

My head bounces between each woman like a hacky sack making its way around the circle, trying to follow along.

They've all caught on. I seem to be the only one left in the dark.

"Not that we were really up to anything…at first," Sawyer continues.

"At first," Willa scoffs. "Who knows what that bedroom has seen now."

"Willa Mae," Miss Belle chides. "You have no room to talk, young lady. I have said it before, and I will say it again, do not think for one second that I am unaware of what my children are doing. Or I suppose in your case, it was *who*."

My mouth drops, hanging wide open so I could catch flies, as my mama would put it. Because of all the people on this planet to call out Willa Hayes on her behavior, there is really only one. And that is her own mama.

"You didn't actually know we were sleeping together, just that I secretly had feelings for him," Willa replies, trying to defend herself.

"Ewan knew though," Brenna quips.

I whip my head to her. Say what?

Brenna nods, then launches into the story, or at least the version she heard from Milo. Each woman takes a turn adding in details from the version of the story they got, Willa trying to defend herself along the way, until I have a perfect picture in my mind. Suddenly the idea that Ewan might be itching for payback makes a lot more sense.

My insides clench, much like they did earlier today, at the thought of Ewan's mouth on me again. Heat crawls up the back of my neck, and it's all I can do to hope and pray that I'm not blushing as I sit here and think about how good it felt to have his hands all over me. About how I can't wait to try other things with him.

Things I've been waiting a long time for.

"Just remember, Wills, payback's a bitch…" Margeaux coos.

Willa shrugs, as if she's not worried about it. "Bring it on, Maisey."

I nod, not knowing how to react to that. Especially with their mama right there. Although, to be fair, Miss Belle does not seem to care one single lick that we've sat here for the last few minutes discussing the sex lives of her children in front of her.

"Oh, did I tell you what I'm making for the welcome party for Reel Madness?" Dolly asks, shouting out her question to no one in particular. "It's so on brand."

From sex talk to fishing tournaments—if that's not the randomness of girl time, I don't know what is.

"Did you figure out how to make a big mouth bass out of pastry?" I quip, not sure how food can be on brand for a fishing tournament.

"Not yet, but don't tempt me," she snarks. "Plus, Alice has the bass on the rod cookies, so that might be a little too much."

Bass on the rod...

The light bulb goes off in my head and I look at Brenna, her wide eyes telling me she had the exact same thought I did. How no one has ever made that joke for all the years Ewan has owned the shop, I have no idea. Especially after he named it The Booby Trap.

I guess that's what I'm for. To make all innuendos.

"How fast can we have shirts made?"

"Ummm, depends on what kind and how many," Willa says, her boss babe brain kicking in. "And if you have a design ready. Why, what do you need?"

"Think we could get some ready by Reel Madness?"

I hold my breath, my heart rate kicking up as I wait for Willa to reply. We have two weeks until the event, so that might be pushing it. If I can get a design worked up, and something rushed through though, even conceptually, then I'll make it work.

Because this will be a hit.

I don't have to have enough to stock the whole store. Just enough to get everyone talking.

"I'm sure Bronwyn's got someone up her sleeve that can produce something in that amount of time. What are you thinking?"

I smile, feeling so alive that I could burst. The design is already forming in my mind, so all I need is someone with some actual artistic talent to draw it out. Should be simple. I hope.

"Can y'all keep a secret?"

14

———

EWAN

"TAB A GOES INTO SLOT B."

Fuck, yes, it does...

Aluminum poles clatter against each other as they hit the ground, slipping out of my hands. The beautiful, melodic giggle that accompanies that borderline dirty innuendo sends a shiver ripping up my spine, almost making me forget I just dropped what I needed to erect this tent.

Erect. Ha.

Walked right into that one. Because thanks to her, that's exactly what I am.

"In this case," I say, picking up the pieces I let fall to the ground. I turn to look at Maisey, locking my gaze with hers. "It's more like the pole slides into the sleeve, nice and easy, and fits perfectly."

Maisey swallows hard, the muscles in her neck contracting, her eyes never leaving mine, as she saunters across the camping showroom floor toward me. I'm at work, and I know I should behave, but that's not easy, watching a shudder course through her when she stops in front of me.

Licking her lips, she lets out a long exhale, and I can't help but smile.

"Oh."

I toss the partially built tent to the ground, wrapping an arm around her and pulling her in for a kiss. She melts into me, kissing me back like it's been years since we've seen each other rather than days, letting her lips linger against mine.

To be fair, we have been like two ships passing in the night over the last few days. Thanks to her taking on the new shift with the EMTs, plus my gearing up for Reel Madness and the summer in general, it's been a busy week. It's almost closing time though, and I've been counting down the minutes until I get to go home to be with her.

Guess I don't need to do that anymore.

"Hi, beautiful." I press my lips to her forehead, inhaling the sweet scent of her shampoo. I've missed having that on my pillow the last couple of nights, and need to get her back in my bed. "To what do I owe the honor? I can't imagine you're here to help me set up the new camping display."

"Is this your way of telling me you need help getting it up?"

Ugggggh....

I groan, simultaneously proud of her pun and unable to believe she went there. Gotta admit, though, it was a good one.

"When it comes to you, baby, I promise you, that's not a problem."

My comeback is thankfully locked, loaded, and landed almost without thinking. Because if I took the time to think, then all the same insecurities from this past weekend would creep back up. Actually, that's not true. They never went anywhere. They've been front and center in my brain since Sunday dinner. Leaving me wondering if she was as satisfied as I thought.

Or worse, if I'm going to live up to her expectations. Small-town life can have its charms. But small-town sex? What if that isn't what she's after?

Maisey crouches down, reaching for the tent, handing me the set of poles that I dropped. I take them from her, continuing to slide them through the fabric, as she picks up another set, starting to snap them together. I smile, loving how natural this feels.

"I know we've had a busy week, and we haven't really seen each other, but you've been all up in that head of yours since Sunday. Wanna tell me about it?"

Just like it comes natural to her to call me out on that.

I glare at her for a second, taking half a heartbeat to consider telling her that there's nothing going on up here and that it's all in her head. But she's known me long enough to know that's a lie. I could tell her no, I don't *want* to talk about it, but then she'll opt for what I call the tornado tactic —where she holds an entire conversation with herself, rambling on and on, winding herself up like the Tasmanian Devil until you finally break down and spill whatever it is just so she will stop.

Looking down at the gear in my hand, I make sure everything is secure, trying to buy some time, and find the right words before proceeding. My insides tense, a knot forming in my chest as I work up the courage to say this.

"Was it Anton's comment?" she asks, trying to prompt me.

"Fucker…" I mutter, taking the set of poles from her.

Grabbing the other side of the tent, I start to push them through the fabric, my heart banging against my chest. I need to tell her. I know I do. It's not like any of this is a secret. Or anything I'm ashamed of. I just want everything to be perfect for her.

"His comment wasn't entirely accurate," I defend. "I've been on the pub crawl. I'm not a…"

I arch the last two poles, snapping them together with a loud click. Feeling triumphant, I hold up my arms like I just won a gold medal.

"Virgin?" Maisey finishes my sentence for me.

Yeah...that...

Nodding, I round the tent and sit down just inside the unzipped front. I pat the spot next to me and wait for Maisey to come join me. It's a tight fit, my large frame taking up a good portion of the two-person tent, but she squeezes in, snuggling up next to me.

"Not a virgin," I say, softer this time. "Cashed it in with Laura Suttle when I was twenty-five after a drunken night at The Giddy Up with Hux, for no other reason than I didn't want to be a virgin forever. We hooked up once or twice after that, but I was clearly not what she really wanted. That said, unlike my brothers, my uh...dance card, as Jace would put it, isn't very full. Other than Laura, and a couple of miscellaneous blow jobs—"

"Miscellaneous blow jobs?" she scoff-laughs, cutting me off. "With who?"

"What do you mean with who?"

"You name-dropped Laura."

I pause, narrowing my eyes, trying to determine whether she's serious. The expectant expression staring back at me says yes, so I opt for the coy answer.

"A gentleman doesn't kiss and tell."

Maisey scoff-laughs again, shaking her head, the smirk on her face so kissable it's distracting. "Miscellaneous blow jobs..."

I ignore her remark, pushing forward, afraid that if I don't, I'll never get this out.

"Other than those, my only other real experience is you."

There's a beat of silence, and the only sound I can hear is my pulse rushing through my veins, growing faster the longer Maisey takes to respond. The knot in my chest tightens, multiplying into more and more knots that continue to turn in on themselves.

Then she squeaks.

Yes, squeaks.

I look at her, not sure that I heard her right.

She smiles up at me, her squeaks turning into a giggle, those bright blue eyes shining like someone set a pair of aquamarine gemstones in the sun.

What the...

"Are you..." I start, the knot tightening to the point it cuts off my ability to breathe.

Maisey giggles again, and this time, there's no mistaking it. Nor the growing smile on her face.

"I don't know what you're laughing at, Maisey. I'm trying to tell you how I feel. That I'm actually kinda insecure about this," I blurt out, my voice louder than I intended. "That there's no way I'm going to measure up compared to all your international lovers!"

Clapping her hand over her mouth, Maisey closes her eyes, and it's clear that she's trying to hold back laughing even harder.

Fuck me...

"Ewan Porter Hayes, I love you so damn much."

Errr...what?

Cupping my face with her hands, she holds me for a second, her skin soft and warm against mine, her thumb brushing gently against my cheek. The gesture is tender, comforting, and loving, but is nothing compared to when she leans in to kiss me. Her lips are just as soft, if not more so, but the power behind them is everything.

The brief contact sets me on fire, igniting me from the inside out, soothing every part of my soul that had been aching just a moment ago. I reach for her, trying to pull her closer, wanting all the space between us to disappear, but she pulls back, holding on to my gaze and letting me know that she has me.

And she isn't letting go.

"I have no idea what thought process got you to *international lovers*," she says, trying to hold back her giggle with my made-up term. "Or what makes you think that men all around the world have sex differently."

"They might…"

She cocks an eyebrow at me, her judgment not so silent. "I can tell you, as a nurse, the basic mechanics are the same everywhere."

Shifting, she crawls into my lap, straddling me and resting her forehead against mine. I grab on to her hips, yanking her down to me, enjoying the moan she lets out as her core makes contact with my hard-on.

"I also don't know why you seem to think I took a lover in every new country I was in. Because that is not at all the case."

I pull back, sweeping the hair out of her face and tucking it behind her ear. Maisey sighs, all the mirth slipping away as she stares back at me, leaving only love. My heart squeezes, the series of knots loosening, feeling like they start to flow out of me and toward her, enveloping her in a whole new bind. One that contains the two of us—together.

"It's not unreasonable for me to believe that you've had relationships in the last ten years."

"Just as it wouldn't be unreasonable for me to believe that about you."

I lift a shoulder casually. She's not wrong. It's not an unreasonable assumption. It's just also not who I am.

"I've been focused on other things."

"Same," she whispers, grinding against me, making my dick throb. I groan, digging my fingers into her hips, wanting her to do it again. "There was one—once—nine years ago. That was it. No miscellaneous blow jobs..."

I laugh, her little taunt there at the end almost too much to handle. Especially paired with the wiggle she adds in for effect. My dick strains against my jeans, desperate for attention, but more than anything, I want to taste her again. To hear the little noises she makes.

I want to make her mine.

"I'd say that I might need to up my game to make you forget those, but I have no game, soooo..."

"They're already forgotten, baby."

"Good."

Running my hands up her sides, I breach the hem of her tee, her warm skin greeting me as I venture up north. Maisey leans forward, pressing her lips to mine, and I lose myself, my mind going blank as we kiss.

"Tell me, baby," I whisper, kissing along her jaw. My hands reach her breasts, running over the thin fabric of her bra. "You said *once*. Did you really mean—"

"*Once*," she cuts me off, arching into my hands for a second, then pulling back. "I let it slip to one of my fellow nurses that I was still a virgin, and she told me I was putting too much weight on it, and that once I got the first time over with it was no big deal and dating would be easier. So, she set me up with this guy she knew so I could get it out of my system."

What the...

Despite my best efforts, my shock shows on my face, because Maisey giggles, kissing me again to reassure me.

"That makes it sound worse than it was. He was a nice guy, I promise. We went out a couple of times, and there was no pressure or anything, so I thought, *yeah, maybe I do just need to get it over with*. Turns out, the whole thing was just okay. I give myself better orgasms. So I turned my focus back on work and—"

Errr...excuse me?!

"Did you just say that you give yourself better orgasms?"

Maisey nods, a devilish smirk spreading across her face. If I thought my dick was hard before, fuck me, I was wrong. It's solid concrete now. The thought of her playing with herself, making herself come, is making it almost impossible to think.

At least about anything other than making her come.

"Fuck, Maisey...you have no idea how badly I want to fix that."

"No time like the present."

Yanking her down into me, I make sure she knows I'm not kidding. That she has me ready to go. Based on all her wiggling and grinding as we've been talking, there's no way she's been unaware, but still. I am making sure it's crystal fucking clear.

"This is a two-person tent, right?" She giggles.

Sure the fuck is.

15

MAISEY

EWAN HAYES BRINGS out a side of me that I swear to God didn't exist. Until now.

One that no one else has ever managed to even remotely come close to accessing.

Yet, somehow, around him, it all seems so normal. Natural. Like this is how it's supposed to be. How *I'm* supposed to be.

Coy. Flirty. Sexy.

Horny.

I wrap my arms around Ewan's neck, leaning forward, changing the angle at which our bodies meet. My core runs along the bulge in his jeans, and I whimper, the brief moment of contact more than enough to rev the already idling engine inside me. I try to fight the shudder taking over me, but my body has a mind of its own.

As does Ewan.

His strong hands grip on to me tighter—one hand palming my ass, the other splayed across my back—as he pulls me into him, capturing my mouth with his. All my resolve fades away as I melt into his kiss, the perfect taste of him taking over, reminding me that this is where I belong. With him. Specifically, in his arms.

"So, about these orgasms…"

He nips at my jaw, and his hands move around to my sides, sliding upward and taking my shirt with them. Cool air hits my skin and my nipples contract, Ewan's eyes going directly to my cleavage.

"W-w-what about them?" I ask.

Kissing his way down my neck, stopping only to nibble at my collarbone, Ewan unhooks my bra, stealing my breath in the process. My insides clench, and I don't know if it's from the temperature change, the idea of being half naked in the middle of the camping display while the store is open, or all the dirty things Ewan is doing to me. Probably all three.

But mostly Ewan.

"Tell me about them."

Everything stops. Well, everything except Ewan. He's rolling my nipple between his thumb and forefinger, like he's trying to tune an old car radio, somehow knowing exactly what my body wants. And how to erase all my thoughts.

"I…errr…they're…" My breath hitches, Ewan giving my other side the same treatment, sending sparks straight to my center. I squirm, trying to find that same contact as earlier. Chuckling, Ewan ups the ante, pinching me gently, causing me to cry out. "They're…good…"

My words are inadequate, but I can barely think, much less string together any sort of coherent sentences as he teases me like this. The longer he continues, the more amped I get. I can feel myself getting wetter and wetter with each move of his fingers, and I just know these panties are ruined. No idea which pair I'm wearing, but they are done for. We can hold a funeral tomorrow.

"Just good, huh?"

He pinches me again, my hips jutting forward as if on some sort of catapult.

"Mmmm-hmmmm…"

"But still better than what anyone else has given you?" he asks, reaching for the button on my pants.

"N-no…" I whisper, biting down on my lip, watching as he skillfully undoes my jeans single-handedly. Looking up, I lock eyes with the boy who stole my heart all those years ago—the man who's still holding it today—my pulse jumping as I get ready to make another confession. "They're better than his. Not yours."

A wicked grin like I've never seen spreads across Ewan's face. It stretches from ear to ear, lighting up those cerulean-blue eyes like the sun dancing across the Caribbean sea, and is easily the sexiest thing I've ever seen. Even more so than the infamous Hayes smirk that every member of his family has.

Because this grin, it does things to me. Dirty things. Body chemistry altering things.

My pussy throbs, wetness pooling at my core, my entire body overheating in an instant. All from a smile.

"That's my girl." He unzips my jeans as much as he can in this position, sliding his hand between us. It's an awkward fit, but he manages, toying with the lacy trim of my panties. "But you still didn't answer me."

Answer him? What didn't I answer?

My pulse kicks up as he dips his hand down farther, my breaths coming faster, willing him to continue. To go where I want him. Where my body is calling him.

"Tell me about them, baby."

His hand stops, a rough, callused finger dragging against my skin, sending goose bumps up me. I want him to touch me so badly I can taste it. But I know he's not going to. He's making it perfectly clear that he's enjoying this.

Shifting, I try to take matters into my own hands, searching out that delicious friction all on my own. I lean forward, kissing him, soft, slow, then drag my hips forward, but Ewan catches on, yanking his hand back.

"Tsk, naughty girl..."

Fuuuuuck...

"I mean it, Maisey," he says, his voice low and deep. It sends a rumble through me, one I feel deep in my soul, settling where I need it the most. "I want to hear all about how you touch yourself. What gets you there. What makes your toes curl and that perfect pussy of yours wet."

You...

I swallow hard, buying time to catch my breath to answer him. Sliding my hand down my body, I slip it into my panties, right where his was, but unlike him, I don't stop. I go all the way, my fingers finding my wet curls, sliding through my slickness to the part of me that is aching to be touched.

Ewan groans watching me, letting me play for a second, fire flashing in his eyes.

"I like to start slow," I say, my voice barely above a whisper. Sucking in a deep breath, I shift again, trying to get a better angle.

Until Ewan stops me.

Grabbing my wrist, he lifts my hand, sliding it out from between us and lifting it to his mouth. One by one, he takes my fingers in his mouth, sucking them clean—savoring the taste of me right off them.

Oh, holy hell...

"Show me."

In a flash, he flips us over, easing me onto my back on the floor of the tent. He looms over me, his large frame blocking most of the light from outside the tent, the fluorescent glow just enough to crack through the moment and remind me where we are.

The Booby Trap.

"Here? Now?" Panic whips through me, the reminder that the store is technically still open suddenly flashing through my brain like a neon billboard. "What if someone comes upstairs? Dennis?"

Ewan winks, turning around and zipping up the door flap to the tent, closing us in. I laugh, my heart soaring at his ingenuity. There's a part of me that still wants to argue that Dennis or a customer could walk upstairs and see that something is going on in the tent, but if Ewan isn't bothered, then neither am I.

"Now, where were we?" he asks, turning back to me, hands on my hips, yanking my pants off me. "Oh, that's right. You were going to show me how you play with your pretty little pussy."

I've never understood the appeal of dirty talk, all of it sounding silly whenever my friends have talked about it. But here, now, listening to those words come from Ewan, I'd do whatever he asked to make him say them again and again.

"You wanna see?"

I prop myself up on my elbows so that I can see Ewan, spreading my legs so that all of me is on display. A new set of nerves reveal themselves as Ewan's eyes dance over my body, slowly drinking me in. It may not be the first time he's seen me naked—or even the first time he's touched me—but it's the first time I've ever offered myself up like this. Shown someone this side of me and allowed them into this space. Let myself be vulnerable.

I can't imagine it being anyone other than Ewan.

He nods, eyes still glued to me, like I'm the Venus de Milo. Or the Mona Lisa. Or some other priceless work of art.

"I like to start slow. Gentle, light touches, working my way from my outside in," I tell him, reaching in between my legs and starting to trace along the outside of my pussy. "I'll play up here sometimes, but mostly focus down here."

Slowly, I circle my clit, trying to avoid direct contact, knowing that I'm not ready for this to be over. My heart pounds in my chest, each beat of it felt throughout my body, the rhythm of it setting a pace for me as I move. I get lost in the beat, in my movements, the pleasure starting to take over, keeping my eyes on Ewan the whole time.

There's something new and erotic about him watching me do this. Something that has always been so private. So intimate. Now it's something shared.

Letting out a groan, Ewan's eyes darken and he moves, breaking our eye contact for a second. I gasp, but he's right there a second later, swallowing that gasp with his kiss, covering my hand with his.

"Tell me, baby," he says, his mouth right at my ear, his voice sounding borderline feral. "What are you thinking about when you do this?"

I swallow hard. Truth time.

"You. Always you."

Ewan growls, the sound no longer borderline. It's full-on feral. Like a man possessed, his focus dialed all the way in, he takes my wrists and pins them above my head, holding them in place with one hand while the other skims down my naked body. The move unlocks something in me, eliciting a shiver somewhere deep, my soul cracking open.

Ready and willing to do whatever he wants. As long as he keeps touching me.

"Fuck, you are gorgeous, Maisey."

His kiss is potent, powerful, and full of so much raw emotion I can't help but reciprocate, pouring everything I have into this moment. Into him. Wanting to make it last.

"The thought of you playing with yourself, thinking of me...fuuuuck," he growls, nipping at my earlobe. "But here's the thing, baby, all those *better orgasms*, are about to move down the list. There's a new sheriff in town."

I have no doubt...

I start to respond—make a smart-ass comment about the new sheriff—until Ewan moves his free hand, slipping it in between my legs and sliding a finger inside me.

"Faaaa!"

I cry out, new sensations taking over as Ewan works his way down my torso, branding my skin with hot, wet, open-mouth kisses. He moves his finger slowly, teasing my entrance, and I start to go dizzy, not sure which pleasure to focus on, his mouth or his hand. Or maybe that swirling feeling that is starting to build in my belly, the more he moves, the more it grows, like a hurricane generating its power.

Power that feels as if it could ignite at any moment.

I am so turned on—so on edge—from everything Ewan has done and said, I feel like I'm going to combust. Like at any moment, the next touch could be the one to send me flying.

A live wire ready to spark, I whimper as he moves his kisses to the insides of my thighs, his scruff tickling my skin. Dragging his finger through my wetness, he cuts the trail short, avoiding my clit, continuing the taunt.

"I think you might be sweeter than you were the other day," he says, licking me from his finger. "But the only way I'm going to know is a taste straight from the source."

Warm breath skirts over my bare skin, my eyes fluttering shut from the sensation. One that is quickly replaced by something else. Pure, unadulterated, carnal pleasure.

Ewan drags his tongue through my folds, licking from one end of me to the other, like I'm an ice cream cone on a hot summer day. If my eyes weren't already closed, they'd be slamming shut, the inability to focus on anything other than each new flick and swish taking over.

Holy shit...

He continues, not letting up. If anything, I think the more noise I make, the harder he goes, spurred on by my cries. The swirling in my gut speeds up, spreading through me, threatening to take over. I'm ready to give in, to let this feeling have its way with me.

"Come for me, baby..."

Ewan's words are somewhere between a demand and a prayer. Rough, but revered. Soft, but powerful. Paired with the two fingers that slide inside me, swiping against the spot that he found so easily, there is no other option but to comply.

For someone who hasn't done this but one or twice, the man certainly seems to know his way around a woman's body. *Specifically, my body.*

Pleasure hits me hard and fast, lightning zinging down my spine. I reach for Ewan, needing something to hold on to, not wanting to lose contact. He grips my thighs harder, doubling down on his efforts, making sure to leave no part of me untouched. Fireworks flash behind my eyelids, and I scream.

The sound is loud enough to be heard halfway to Atlanta, much less downstairs. If anyone is still left in the store, there's no question what's going on up here. But I don't care. Right now the only thing that matters is Ewan.

And getting him inside me.

Pushing his head back from between my thighs, I scramble to grab ahold of him, trying to yank him up my body. He chuckles, getting the message, slithering his way along my naked form, my extra sensitive post-orgasm skin not sure how to react to the feel of his clothes.

Why the fuck is he still wearing clothes?!

I grab at his shirt, struggling to pull it over his head. My fingers don't work properly—like I'm all thumbs—the soft cotton almost too pliable in them at this moment. They won't grip. Fuck it, focus on the pants. Those are the important part. He can fuck me with a shirt on. Pants? Not so much. Those have to come off.

That's nonnegotiable.

As I move my focus to the fly of his jeans, Ewan puts his hands on mine, stopping me. I look up at him, letting out a frustrated huff. What is he doing? I need him naked. Now.

"In a hurry?" he chuckles, kissing me gently.

My taste lingers on his lips—sweet, tangy—slowing me down as he steadies me with his kiss. My pulse skips, taking a breather, then returning to normal, the whole of me getting lost in him.

"I need you inside me," I whimper.

I need you inside me. Words I've never understood until now. Words that always sounded so cheesy. So made-up. How could anyone *need* someone else inside them?

But I get it now. I understand this feeling. This craving. This…*need.*

The realization that something is missing and that the only thing that is going to fill it is a specific person, in a specific way.

Because I *need* Ewan.

"You have no idea how long I've wanted to hear you say that."

"About as long as I've waited to say it."

His eyes flash dark again and he reaches behind his head, whipping off his shirt. I take a moment, drinking in his broad, muscular chest. Running my fingers across his pecs, I suck in a breath, watching as he leans back on his haunches, shimmying out of his jeans and skivvies in one move.

Leaving him just as naked as I am.

Only more magnificent.

I can't take my eyes off him, his hard cock standing at attention, begging to be touched. Reaching up, I run my hand along his shaft, circling the head with my thumb, a move I learned the other morning drives him wild.

"Maisey," he groans through gritted teeth.

Yeah, just like that.

"Fuck me, Ewan...please."

Fire flashes in his eyes, followed quickly by a moment of hesitation. He swallows hard, pressing his lips together.

"I don't have anything on me. I'm not the guy who carries a condom in his wallet just in case."

I smile, gripping him harder and continuing to stroke.

"I'm a nurse who tests herself for everything once a month, just in case. Straight negatives ten years running."

"Doc Galindo automatically tests every unmarried guy in town as part of the yearly physical, and I'm also in the clear there. But that's not where my mind was going."

Be still my heart, Ewan Porter Hayes. You are too much...

"I have an IUD, so we don't have to worry about that part until we want to."

The fire returns to his eyes, but this time, it's bigger, brighter, and accompanied by his dick twitching in my hand. Ewan mutters something I can't make out, but it doesn't matter. Because the talking portion is over.

Ewan's mouth is on my lips a split second later, his tongue seeking out mine like he needs this kiss to breathe. I moan, pulling him close, the heat from his skin making me want him as close as possible. Swiveling my hips, I try to make contact, seeking out his dick, still desperate for it.

Reading my mind but never letting up on the kiss, Ewan shifts, his cock sliding through my wetness, the head hitting my clit just right.

"Fuck!" I cry out, unable to hold back. Stars outline my

vision, my chest constricting as the hairs on the back of my neck stand up.

"If you like that, baby…"

Taking a second, Ewan lines himself up with my entrance. I suck in a breath, waiting for it, not sure what to expect. Nerves bubble up again for a brief second, but they dissipate as Ewan looks at me.

"Eyes on me, baby."

Slowly, he pushes forward, entering me.

And everything stops. Really, truly stops.

I hold my breath, afraid it might get in the way of this incredible feeling. Of this glorious, beautiful fullness. I can feel my body stretching, adjusting to him, so I exhale, all of my nerve endings suddenly standing at attention.

Then he moves.

If anything still existed in this time-stopped world, it fades away. Nothing remains but Ewan and me, and how full I feel. How right this feels. How perfect it is.

How perfect he is.

"Oh, fuck, you are so tight."

We continue to move, just the two of us, a jumble of limbs and kisses, finding a rhythm that works for us. One where it doesn't matter that we're as uncoordinated as can be in this unchoreographed symphony, because our bodies are doing all the talking. And they are screaming. Loudly.

The swirling feeling in my gut returns, this time with a vengeance. There's no stopping it, the storm brewing inside me ready to clash and take me with it.

"I'm…I'm gonna…"

"Yeah, baby…" Ewan says, reaching in between us, finding my clit with his thumb. "Come for me."

Again, that's all it takes.

Thunder booms within me, rocking me to the core. All my synapses are firing at will, taking over, a beautiful chorus of rests and beats. My eyes slam shut, fireworks blinding me as the pleasure takes over.

In the distance, I hear Ewan roar, his pace picking up, his thumb never leaving my clit, his own climax rushing through him. Collapsing on top of me, he heaves out a sigh, then wraps me in his arms, rolling us over so that I'm resting on his chest.

The heavy, steady beat of his heart against his ribs lures me into a trance, and I lie there, drifting away in a bliss I can't name, happy and secure in my new confirmation.

Ewan is mine. All mine.

And I am his.

As it should be.

"Guess I'm going to have to keep this tent," he says with a chuckle after a long moment.

I consider lifting my head to look at him, but I'm enjoying the movement of his chest from his breathing too much to move. Instead, I shift, snuggling into him more.

"Don't you keep all the items?" I ask, realizing halfway through my question it might be a stupid one. I suppose just because he owns the store doesn't mean he keeps all the display merchandise.

"Depends on the items. Really popular items I keep a display on hand at all times. But usually with the camping gear, something new comes out every year, so I sell off the store display for a discount at some point."

Oh. *Oooops...*

"No one will ever have to know," I offer, guilt creeping in that he might lose a sale over my impulsiveness.

"But *I'll* know. And there's no way I'm letting the tent I first fucked you in go home with someone else."

I laugh. I don't think he meant for that to be as funny as it came out—actually, I know he didn't—but the seriousness in his tone, paired with the pride on his face is too much. My heart can't handle it.

How did I ever walk away from this?

"Sorry, unsuspecting customer," I mimic. "You cannot have a souvenir from our first time together."

"Exactly."

"Oh, Ewan," I sigh, pushing up to look at him. "What am I going to do with you?"

"You could fuck me again."

Yes, absolutely.

"How 'bout our second go be in a bed?" I suggest, waggling my eyebrows.

"Gladly."

My stomach gurgles, cutting into our conversation, weighing in on what comes next. Dinner was always part of my plan—I almost stopped at Little Slice of Heaven on the way here—so it's no surprise I worked up an appetite.

"And maybe a pizza?"

Ewan chuckles, sitting us up and kissing me. Wrapping my arms around his neck, I let my lips linger against his, not rushing the moment. I want to savor this—this feeling, his taste, our own private cocoon—for as long as I can.

Then again, he's all mine. So I get to do this again.

"And a pizza." He nods, tightening his hold on me. "Do you have shifts this weekend?"

I pause, taken aback by the sudden change in subject.

"I do…"

"Think we could talk Landon into letting you out of them?"

Errrr…

I don't answer him, not sure where he's taking this. Could I talk Landon into that? Yes, I could. Probably wouldn't even really take all that much talking into. More like a *sorry, can't work this* text. But I just started with the department, and I don't want to be that person. I've never been the type to call out for no reason, and I'm not sure I want to start now.

Ewan smiles, his ability to read me as good as mine at reading him. He can see the gears turning in my head, and is ready with an explanation to help me get there.

"We should take our new tent camping. Sneak in a couple of nights under the stars just us before the summer starts and we're too busy to do anything but catch our breath."

He makes a good point. The weekend after is Reel Madness, followed by my Grandmother's hundredth birthday party two weeks after that, and then we'll blink and it'll be Memorial Day. Once summer hits, Ewan will be so on the go hosting fishing and camping trips, plus whatever it holds for me with the fire department, we might end up even more like two ships passing than we have been this week.

"Well, I do have an in with the fire chief," I joke. "So I'm sure we can work it out."

"Maybe leave out the part about how we acquired the new tent."

I throw my head back, a bark of laughter erupting. That comment I really know he didn't mean to be funny.

"That's how I was going to start the conversation with my daddy, c'mon…"

"Hmmph." Ewan makes a face, not appreciating my joke. "Leave Friday morning and be back by Sunday dinner?"

"Perfect."

16

EWAN

"ARE YOU REALLY THAT COLD?"

Stepping out from the tent, her arms wrapped around herself inside my old hoodie, Maisey looks at me, incredulous, as if I just asked her to solve a word problem using hieroglyphics. Her beautiful, luscious frame is dwarfed in the old, faded sweatshirt, but looking at her in it, my body can't help but react.

Because she is gorgeous.

"Yes," she replies, a shiver ripping through her. "I thought I was prepared for the temp to drop overnight, and I was fine snuggled up next to you all night, but I feel it never got warm today."

"C'mere."

I hold out my arm, ready for her to slip under it. She's not wrong; it didn't warm up today as much as I expected, making last night's lows feel even harsher. Spring in Georgia can be wild and unpredictable, and this one is proving to be no different. Still, Mother Nature gifted us a beautifully sunny day, even if it was on the cool side, perfect to spend playing in the river, fishing, and not having a care in the world.

Now back in my favorite clearing in the woods, I've got the fire going and dinner pretty much prepped, ready for a cozy night curled up with Maisey. Who is apparently as cold as if we were hanging out on Antarctica.

I scoot her in front of me so that she's directly in front of the fire, and wrap myself around her. Letting out a sigh, she melts back into me, her muscles releasing under my hold.

"Do I need to go get the big blanket from the truck? Or are you gonna be okay?"

"Depends. Are you going to let go?"

I roll my eyes, shaking my head, but tighten my grip, nonetheless. Because when it comes to this woman, I'm a goner. I am putty in her hands, ready and willing to be molded into whatever she wants.

"I do have to make dinner at some point," I tell her, pressing my lips to the top of her head.

The smell of her shampoo fills my nostrils, still potent from yesterday's use, the unique, fruity scent triggering something in my brain. Happiness. It's a smell that I've always associated with her. Any time I get a whiff of it, no matter where I am, my thoughts immediately go to the feel of her head on my chest. Of nights like this when we were teenagers—she complained about the cold then too—or movies on the couch. Now, I get to add a tent display in my own store to that list too.

"I hope you packed something good, since we didn't catch anything today. At least not something you were willing to keep."

"Don't worry, I came prepared."

I give her a squeeze, then let go, stepping back. Maisey squeaks in objection, turning to follow me as I reach for the camping chair behind me. Motioning for her to sit, I reach for the cooler and the bag of camping cooking utensils, pulling them closer to us.

Then, I hand her the roasting stick.

"We're having s'mores for dinner?"

"Better."

"What's better than s'm—"

I open the cooler, pulling out the pack of hot dogs. Maisey stops, eyes going wide, hands clasping over her mouth.

"Hot dogs…" She sighs. "I don't think I've roasted hot dogs over a fire since…"

Trailing off, her face morphs as she tries to think. To be fair, I can't remember the last time I did it either. Hot dogs are not a go-to food for me. I'll grab one if I'm at a baseball game, or maybe at the Fourth of July picnic—although even then I'll opt for a burger if I have the choice—but that's about it. Truth be told, I think the only reason we were roasting hot dogs that night when we were teenagers is because we happened to have some in the house.

"You know, I feel like that night couldn't have been the last time, but for the life of me, I can't think of another moment."

I cut open the package, pull out a dog, and hold Maisey's roasting stick steady as I slide it on. Trying my best to keep my composure, despite all the dirty jokes I could make right now, I look up at my girl, her lips pressed together as she watches me. It's clear that her mind is moving the same way mine is.

Fuck, she's amazing.

"Because you eat a lot of hot dogs?"

Maisey shakes her head, sticking her roaster into the flame. "Not even close. Very much an American food. In Europe, there are lots of wursts and sausages, but a *hot dog*, that's pure 'Murica."

I laugh, plopping down into my camp chair next to her and following suit, lining my roaster up next to hers.

"And don't worry, I have the ketchup too."

"I prefer mustard."

What?!

Maisey makes a face, shrinking into herself, suddenly embarrassed by her admission.

"Depending on the country, ketchup was tough to find. And I never took to the whole mayo on my fries thing." She shrugs. "So, I developed a taste for mustard. Fancy mustard, actually, but really, any kind works. So, that's what we're putting on this baby. Keep the ketchup for pacts."

Smiling, I reach back into the cooler and pull out the small baggie I shoved in there earlier, holding it up to show it off. The little white packets with red and black writing are a bit hard to read in the dark, reflecting the light of the fire as the flames flicker, but there's no doubt what they are.

"Packets!"

"You were the one who liked it, not me, so I didn't want to bring a whole bottle. Instead, I stole some packets from the cafeteria at Hayes headquarters."

"But you have mustard, right?"

I scoff. Do I have mustard. Taking a minute to rotate the dogs, I reach back into the cooler, pulling out the bottle of stone ground mustard, showing it off like I belong on QVC.

"You know, this whole you and me thing might just work." Sticking her tongue out at me, she takes the bottle, along with a bun from the bag I laid at our feet.

"You'd break up with me over the same condiment that was the whole reason you came back?" I quip, knowing it'll get a rise out of her.

Only, it has the opposite effect.

Maisey's face turns serious. She looks away, but not before I catch a softness in her eyes that tells me there's something more there. Something that she's been keeping to herself.

"That wasn't the whole reason," she says.

Her voice is so soft, and she's still facing away from me, so I almost don't hear it. Crackles and pops from the fire fill the silence, swallowing her statement whole, never letting it make it into the evening sky.

My stomach knots, tension moving through my muscles like sand through a timer, waiting for her to continue. I don't doubt her feelings for me, and we've already discussed how bad our communication was back then, leaving me curious as to where her mind is. As much as I want to know what she means, I don't want to push her.

Instead, I turn my focus back to dinner, silently taking her roasting stick from her and giving it another turn to make sure there is the perfect amount of crispiness to her dog. Once I'm satisfied, I remove it from the fire and load it into the bun.

Handing it to her, my fingers brush along hers, sending sparks flying. It doesn't matter that she's been my best friend since forever or that she was gone for years. Touching her—no matter how briefly or innocently—ignites my soul. I would burn the entire world down if it meant getting to hold her hand, even for a few minutes. Because that would be enough.

"This is the real reason. This whole moment," she whispers, stopping me and interlacing her fingers with mine. Looking around us, she shrugs gently, as if she isn't sure she's making sense. "Because in a whole bunch of years, I want our kids to be weirded out, yet oddly accepting, by us having a sex tent, the same way y'all are that Auggie and Miss Belle have a sex boat."

Our kids...

My heart stops, all of the oxygen sucked straight out of

the universe with those two words. I know I need to react. Say something. Do something. But I'm too dumbfounded by how casually she throws out that future. A future I want so badly I can taste it.

"You get over the weirdness of *Fishy Business* pretty quickly as long as you don't think about it as the sex boat," I tell her, trying not to think about what my parents do on that boat.

The thirty-three-foot cabin cruiser was a gift from Auggie to Miss Belle when Willa graduated from college, since they were officially empty nesters and all seven of us were on the legit Hayes payroll and not his personal one. As far as yachts go, it's small and rather unassuming, with enough room for all of us to hang on it for a day, and a cabin that is big enough for basically one purpose. A purpose that all of us adult children are well aware of.

Anyone who has ever met my parents knows they are still very much in love, even forty-plus years of marriage and seven kids later. They've never hidden their PDA, flirting, or adoration of each other from us, always wanting to be a model of a loving, healthy relationship. Something they very much are. Which is why we can tease them about their "sex boat" or "grown-up naps," despite not wanting to think about my parents that way.

"Besides, we have our own boat for that," I add.

Maisey blushes, the glow of the fire showing off the tinge in her cheeks just enough for me to see it. Squeezing her fingers with mine, I lean in, kissing her knuckles, loving that my vibrant, confident girl turns pink at the offer of getting frisky on the boat.

Definitely add that to the to-do list.

"So, sex tent, check. Sex boat, check. If you're really feeling adventurous, we can add deer stand and duck blind to the list," I offer, trying to be funny.

Maisey gives me the side-eye, and for a second, I think my joke didn't land. Shit. She's going to think that's all I'm thinking about now. Or that I'm not taking her seriously. Because I am. I want the same kind of relationship, and more than anything, I love that she's thinking about our future together this way.

Her side-eye morphs into an eye roll, and then laughter. Phew.

"Oh, no, I draw the line at deer stands and duck blinds. Those can remain unchristened."

"Fair."

"I mean it," she reiterates, letting my hand go so she can dress her hot dog. "I want it all."

Taking a big bite of her hot dog, she slowly chews, letting her bomb explode. Or well, fizzle out. Because that reaction isn't surprising to me. It's relatable.

"Same."

Maisey stops mid-chew, her eyes going wide, waiting on me to elaborate. There isn't anything left to say though. I want it all, with her.

I want late nights and shared secrets—inside jokes that only we understand and couldn't explain if we tried. I want the wedding where our mamas fuss over details that I won't give two shits about, while Maisey tries not to have a meltdown over everything being perfect. I want sleepless nights filled with crying babies and family camping trips. I want to spoil her on birthdays, anniversaries, Mother's Days, Christmases, and every other stupid holiday—made-up or otherwise—that someone can think of for the rest of our lives.

I want her to be the one I wake up with when we're both old and gray.

"Tell me something, Mais…"

"Anything."

"You mentioned our kids; what else do you see in this future of ours?"

Maisey stops, hot dog partway to her mouth. "Well, I mean…"

She trails off, pressing her lips together as she looks for the answer that is going to sound the least presumptuous. I let her panic, just for a few seconds, loving how cute she looks like this with her eyes darting back and forth, searching for the answer in the campfire smoke.

Clearing her throat, she turns back to face me fully, popping the last bite of her dinner into her mouth.

"If I'm being *that girl*, and just letting all my fantasies run wild…" Her eyes sparkle, and I know it's not just the firelight dancing in them this time. "Two kids, a matching pair. None of this one of each nonsense. Whatever the first one comes out as, that's what I want the second to be."

I nod, not sure how to respond to that oddly specific detail. She's a nurse, so it's not like she isn't very aware that's not how the process works, but it's her daydream, so who am I to stop her.

"Plus a dog. But not like a golden doodle or something like that. I mean like a beagle or a blue heeler or something that you can take hunting and camping and fishing."

Shaking my head, I reach for the meat in the cooler again, slipping round two onto the roasting sticks. I hand her one, not bothering to hide the silly grin on my face.

"What's that look for?"

I shake my head, still not hiding my smile. "When you said you were going to be *that girl*, I thought I was going to get an earful about a wedding and a house, and maybe even the names you have picked out for our kids, not the very specific dog breeds you want us to have."

"I have a whole list of names, don't you worry," she mutters, yanking a roasting stick out of my hand.

I throw my head back laughing. The last thing I was worried about was her having a list of baby names.

"Laugh all you want, but I've been thinking a lot about it. And not just since I've been back. It's all part of *why* I'm back. Of why..."

She pauses, holding on to her breath.

"Why what?" I press.

"Do you know what my first, gut, knee-jerk reaction was when Dolly texted me last year telling me that she and Hux were together? I was jealous. I mean, I was happy for her too. Because everyone knows those two belong together. But... but at the same time, it made me start thinking about all the things I wanted from life." She exhales loudly, letting out all the air she'd been holding on to. "How I wanted both the career and the family. And while the career part was going well, the other parts—all those things—were back here, with you. I'm not trying to make this all heavy, but...for all that time I spent growing up thinking about getting away from here, now, this is the only place I want to be."

"That's because growing up we didn't realize we could have a sex tent," I comment.

Maisey side-eyes me again, and this time I'm sure I'm gonna get it.

"Oh no, I thought about us having sex in a tent," she admits. "Senior year in high school. That trip we took the weekend before Rhythm and Brews, when our parents actually agreed to let us go, just us? When you only brought the one tent, I thought maybe something might happen, and kept waiting for you to make a move. But you were a perfect gentleman all weekend."

I groan internally, remembering every minute of that weekend like it was last week. What had inspired both the Phillipses and the Hayeses to suddenly waive the "no unchaperoned boy-girl overnight trips" rule is still beyond me, but Maisey and I jumped on the chance to get away, sans parents. Looking back on it, I can't help but wonder if that was their way of condoning more than a friendship between us, thinking that we would cross the line if left alone.

Except, Maisey's right—I left the line completely untouched.

Something that took a level of self-restraint that I still think is worthy of a gold medal.

"You have no idea how much I didn't want to be. Had I known you didn't want me to be either…"

My dick twitches at the memory, my hands itching to hold her right now just thinking about all of this. I need something to cool my ardor. A change of subject.

"Want to know what I want our future to look like?" I ask, hoping it's enough to distract her.

"More than anything."

"I want to hire someone else to help me run the store. Dennis is great, but he works for exactly two reasons. One— so that Abigal isn't always fussin' at him about being under foot all day, and two—so he gets a discount on fishing gear. If it were legal, I'm pretty sure he'd let me pay him in store credit. What I need is someone who can really take over, full-time, and be a retail manager for me."

Maisey looks at me with an intent focus, her interest piqued. "You want to step away from the store?"

"Not completely. I still enjoy getting in all the new toys and helping people learn and be properly equipped. But if I can get someone who is fully focused on that, I can turn my attention to the guided tours and environmental education side of things. I want to grow that portion of the business a lot more. Which I think I can—I've got a few irons in the fire, so to speak. There's a decent market for it, believe it or not."

"I absolutely believe it."

"Plus, it has the added benefit of giving me flexibility to

really be a hands-on dad and work around your ER schedule."

"What?"

The question is out of her so fast, I question if she actually heard me or is just surprised by my answer. Time to double down.

"I presume you want to go back to an ER, which potentially means nights, weekends, and twelve-hour shifts. Not having to do retail, which also has those, means I have extra flexibility for that matching set you want."

Maisey leaps from her chair, dropping her roasting stick onto the ground and tackling me in a hug. The force from her landing in my lap is enough to make the chair rock, but thankfully not fully knock us over. I wrap my arms around her, pulling her in close as she buries her face into my neck.

"You're gonna burn your hot dog."

"I don't care about that."

She squeezes me tighter, head still buried, and I feel tears against my neck. Damn, I hope those are happy tears. I squeeze her back, holding on tight and cherishing this moment. I spent too long without her not to hold on every chance I get.

"Fuck the hot dog..." she mutters.

"Not gonna do that. Not even sure how that would work." I chuckle. "You, on the other hand..."

Maisey sits up, her eyes glossy with unshed tears, playfully shoving me. I shrug, not at all sorry for my comment.

"I love you, Ewan."

"I love you, Maisey. That's never changed."

Shifting in my lap, she reaches down into the cooler. I try to lean over to see what she's after, but can't get a good look from this angle without risking us toppling over. A second later, her hand reappears, holding up a ketchup packet.

"What's that for?"

A sly smile tugs at the corner of her mouth, her tears gone and replaced by an impish look that only Maisey can pull off. Ripping the packet open with her teeth, she takes my hand, squeezing out a portion of the red condiment, then following suit on her own hand.

"We already made the pact about no more secrets, but we didn't swear it in ketchup."

"We said we didn't need to," I remind her.

"I know, but I'm adding to it, and I think it's important that we do it properly."

"Okay…"

"And I'm very, very serious about this. Promise me you won't laugh."

Pressing our hands together, she looks me in the eye, as serious as I've ever seen her.

"If we have girls, and they want to learn, you'll teach them to shoot and hunt and all that just like you would the boys."

I wrap my hand around hers, completing the handshake hold, and squeeze. This is the easiest thing I've ever promised.

"Of course."

"And if genetics works against us, and we end up with one of each, we curse the universe, but we don't go for the third."

There is determination in her declaration, leaving no room for doubt that right here, right now, she means this. My stupid own sly smile starts to form and I have to fight it, afraid that it'll look too much like a laugh—something I promised I wouldn't do.

Nodding, I reach deep inside and keep my face as straight as possible, knowing that I won't keep that part of my promise the day she looks at me and tells me she wants more. Because there is no way I'm ever going to be able to deny her what she wants.

"I swear it in ketchup," I say.

"Most sacred bond there is," she says with a giggle.

I kiss her, softly at first, then deepening it. At least as much as I can with our hands still clasped together between us, oozing with ketchup. Turns out those packets came in handy after all.

"You're gonna need another hot dog—that one is ruined," I say as she pulls back.

Maisey nods, that impish look still in her eyes. "Can we toast the buns this time?"

My dick twitches again, my mind instantly filling with dirty thoughts. All because she said *buns*.

"Oh, I'll toast your buns…"

"Save that for after, please." She drags her core against my crotch, wiggling as she climbs out of my lap and back into her own chair. "That's what the sex tent is for."

Hell yes.

MAISEY

"Ta-da!"

Dolly does a little shimmy, showing off the back of her T-shirt, arms outstretched like she's Simone Biles balancing on the high beam. I smile, not only thrilled to see the idea come to life, but that they made it in time.

The basic heather-gray tee has The Booby Trap logo across the front, looking fairly unassuming from this angle. Until you turn around. Across the back is a largemouth bass partially encircled by a rod and reel, with the tag line *I like a big mouth on my rod* printed alongside the curve of the fishing line. The double entendre makes me giggle—again—same as it has every time I've looked at the design.

"It's perfect!" I tell her, taking a big sip of my coffee. And then another.

We have a long day ahead of us, and it's only just starting. At barely five thirty.

The second annual Reel Madness, a charity fishing event The Booby Trap is hosting to raise money for Hayes Cares, the charitable arm of Hayes Industries, is up and running, with Silver Lake's parking lot already full of tents, trucks, boats, and people. The volunteers finished up their safety meeting not long ago, and registration will officially open shortly— getting this show on the road for the more than one hundred and fifty teams that are registered.

As one of the EMTs on for the day, all I can do is hope that it's a calm, uneventful day. At least for the humans. The fish are on their own.

"We've already sold six," Bronwyn Ainsworth-Keller, Hayes's Director of Marketing says, rounding the merch table. "We are absolutely going to sell out of the tees and the stickers and the koozies. I should have bought more stuff with that design on it."

I laugh, excited that she's excited. "I'll make sure that Ewan stocks it in the store. I honestly don't know how he and Milo didn't come up with it themselves."

"Because as smart-ass-y as all those boys are, they don't think about using that skill for marketing. Actually, they just don't think about marketing," Bronwyn says.

Dolly and I look at each other, unable to argue that point. Neither of our Hayes men put any kind of effort into marketing. To be fair, Hux is over lumber and paper, so not an area that traditional marketing really applies to, but even if it did, zero thought would go into it. Ewan, though, does nothing. I know this for a fact because I've asked. Very specifically when I showed him the largemouth design and told him all about making shirts and stickers and how we could sell them.

He looked at me like I was an Oompa Loompa escaped from the chocolate factory, before asking, "People will buy stickers with my store name on it?"

That was the point I knew I needed to get Bronwyn fully involved.

"I'm working on hiring a social media manager who can focus on building an online presence and personality for

Southern Brothers and The Booby Trap, so any other ideas like this you have up your sleeve, let me know. Unless you're interested in the role?"

"Absolutely not," I answer without thinking. "I'll take an open wound to dance trends any day."

Bronwyn laughs. "You can keep the blood and guts, but I'm with you on the dance trend part. Which is why I need someone who is good at all that stuff. I know a gal from my days at Coffman Witte who always had a pulse on hot trends, but if you guys know of anyone…"

She looks between Dolly and me, as if the two of us are going to be a wealth of knowledge in the area and have a ready-made list of names for her. Truthfully, Dolly might, since she knows people in this town still. Meanwhile, I'm over here wondering if it would be rude for me to Google Coffman Witte to figure out what that is.

"Here's what I know. If I don't make it back to the food tent, I run the risk of Huxley Hayes eating all the cinnamon rolls before the guests arrive," Dolly says.

"Please don't let that happen," I say, my pulse jumping at the thought. "Ewan would lose his mind."

"Have you seen him recently?" Bronwyn asks. "He was supposed to be bringing me a list of team names but then he disappeared."

Sounds about right. He's been running around like a chicken with his head cut off since the alarm went off this morning. I swear he hasn't stopped for a single second, barely slowing his truck long enough for me to get out, or for him to kiss me goodbye when he dropped me off at the fire station this morning. Good thing I've practiced my tuck and roll. I think I've seen him maybe twice—both times in passing—since Landon and I arrived in the ambulance.

"Not recently, but I'll text him and let him know you need him," I tell her, pulling out my phone.

My fingers fly across the screen, my text thread with Ewan on top of the list, tapping out a message for him to head to the merch tent whenever he gets a chance.

Saying our goodbyes to Bronwyn, I loop my arm through Dolly's and head back toward the food tent. Jace Hayes's voice carries through the early morning air, his safety first reminder to the volunteers hopefully not landing on deaf ears.

"Sooooooo…" Dolly prods, her single word drug out for multiple syllables. I look over at her, our arms still linked, and there is no mistaking the smirk on her face. She's up to something.

"Soooo, what?"

"You finally got what you really wanted," she says, her shit-eating grin growing. I start to respond—to make a smart-ass comment about *how does she know*—but she cuts me off. "It's written all over you. If we thought you were glowing at that Sunday dinner, you've been radioactive this last week."

Well, shit…

I feel the heat prick at my cheeks, despite the coolness still lingering in the morning air. Nervous laughter builds in my chest, like I'm thirteen all over again, ready to burst because my crush nodded at me while walking to math class. Only, this was better. Looking away, I try to think of something to say—a way to put this feeling into words—but Dolly simply giggles.

She gets it. I know she does.

"Just tell me this, worth waiting for?"

"There you are! Well, two out of the three…"

Aunt Hattie's shrill exclamation stops us in our tracks, right in front of the food tent, a table filled with precisely lined-up cinnamon rolls behind her. I blink hard, doing a double take, making sure it's actually her. Aunt Hattie, at a fishing tournament at o'dark-thirty in the morning. I might as well be looking at the ghost of Christmas past for all the sense this is making right now.

"Aunt Hattie. Morning," I greet, managing to get the words out.

Behind her, Hux mouths the word *sorry*, with a big shrug. Not that I have any idea what there is to be sorry about. Not like he was going to be able to stop her. She was going to find us, one way or the other.

"Good morning." She purses her lips, the greeting somehow sour on her tongue.

"Would you like a cinnamon roll?" Dolly offers.

"What I would like, no, what I *need*, is your RSVPs for the birthday party. And Emily's, wherever she is."

Seriously? She needs that now? Can't she see we're a little busy at the moment? Wait, no, never mind. I'm not going to bring logic into this. I know better than that. That has no place here.

"I need to RSVP for the party?" Dolly asks, braver than I am.

Oh boy...

"I need a head count for the food."

"*I'm* catering it!"

I look over at Hux, my eyes wide, hoping he can read my expression as the distress signal that it is. In every ER I've worked in, the nurses have had a series of hand gestures to secretly communicate with one another—something that I desperately need in the moment. However, there is no way crossing my fingers in a particular pattern is going to look like anything other than me trying to throw gang signs right about now.

Thankfully, though, Hux is on it. Swooping in, he drapes an arm around his wife, working on sweet-talking our aunt. Something that also makes him braver than I am.

It's also my cue to exit.

Grabbing the bag of cinnamon rolls set aside for the first aid tent, I weave my way through the crowd back to the ambulance and first aid area. I stop to look out over Silver Lake as I wait for a large, dually pickup to straighten itself out on the launch ramp. The sun is starting to peek over the water, turning the sky from pitch black into muted grays and blues, and it won't be long before we start to see pinks and reds.

I have no idea how many sunrises I've seen over this lake —hundreds, probably—but there is something about this one that hits me. That makes me realize how much I've missed them. The simplicity of the light moving over the water and all the stillness that goes with it. Even with all the chaos churning around me with the tournament.

Or maybe it's nothing more than a simple reminder that I'm exactly where I belong.

"Hey, I grabbed the cinnam—"

I stop, snapping my mouth shut, caught off guard by the sight greeting me as I approach the tent. Sitting on the back bumper of the ambulance, the doors wide open, are Landon and Emily, huddling together, both of their heads bent over Landon's phone. They're looking at something intensely, whispering almost conspiratorially.

Now that's a sight.

Landon and Emily sittin' in a tree...

I lean against the metal pole of the tent, my eyes glued to the two of them, the cuteness radiating off of them in waves. The pole shifts under my weight, moving the entire pop-up shelter, causing me to lose my balance and distract both Emily and Landon.

"That was graceful," Em snickers.

"You okay?" Landon asks, feigning concern. At least one of them is willing to.

"Fine." I straighten myself out, shrugging it off and pretending like it never happened.

No one saw that. Not my cousin, or my boss, or any one of the dozens of strangers who are hanging about. Nope.

"Whatcha watching?" I ask, changing the subject.

"Oh, just this cat video Landon wanted to show me," Em says, hopping off the ambulance. Landon looks slightly crestfallen as she moves away from him, his brown eyes dimming. "Those cinnamon rolls?"

I nod, holding up the bag. "I'd avoid the food tent for a minute though. Aunt Hattie was over there."

Em makes a face, her features scrunching as if she's in pain, and I know without saying anything exactly what she means.

"Right, so, back to my assigned post. I'll see y'all…at some point."

"You know, Emily, if you were planning on heading to the fish fry tonight, I could pick you up."

Emily scoffs, dismissing his offer. "Land, just because it worked for Ewan doesn't mean that you will find yourself a girl because you bring me to the after-party."

Emily Minerva Barrowcliff! I scream in my head, fully aware that I sound like my mother, grandmother, and all of my aunts combined right now. But there's no helping it. She did not just say that.

"Well…I…" Landon stammers, equally taken aback by her comment. "That had not been my thought."

"Although, maybe we try it and see if it works? I could start marketing it as a skill? Make it a side hustle? Take the whole *always the friend never the girlfriend* to a new level," Emily quips, laughing at her own joke. "Could you imagine Aunt Hattie's face if I started putting it out there that I'm the one before the one?"

I sigh, shaking my head. As one of the most self-assured

people on the planet, I know that Emily is not bothered at all by her single status, and relishes any chance to make that weird for our older relatives who keep trying to marry her off. This stunt would only help that. Actually, I would love to see their faces.

Landon's face right now, however, is breaking my heart.

"Anyway, I really should get back. I'll catch y'all later."

Trotting off, Emily gives us a little wave, clearly not thinking anything more about her comment. Truth be told, had I not stumbled across the smile Landon was trying to hide as they were huddled over his phone, I wouldn't have either. I know now though.

"A cat video? Really?" I tease, unable to help myself.

I have so many questions I want to ask—the biggest of which is just how long this has been going on—but I don't. I keep them all to myself. I tamp down the urge to be the small-town girl who plays into all the gossip and the need to be in the know. Despite how fun being the keeper of this secret is going to be.

"So, the cinnamon rolls?" Landon points to the baggie. Damn it, he's back to all business.

I hand it to him, ready to dig in. I'm starving.

"So, I was over at Knox Regional Medical Center the other day," he says, completely changing the subject.

I nod, not sure what him visiting the county's hospital has to do with anything. Other than maybe that it's a ways away from here. As in, almost an hour, since it's on the other side of the county, designed to serve a wider rural area than Knox County alone. It's always been a little bit of a sore spot with some of the folks in town, since Hickory Hills is the county seat, and yet it's faster in most emergency situations to head to Tifton than our own county's regional medical center.

"Apparently," he continues, "their head of nursing retired.

And the replacement they hired is someone they stole out of the ER in Tifton."

My ears perk up. Is he saying what I think he's saying?

Landon nods, confirming my unspoken question. The corner of his mouth slyly turns upward, an *I know something you don't know* smile starting to appear. If I didn't know any better, I'd think that being besties with Hux Hayes all these years was starting to rub off.

Hope bubbles inside me. I technically still have an employment agreement with InterCon MediTrust until the end of the summer, making applying to work with another hospital a little difficult. Then again, they haven't found me another contract since the one in Nicaragua was abruptly canceled either, so at this point, my asking for an early opt-out shouldn't come as too much of a surprise.

A round trip to Tifton every day isn't ideal, but it means permanency here. The final step in making Hickory Hills home again.

If they hire me.

Let's not put the cart before the horse.

Actually, for once in life, let's. Because that's what I want to picture. What I want to daydream about. Spending my days in the ER, and then coming home to Ewan and—

The high-pitched sound of an alert pierces through our walkie-talkies, cutting off my thoughts. Landon and I both react—instantly going on high alert, ready to jump into action.

"Hickory Hills EMT, what's the emergency?" Landon says into the radio, his deep voice in full command mode.

"Uhh, we need medical attention over at the *Hooked on a Reeling* right away. ASAP. Errr…" the volunteer's voice crackles. "STAT. Is that the medical term? STAT?"

The *Hooked on a Reeling*. My heart sinks. That's Ewan's boat.

Fuck.

18

MAISEY

Fᴜᴄᴋ…

I don't think. I just move. Grabbing my EMT bag, I take off, running faster than I think I ever have in my life. My legs move as if they are semi-detached from my body—like two little fidget spinners attached to a torso.

The crowd parts like the Red Sea—either because they see me coming or because I'm screaming and I don't hear myself —making a clear path as I run toward the jetty.

My instincts tell me where to go, leading me toward the same slip that the *Hooked on a Reeling* is always parked in. Thank God for Ewan's habits. Skidding to a stop, I suck in a breath as I elbow past a volunteer, ready for whatever I find.

I think.

"FUUUUUCK!"

It's the loudest curse I have ever heard in my life, and there is zero mistaking that voice. If there is someone in this town who wasn't awake, they are now. All because Ewan dropped an F-bomb that could have leveled Australia.

I jump into the boat, not giving myself a moment to get my sea legs under me before rushing to the front, my heart slamming against my chest, pure panic filling my veins, especially now that I have confirmation that it's Ewan that is hurt. Scanning around, I don't see any blood and am not sure if that's a good sign or not right now. Until I get around the captain's chair.

Holy...

Ewan is splayed out on his back, eyes shut, face contorted in pain, legs spread out in front of him. Wait, no. Only one leg is. The other leg is...

The other leg is in the fish box.

"Ewan!"

I rush to his side, kneeling down and starting to examine him. He groans as I run my hands along his body, lightly applying pressure to check for any open wounds or contusions. I press gently against his ribs, earning me another groan, and he opens one eye, halfway glaring at me. Shaking his head, he tries to push himself up, but I stop him.

"Don't move."

It's an order. One I expect him to follow. One I also expect him to fight me on. A fight he's going to lose.

"I'm fine, Mais," he croaks, his voice thick and gravelly. "Although I like the bossy tone."

Called it...

"Well, you're about to get a lot fucking more of it, and you are not going to like it if you move," I snap, my panic still in overdrive. Landon slides up behind me and I hear him let out a single chuckle, no doubt over wondering how this happened, but I ignore him, focusing on doing all the necessary checks to verify we're not dealing with a major spinal or head injury. "How many fingers am I holding up?"

"Three," Ewan answers correctly. "Although behind you I think Landon is making me an offer I'd prefer to refuse."

I spin around, catching Landon flipping him the bird.

Swatting at Landon's legs, and earning more laughter from both of the guys, I turn back to Ewan.

"What happened?"

"Am I allowed to sit up to tell this story?"

"No."

"I tried." Ewan lets out a long exhale. "I grabbed ice for the fish box, and was bringing it on to fill it up and didn't realize the door was open..."

I look down at his leg, half hanging in the cooler that is built into the hull of the boat. Sure enough, there is some ice already down in the fish box, but not enough that it's flush with the floor of the boat. If the lid was open...well, it doesn't take much for my mind to put the rest together. The open bag and ice chunks scattered around the boat deck also corroborate said story.

Two and two are definitely four here.

"My hands were full, and I stepped right in it, and down I went."

"Did you hit your head?" I ask.

That's my biggest concern. Because if we're dealing with a head injury...

My pulse skips, nurse brain taking over, trying to remind myself that Ewan is exceptionally coherent at the moment so the likelihood of a TBI is probably pretty slim. Then again, I've experienced patients participating in a full-on conversation with me one minute, and then be out cold the next, so never say never. I know better.

"I hit my ass. It's my foot that fucking hurts. I laid down after the fact."

Looking up at Landon, I search his eyes for confirmation that he's thinking what I'm thinking. He nods, the two of us secretly agreeing that we aren't going to need the backboard that he carried over here. A CT scan—without question, because mama here isn't messing about—but I'm confident we're not at risk for paralysis.

I turn back to Ewan, helping him sit up slowly. His face is still bright red, the pain clear as day, so I cup his cheek, hoping it offers a little comfort.

He places his hand over mine, holding it against his cheek. The contact is both soft and sharp, a weird mix of exciting and calming, making my racing pulse ease. Ewan is okay. Well, bruised and potentially broken, but overall okay.

"You fell through a hole in the boat." I giggle. "Jace is going to have a field day with this, you know that, right? You're about to become one of his what not to wear videos."

Ewan rolls his eyes, letting out another very annoying noise. "Do we have to tell him?"

"I'd be willing to keep your secret, buddy," Landon says as he lifts Ewan's injured leg out of the fish box and rests it on a rolled-up towel. The disturbed ice settles underneath him, the crunching sound filling the air.

"Fuck!" Ewan's curse is sharp and loud, no doubt from the pain the movement caused.

"But this is gonna require X-rays, so we're gonna have to carry you outta here and—"

"You're not carrying me anywhere. I'm fine."

Excuse you?!

I shoot him a look. "I don't think so. You are going to listen to the medical professionals."

"I'm fine," he reiterates.

The fuck you are...

"Best I can offer is to hold you up and let you hop your way to the ambulance so we can—" Landon starts.

"Absolutely not. Just wrap it up and it'll be fine. We can go after the tournament is over."

Fire rises in me. I know this man is stubborn—it's how we've gotten ourselves into many situations in the past.

Including spending ten years apart. But if he thinks for one second that he's going to get away with refusing medical treatment so that he can hang out at a fishing tournament… Well, Ewan Hayes—think again.

"The fuck we can." My voice is louder than I intend, but I don't care. Landon reels back, hands flying up in surrender, giving us space. "Your ass is going and it's going now. Landon might be willing to make deals with you, but I am not. Is that understood?"

Ewan's eyes darken, his mouth morphing into a smirk that a few minutes ago would have seemed impossible. Reaching for me, he wraps an arm around me, tugging me into him. I go willingly, my heart so happy that all we're dealing with is X-rays and a CT scan that I can't even put it into words.

I collapse into him, burying my face into his shoulder, inhaling his scent, and letting myself get lost in him. His breath tickles my skin, and I can tell he's getting lost in our embrace as well.

"Okay, baby. Okay," he whispers. Loosening his grip on me, he presses his lips to my forehead, making the knot I didn't realize had formed in my chest unfurl. "Also, Mais?"

"Yeah?"

"I really love watching you in action."

19

EWAN

"Faaaa…"

I crash down on the couch, my entire body aching in a way I didn't know possible. Which means that tomorrow is going to introduce a whole new level of sore. Something that is hard to wrap my brain around right now, since this bone-deep throb is already overwhelming.

Propping my injured foot up on the coffee table, the plastic of the walking boot making a loud thud as it hits the wood, I suck in a breath, trying to ignore the hurt. To both my body and my pride. Because that second one definitely took a hit. Maybe a harder one than the first.

Definitely harder than the first.

My foot will heal. Detaching the muscles in my foot was not how I wanted today to go, and healing from this is not going to be a fun process. I'm stuck in this damn boot for weeks according to the ER doc, although I'm hoping that a visit to Doc Galindo here in town will provide a better update on Monday. It's the living down the teasing from my brothers about falling through a hole in my boat and having to be carted away by my girlfriend at my own event that is going to hurt the most. Because those fuckers will never let me live it down.

Hell, they've already started.

Once they got the all clear text from Maisey while we were at the ER that nothing was broken, it was game on. Everything from that point on was fair game. By the time we got back to Reel Madness, I had more than fifty unread messages in the sibling group chat—that was on top of the twenty-plus I had already read. Five older brothers and a younger sister isn't a blessing when it comes to group texts.

"Let's get this bad boy off and see what kind of pretty colors we can see, huh?" Maisey says, sauntering into the living room.

I perk up, my weary body coming back to life with her choice of words. She's changed out of jeans and her EMT T-shirt into a pair of cotton shorts and a tank top that is not helping matters either, showing off all of her curves and more than a little cleavage, making my dick twitch.

Parking herself on the coffee table facing me, she leans forward to grab a throw pillow, showing off even more cleavage, and it's like I'm a teenager all over again, sneaking looks down her shirt. Doesn't matter that I know just how perfect those tits are and how even more perfect they feel and taste—stealing a glance like this feels forbidden. My mouth waters and my fingers tingle, wanting to play, but I need to behave.

Maisey runs a hand down my leg, testing my ability to control myself, then starts to unbuckle the boot. The Velcro makes a harsh noise, filling the silence of the apartment, but only barely registering over the blood rushing through my veins.

"Ooof, now those are quite the shades of purple and green…"

I look down, and sure enough, my foot and ankle, which

are about three times the size they normally are, look like I stepped on a tube of purple paint, with a mysterious shade of green mixed in. There is no question that I lost the fight here.

"Would you believe if I said you should see the other guy?" I joke.

Maisey laughs, her boobs jiggling under her tank top, stealing my attention for a second. But only a second, because then she runs her hand down my leg again, and my dick reacts as if on cue.

"Problem is, I've seen the other guy—he looks unharmed." She continues to stroke my leg, making it harder to breathe, every inch of me wishing it were a different part of me receiving that treatment.

"Not true. Pretty sure one of the gas shocks on the fish box lid is busted."

"Not quite the same thing as muscular detachment and a trip to the ER."

No, no it's not. A gas shock is a standard part that you can buy in any number of stores, including my own. Fixing it will take fifteen minutes at most. Maisey's right—all the real damage done here was to me.

"When the call came over the radio, and they said *Hooked on a Reeling...*" Maisey's voice cracks, her hand stilling on my leg. "I thought I was going to throw up. I know it could have been anyone, but..."

My stomach sinks, the realization hitting me of what that must have been like for her. Maisey was such a professional, handling the call today the same way she did with Kendall that day in the parking lot—although her bedside manner with Kendall was a little gentler than it was with my stubborn ass—that I didn't think twice about it. She was in nurse mode. At least on the outside. But inside, girlfriend mode was still there. Freaking out.

"Oh, baby, I'm sorry. I didn't mean to freak you out."

"I'm not saying you fell in the fish box on purpose." She giggles, squeezing me before going serious again. "Just that I couldn't turn off that part of my brain. Had you been severely injured, poor Landon would have been on his own."

I nod, understanding completely. "I get it. But I'm thankful you were there. And I meant what I said; I loved getting to see you in action. I loved watching you that day with Kendall, and I loved watching it today on the boat and at the hospital."

I pause, taking another second to allow myself to be distracted by her cleavage again. Her fingers strum lightly against my skin, making it zing with each new touch.

"Especially the hospital. I thought I'd seen you in your element helping Kendall, but that was nothing compared to this afternoon. And you seemed to really hit it off with the staff."

Maisey's cheeks tinge and she looks away. "I was worried there for a second that I was overstepping. Some ERs get really touchy about EMTs jumping in, and I get it, because I was that way. There are moments you just want to tell people to stand back and let you do your job, you know?"

I do. Well, I don't, not like that. But, conceptually, I get it.

"If I were on shift and this whole situation had come in," she gestures between us. "Female EMT brings in her boyfriend and then tries to start helping, I would have sent me packing. Probably with an armed escort."

"You're mean," I tease. She nods, owning up to it with a guilty smile. "But Allison, was that her name? She didn't seem to mind."

Maisey nods, lighting up. "No, she was actually really happy to find out that I'm a fully licensed nurse paramedic in the state. Since they are short-staffed at the moment, having me there with you meant that she could get away with having her nurses focus on other patients."

"Aren't I lucky."

Maisey scoffs, slapping the side of my leg. "You are. You got very personalized attention."

I laugh, knowing that I got the best attention and care possible today. Not only from Maisey and the team at Tifton Regional, but the entire town once we got back to Reel Madness. I became an instant point of interest, people stopping me what felt like every ten feet to ask me how I was feeling, if I was okay, did I need anything, could they get me something, or some other annoying but intended to be helpful question. Didn't matter that I needed to work and that I had left a pile of things undone thanks to my fall—I had to attend to assuring everyone I was fine.

"What were you two all whispers about when I came back from my scans?"

Maisey swallows, an impish smile tugging at one corner of her mouth. Okay, now I'm intrigued.

The question has been nibbling at the back of my mind all afternoon. I asked her while we were in the ER, but she'd brushed me off, telling me we'd talk about it later. I tried asking again on the ride back to Hickory Hills, but was once again given the proverbial Heisman stance, with nothing more than "later, once we're at home."

Well, we're home now.

"So, earlier today, actually, not all that long before we got the call about you, Landon had mentioned to me that he had heard through the small-town, rural Georgia grapevine that there was an opening in the emergency room in Tifton. I was trying to casually deduce if that was true."

My ears perk up at the thought of a job opening locally for Maisey. No, that's not true. My *whole body* reacts. In the back of my mind I've secretly been waiting for the other shoe to drop. Waiting for her to get a call and leave again. But if she had a job offer here...

"Really?"

That impish smile grows, taking over her face, making her eyes light up.

"Yup."

Her single-word answer doesn't help much. I don't know if she's confirming that is what they talked about or if they have the opening. Her face isn't giving anything away either. Other than that she's loving the tease.

Leaning forward, she runs her hand along my leg, resting her hand on my knee, showing off even more of that perfect view. Fuck me…I swear she knows what she's doing.

"And do they?"

"They do. I have an interview scheduled for later this week."

Holy shit!

I lurch forward, only reminded that I can't jump up and grab her as she holds out a hand to stop me. Giggling, she leans back, licking her lips.

"Maisey, that's incredible."

"Not that working for Dad and Landon isn't nice, but I want to be back in a hospital. That's my world."

"They'll understand."

"I know," she agrees. "Landon's the one who told me about the position, so…"

She shrugs, the thin strap of her tank top sliding off her shoulder. She doesn't bother to adjust it, letting it hang there, the top curve of her breast peeking out even more. My dick twitches, and I don't know how much longer I'm going to be able to hold back. I'm too worked up.

My hands ache to hold her. To show her how much she means to me, and to take care of her the way she's taken care of me today. To repay her for being there. To convince her to stay.

"You know, after today, once again seeing how sexy it is

to watch you in action, I might just have to start injuring myself more."

"If this works out though, I won't be an EMT for much longer. You'll be stuck with Landon coming to your rescue all the time."

I shake my head. "Nope. I'll put in a request. Only hot blondes."

Maisey giggles. "Depending on which dispatcher you get, they still might send you Landon."

Touché…

"Okay, fine. But I would still get to have you as my own personal nurse when we're home."

"Ohhh, is that how you think this is going to work?"

20

EWAN

"OHHH, is that how you think this is going to work?"

Her taunt echoes off the walls, reverberating through me, straight to my dick.

Pushing off the coffee table, Maisey nudges my legs apart and steps in between them. Placing a hand on either side of my head, she leans down, giving me a full view down her tank top. *Fuck me.* "You think I'm going to nurse you back to health?"

I swallow hard, trying to peel my eyes away from her boobs so I can look her in the eye as I reply. Only, I can't. She has me hypnotized.

Yeah, she knows what she's doing…

"A man can hope," I tell her, grabbing ahold of her hips.

It's all I can do not to bury my face in her cleavage right now and motorboat the fuck out of her. My dick throbs, the desire flowing through me like rain through a gutter after a storm, and I'm not sure how much longer I can hold back.

As if she can read my mind, Maisey smiles. But not just any smile. A shit-eating grin that makes her whole face light up like the Fourth of July, letting me know that I'm in trouble.

"Well..." Tossing her head back, Maisey climbs onto the couch, a leg on either side of me, settling into my lap. Placing her palms flat on my chest, she runs her hands up and down, heat building underneath, traveling straight down south. "As a professional nurse, there is something I think I could do that might help."

"Oh, yeah?"

I run my hands up her sides, sliding under her tank, her warm skin greeting me like an old friend. She shudders under my touch, eyelids fluttering shut.

"I'd want to make sure I received proper payment though."

Sliding my hands around to her front, I cup her breasts, running the pads of my thumbs over her nipples. Inhaling sharply, Maisey rolls her hips against me, her core brushing against my hard-on. The contact is glorious, fleeting, and leaves me craving more. So much more.

"That can be arranged."

"You sure?"

I pause, wondering why she would question that. What she could possibly think I wouldn't do for it. Because there's nothing on this earth I wouldn't do if it meant making Maisey Phillips happy.

"Positive. Whatever you want, Maisey. I mean it. Anything, absolutely anything."

That grin returns—the one that tells me I'm in trouble—setting off the drumbeats in my chest. I can't wait to hear her request.

"Talk dirty to me. As dirty as you want. Call me names. Tell me what a slutty little nurse I am, or a whore or—"

"You want me to call you a whore?"

That's it? That's what Maisey wants? For me to talk dirty to her?

Maisey nods, her cheeks tinting pink as she bites her lip. It's taking a lot for her to admit this, but it's making me fall for her even more. I love that she feels safe enough to tell me this. That she wants to explore this with me.

"Yeah…" Her admission is soft, breathy. "In the moment, yeah. The idea is kind of a turn-on. As long as I know it's coming from a place of trust and intimacy. Because I'm *your* slutty nurse."

My dick strains against my pants, screaming to break free, all the blood in my body rushing straight to my groin. It's taking everything in me not to maul her right now. Not to show her exactly how *mine* she is.

"Oh, baby…" I swipe my thumbs across her nipples again, chuckling as her breath hitches. "Has me telling you what a pretty pussy you have not been enough? Or just how much I like tasting that pussy?"

Thrusting up into her, I tighten my squeeze on her boobs, rolling her nipples in between my thumb and forefinger. Maisey squeaks, swiveling her hips, trying to make better contact with my bulge. I hold still, letting her use me, as I continue to toy with her.

"You need more?"

I let go, and Maisey's eyes fly open, meeting mine. There's a fire in her baby blues that is unmistakable, and I know I've tapped into a new side of her. A side that she's waited forever to share, unsure that she'd ever get the chance. One that I'm going to treasure for the rest of my life.

Gripping the nape of her neck, I yank her into me, kissing her hard. There are so many things I want to tell her. Things that I know words won't be able to express. So this is going to have to suffice. The unspoken feeling of our lips meeting and our tongues tangling as she straddles me on the couch.

Pushing back, she reaches for the hem of her tank, pulling it over her head. My breath stalls in my chest, my eyes feasting on the vision before me. Maisey doesn't give me long, though, before climbing out of my lap and pushing my legs farther apart, then turning her focus to the waistband of my pants.

"Now, from my understanding, you've experienced this treatment before," she starts, teasing the elastics of my briefs. "And I'm a little inexperienced, but I'm hoping to rank better than the *miscellaneous* category."

Oh, fuck me...

I should have known those words would come back to haunt me. I had been trying not to be a jackass in mentioning that I'd been a complete jerk—more than once—drunkenly letting someone go down on me without reciprocation. Turns out, there isn't a way not to be a jackass about it.

"Maisey…"

"Shhhh." She presses a finger against my lips, her blue eyes so dark they look like the ocean at night. "Sit back, relax, and let me take care of you."

She has my pants off me in a flash, careful not to rough up my injured foot. Sinking down between my legs, Maisey licks her lips, sending a torch through me. My skin feels like it's on fire, the anticipation of this moment making time stop. She's so fucking beautiful—half naked, wanton, and all mine—there's a part of me that thinks I could come just looking at her like this.

Until she takes me in her mouth.

"Fuck!"

Hot, wet heat surrounds me fully, engulfing me in the most intense pleasure I've ever felt. I bolt upright, almost losing my balance. If I thought she was hypnotic before, looking at her between my legs with my cock in her mouth might just be the end of me. Because this is too much. Too overpowering. To the point where nothing else exists.

Just her and me. Us. Our connection.

How much I fucking love her.

Maisey continues, and I fight the urge to let go. It doesn't matter that it feels like she's sucking my soul out straight from my dick. My girl wanted something from me.

So I'm going to fucking give it to her.

"Fuck, baby…you are so good at that. Such a good cocksucker…"

Maisey moans, sending vibrations straight up my shaft that almost make me lose it. She is absolutely going to be my undoing.

"Maisey, you keep that up, and you're going to make me come. Is that what you want?" I ask, reaching down and weaving my hands into her hair.

Maisey moans again, and I can't tell if she's trying to speak or just getting off on my words, but either way, I know it's a yes. But there's still an unanswered question.

Gripping her hair, I pull her off my cock, hating the feel of her mouth leaving me, but loving the little bit of spit that forms in the corner of her mouth. *Oh, fuck, that's hot…*

"I need to know, Maisey, where do you want me to come? In your mouth or on your tits?"

Flames dance in her irises, and she reaches for my cock again, stroking it as she answers. "Mouth. I want to try swallowing." Sticking out her tongue, she licks me from base to tip, like I'm an ice cream cone, sending a zing down my spine. "If that's okay…"

"I told you, whatever you want."

Taking me back in her mouth, she starts up again, working a black magic I didn't know existed. Between her moans, swirls of her tongue, and her hand on my balls, my orgasm starts to build in no time. Starting at the base of my spine, it grows hot and fast, and I know that there's no stopping it.

"Maisey, I'm gonna…"

I roar, gripping her head and exploding into her mouth as a freight train of pleasure slams into me. Maisey doesn't stop though, keeping up her efforts, her fingers digging into my thighs as she holds on. The world goes black for a moment, a faint buzzing noise in the background all I can hear, the aftershocks still zapping me as Maisey pulls back.

"C'mere…" I growl, reaching for her.

Everything is still fuzzy, but my desire to hold her, to feel her against me, is stronger than anything else. Nothing will ever compare to this woman, and being the man who gets to hold her in his arms is the ultimate privilege.

"Was that okay?" she asks meekly, as if she's worried it won't measure up.

"I don't want you to ever ask that question again. Do you understand me?" I tell her, one hand weaving into her hair, pulling her in to kiss me, the other sliding into her shorts. Her lips are swollen and her kiss is slightly salty, the remnants of me still lingering there. More importantly, she's wet. So fucking wet. "Because that was way more than okay. Turns out, you are impressively slutty."

"Only for you."

"Mmmmm." Lowering my hands, I dip my fingers into her, making sure to graze her clit along the way. "Judging by how wet you are, you enjoyed that. A lot. Tell me, baby. You like sucking my cock?"

My thumb finds her clit, circling slowly, her breath hitching, those perfect tits at eye level. Only problem is these damn shorts. Removing my hand, I tug her shorts down as quick as I can, sneaking a taste of her off my fingers, then pull her back into my lap. Her bare, wet pussy grazes along my shaft, bringing it back to life.

"Not yet," I whisper into her ear, holding her back from sinking down on my cock. "You still need to come."

"I will—"

I shake my head, my hand slipping back between her legs. She whimpers, giving in to me. Good—because there is no way she's not getting hers. Not after what she just did for me. Fuck, I'll spend all night making her come over and over again after that.

Sliding two fingers inside her, I angle my wrist just right, rubbing the heel of my hand against her clit. Gasping, Maisey grabs on to my shoulders, moving her hips in time with my motions.

"That's it, baby, ride my hand. You were such a good girl sucking my dick, now be a good girl and come for me."

"Ewan!"

My name is like a curse on her lips as her body goes taut, eyes slamming shut, an orgasm taking over. Capturing her mouth in a kiss, I hold on, not letting her go—never wanting to let her go—trying to make this last forever.

"Inside me, now. Please," she demands, her climax barely finished.

Gripping me harder, she shifts, lining herself up with my dick and easing herself onto my shaft. We both groan, the collective sound of relief, pleasure, and coming together mixing as our bodies join. Her pussy is wet, tight, and welcoming. Like sliding into home.

As amazing as it is, though, I need more. I need her. I need the connection that comes only from us joining together like this.

So I pull out. Not all the way, but enough. Then slam back in. Maisey cries out, throwing her head back, her pussy gripping me tighter. So I do it again. And again.

"Yes!"

We find our rhythm—a mix of hard and fast with slow

and drawn out—both of us losing ourselves in it. We're a mess of limbs and movements, trying to be careful of my foot, Maisey riding me, keeping me hypnotized. Keeping me locked in, right where I belong.

Here. With her.

The two of us. Together. As one.

Maisey picks up the pace and I can tell she's close. She doesn't need to say anything; I've learned her body. Her tell-tale signs. What will make her come undone. And the deep need to do that fills me. To be the one who knows that. Who has the power.

Reaching down, my thumb finds her clit and I start to circle slowly. Maisey whimpers, rolling her hips.

"That's it, baby. Use my cock. I want to make you come." I lean forward, flicking her nipple with my tongue, feeling the tingle of my own climax prick at my skin.

But I need to get Maisey there first.

I turn my focus to her nipples, knowing the combination of that and her clit will be her undoing. Throwing her head back, she thrusts her chest toward me, so I double down. Any moment now…

"Together…please…" she begs.

Together? Fuck, yes.

I shift, changing my angle inside her, getting deeper. I thrust harder, focusing on nothing but our new target. Our destination. Getting us there and tumbling us over that edge. Together.

Maisey clamps down on me, her pussy trying to coax my orgasm from me, so I go harder. I give in to this. To us. Let our bodies take control.

"Ewan!"

Maisey screams out, her pussy gripping me like a bear trap, and she lurches forward, burying her head into my neck. That's all it takes, yanking me over that cliff with her, my climax hitting me like a bolt of lightning, shooting straight through my limbs. I hold on to her tighter, not ready to give this up—to let her go—riding out the waves of pleasure as they course through us.

Hearts racing, we stay like this for a long while, trying to catch our breath and basking in the afterglow. I've never felt calmer or more at peace than I do right now, with her in my arms, after coming together like that. I wish I had a way to tell her how she makes everything inside me still—in a good way. That I want us to spend the rest of our lives just like this.

"Ewan," she whispers, sitting up. A single tear snakes down her cheek, and my heart drops.

"What's the matter?"

She shakes her head, giggling as she swipes away the tear. "I love you."

"I love you. But why the tears?"

"That was just...intense? A good intense, but...still intense. Happy tears are a totally normal physiological response to being overwhelmed and/or intensely happy."

Overwhelmed and intensely happy. I'll take it.

I press my lips to her forehead gently, not wanting to overwhelm her more, but to reinforce that I'm here. That I mean it when I tell her I love her. That she's my future.

"Thank you for not laughing."

Okay, now I'm confused. I lift an eyebrow, trying to figure out what she's getting at.

"What was there to laugh at?"

"My request." She blushes again, looking down at her hands and then back up at me. "I realize it's not very high on the list of kinkiest things ever—in fact, it's pretty mild. I mean, ER nurse, I've seen some shit, but...we hadn't talked about it and I wasn't sure how you feel about talking to me that way, and since this is all so new to both of us…well, thank you for not laughing."

"I meant it, Mais. Whatever you want to try, I'm down. Especially if you actually want to dress as a slutty nurse."

She quirks an eyebrow at me. "Really? Whatever I want? You're open to *anything*?"

"Okay, there will be some things I draw the line at."

She's got me there.

I tickle her sides, drawing a laugh out of her.

"I should get us cleaned up and figure out dinner. Then I want part two of my payment."

Errr…what?!

"There's a part two?"

Climbing out of my lap, she gathers her clothes and leans back down to kiss me.

"Yup. Movie night snuggled on the couch. I'll let you pick the movie. But I'm picking the snack."

I laugh, unable to control myself. Fuck, I love her.

"Deal."

21

MAISEY

"Does that say *I want to fuck?*"

Errrrr....what?!

I whip around, Sawyer's voice carrying through the entire great room of Dolly and Hux's new home. The little white house—picked out from a stack of house plans that Dolly had saved over the years and then built to satisfy her every whim—is a sea of half unpacked boxes, packing material, and who knows what else. I don't know how she's ever going to find anything in this mess, or get it all organized and put away, but she swears she has a system. Something I'm just going to trust her on.

"Sure does!" Dolly confirms, beaming proudly. "Hux carried that around in his wallet for, like, years, trying to figure out a way to use it to ask me out."

Holding it up like an item on *The Price is Right*, Dolly shows off the wooden sign, the words burned into it. My eyes scan across it, laughter bubbling up inside with each new line.

I want to FUCK
Find ways to make you smile
Understand and support you
Cuddle you up and hold you close
Kinda also really want to fuck you too

"I think it's cute," Brenna says, peering around a box she's unpacking on the floor behind the couch.

"I'm still impressed *Hux* came up with that," Emily adds from the kitchen. "I mean, he's better than Grumpy Gus or Ewan's silence, but still. Not the vibe that the tats and ear gauges give off."

"Hey!" Margeaux and I call out in unison, defending our men.

Emily shrugs. "I said what I said."

"Gus is *intense*, not grumpy," Margeaux corrects, waggling her eyebrows. We all laugh, equally loving watching her blush at the mere thought of Gus's *intensity*, and the awkwardness of that too-much-information reveal.

"I'm still not entirely convinced he didn't get Jace's help, even though he claims he came up with it all on his own," Dolly says.

"I believe it," Sawyer says, tying up a trash bag full of packing paper. "I stumbled across some of the suggestions Jace made for Anton's letter to me after our fight, and well… they were a little over-the-top. He really takes that whole *I read romance novels so I'm an expert* thing seriously."

I bite my tongue, trying to hold back a laugh at Sawyer's Jace impression. Easier said than done, because she is spot-on. She might be the newest member of this family, but it's clear that she slipped in seamlessly.

Wait, no. She's not the newest. I am.

I step back from the box I just cut open and take a look

around the large, open concept space. The beautiful kitchen with all the bells and whistles Dolly could ever want, including her massive walk-in pantry and an island with a built-in range, gives way to a bright living room with large windows that overlook a beautiful open meadow leading to a creek on the Hayes property. Around the corner is an office and a set of stairs that leads to bedrooms and a loft that will undoubtedly be a playroom soon enough.

Right now, the house is filled with us girls—Dolly, Brenna, Margeaux, Sawyer, Emily, and me, with Alice and Rose on the way at some point—waist deep in an unpacking party. Something all of us were more than happy to agree to. Because it's about spending time together, as a family.

Three of us actually related by blood.

Five us by something stronger than Gorilla Glue.

Family, nonetheless.

One that I get to be a part of.

"Something the matter?" Brenna asks, looking at me like she can't tell if I saw a ghost or I need a drink.

"Emily's comment got her thinking about Ewan," Sawyer comments. "I mean, the whole I like my mouth on a big rod thing came from somewhere, right?"

I gasp, amazed that serious, no-nonsense Dr. Sawyer Brown just said that. Of all the people, I was not expecting that from her. Had it been Brenna, well, I don't know that I would have thought twice. She's proven more than once since I moved home that she's not the sweet and innocent tween that she was when I left for college—Cummins Cider, anyone? But Sawyer? No. She's the grounding force to Anton and all his antics.

Maybe he's rubbing off on her...

The rest of the group burst into laughter, so loud and unsynchronized, bouncing off the bare walls and echoing through the room. The sound reverberates through me, surrounding me, tackling me like a linebacker in the championship game with everything on the line. Giving in, I let it all out, a roar escaping, until I can't breathe I'm laughing so hard.

"It's *I like a big mouth on my rod*," I correct her, trying to catch my breath.

"Eh, I think my version works just as well."

Her perfectly straight face makes me lose it all over again. Holy shit, I think I just fell in love with Sawyer.

"How do we get *that* shirt made?" Margeaux asks, still laughing.

"Right, because you, Little Miss I'm Going to Take Over the World is going to wear that on a T-shirt?" Dolly teases.

"I'd wear it around the house...for Gus," Margeaux tosses back.

"Ew, no. I don't want to know about what you wear for Gus." Emily sneers. "He's my older brother's best friend. There's a line and that's it."

We all burst into laughter again. If this keeps up, my sides may actually split open.

"Seriously, though," Brenna chimes in. "I think it would be funny. Can you just imagine the boys' faces if all us wives showed up to Sunday dinner wearing that?"

Just one problem there, Brenna...

"Not all of us are wives," I point out.

To be fair, Brenna and Margeaux aren't married yet. But they will be soon enough. There are rings on their fingers. Dates are set. As far as anyone is concerned, they are Hayes women in all but actual on paper legal status. Sawyer and I, however...

"*Yet*," Dolly quips. "Sawyer just caught the bouquet, and do not for one second pretend like you're not halfway to negotiating a baby name list."

I purse my lips. She's got me there. Actually, there's no negotiating that. The list is set. Ewan might get a veto or two if he can provide a valid argument, but the list is made. To be fair, though, I think he'll be in agreement with me, since it does feature plenty of Hayes family names.

"Wait, you're going to allow negotiations on that?" Brenna asks, genuinely curious.

"No," Dolly, Margeaux, and I answer in unison, then burst into laughter again.

My phone vibrates in my back pocket, interrupting the moment. I pull it out, ready to dismiss the call, enjoying my time with the girls too much, when the number catches my eye. InterCon MediTrust. My employer.

My pulse jumps, a lump forming in my throat. This can't be good.

"I need to take this," I say to no one in particular, eyes still glued to the number flashing on my phone.

Stepping away, I walk around the corner into the entryway of the house, giving myself some room to be able to hear.

"Hello?"

"Maisey? It's Cathy Marshall from InterCon MediTrust. How are you?"

"Hey, Cathy."

My insides relax, my muscles unclenching as a mini wave of relief hits. Of all the contract coordinators at InterCon MediTrust, Cathy is one of my favorites. Always so easy to work with, understanding that we are actually humans that have needs rather than robots. She also isn't so hard and fast with all the rules, keeping us boxed in with the red tape like some of the others that I've worked with over the years. Even when delivering the bad news about our contracts being cut short, she was patient and understanding with us—just as frustrated as we were about the whole situation—and worked to make sure that those of us affected were taken care of. Truth be told, if she had any interest in practicing medicine, she'd make a damn good nurse.

"I'm good. Really good, actually." I smile, letting my happiness flow through me and into my response.

"You sound it. Seems like this extended break has been good to you."

"Extremely." Looking over at the girls—my *sisters*—my heart fills again. This extended break, as Cathy called it, has been exactly what I needed.

"Good. I'm glad to hear it, especially after how Nicaragua ended."

The mention of Nicaragua feels like it should be painful. Like it should be accompanied by a sharp pang, or a twinge, something to make me wince or recoil. Instead, there's nothing.

Yes, it sucks that it all went down the way it did, but I had no control over the hospital opting to cancel the contracts, resulting in the termination of me and several colleagues, so dwelling on it isn't going to get me anywhere. Plus, it was what I needed to pull the trigger on the ketchup pact. Something I likely would have left undone had my employment remained intact.

Pretty sure Garth Brooks has a song about this, the little blessings in disguise—or maybe his was about unanswered prayers—but either way, that's exactly what this was. A blessing in disguise.

"Thanks. I assume you're calling about my email?" I ask, not wanting to linger on the topic of my last assignment.

"Partially," she responds, hesitancy laced into her voice.

"Is something wrong? Did I miss something?"

"No, no. We got your request for an early opt-out of your employment, and everything is in order. And since you were part of the whole deal in Nicaragua, the agency has automatically approved it."

Oh, that's good. That makes that easy then. So why the call?

"Buuuut…"

No, no buts…

My stomach clenches. Cathy just said that they had my paperwork. That it was automatically approved. So why a but? Buts are bad. So, so bad.

"You were already on my list of people to call. I was just trying to get my ducks in a row. And I still can't promise that they're in a row, or that one isn't actually a pigeon." She laughs at her own joke and I smile despite the internal panic trying to crawl through my skin. Because I understand that feeling all too well. "And then I looked at your file and I saw your request, and well, I figured I needed to get my butt in gear and call."

"Okay. Is there an issue?"

"Oh, no. Exact opposite. There's an opening…in one of your requested countries. So, I'm calling to see how serious you are about that opt-out."

Oh, well then.

"Very, Cathy." That answer is easy. "I know it might sound crazy, but these last few weeks have made me reconsider a lot of things, and while I've loved working with y'all and all of the incredible experiences that I've had everywhere I've been, it's time to stay put. I'm in the process of applying to a hospital here locally in Georgia, which is why I asked for the opt-out, so—"

"It's Reykjavík," she cuts me off.

Reykjavík? As in Iceland? My stomach flips, the air in my lungs failing to move, the news hitting me hard and fast. There's an opening in Reykjavík. Holy shit.

The one place I never made it to. At least not professionally. I got to visit once, while I was posted to Austria, but only for a quick weekend getaway, instantly falling in love. I put it on top of my requested locations before we'd even left, hoping that something—anything—would come up. But the need never arose. So I kept going elsewhere.

Until now.

"Maisey, you still there?"

"Yeah, sorry, Cathy." I shake my head, trying to clear my jumbled-up thoughts. "Reykjavík. Wow...I...I don't know what to say."

"Does that change things?"

Does that change things? Good question...

I told Ewan that I was done traveling. That he was my future, and that Hickory Hills is our home. All the dreams we've talked about and plans we've started making—I can't go back on those. I don't want to. I meant them. He is my future. This is my home.

But Reykjavík would be a dream come true.

Fuck...

"It...ye...I don't know." I sigh, closing my eyes and wishing that I wasn't thinking about this. "Maybe."

"I thought it might."

"Cathy, I have things in motion here. And...and this is no longer just my decision. I can't give you an answer right now. I need some time to think."

"I get it." As always, her voice is full of understanding. Whether or not she actually gets me and my sudden onset of an internal struggle, who knows. But she can fake it like the best of them. "Contract has an October one start date, but I will need an answer by the twenty-first so we can start the paperwork."

The twenty-first. A week from today. Doesn't give me very long, but then again, how much do I really need? A conversation with Ewan, and…oh, who am I kidding, a week is nothing. Especially since we have my grandmother's birthday party this weekend.

"Yeah, fine," I tell her. "I'll have an answer to you by the twenty-first."

"Sounds good. I'll email over some of the particulars about this hospital to help you make more of an informed decision. Don't hesitate to reach out if you have any questions."

"I won't. Thanks, Cathy."

Ending the call, I slide my phone back into my pocket, inhaling deeply. Reykjavík. Holy shit.

Six weeks ago I would have been ecstatic to get this call. I wouldn't have had to tell Cathy that I needed to think about it or drag out my answer in any way. I'd have been doing my happy dance long before we got off the phone. My bags would be halfway packed by now.

Instead, I'm standing here, a wild mix of emotions too big to name, unsure of everything. Every last thing. Because six minutes ago I thought I had a new plan. I thought I had it all figured it.

Now the only thing I have is a tailspin.

"Maisey, you okay?" Sawyer asks, stopping in front of me as she makes her way to the front door with a trash bag.

I look at her, blinking hard, trying to focus on her question, but I can't. I don't know how to answer that question. My entire world has been turned upside down all over again —for the second time in a matter of weeks. Fuck me.

I need to talk to Ewan…

"Maisey…" Sawyer repeats, dropping the bag and stepping into me. Placing her hands on my biceps, she gives them a squeeze, pulling me back into the moment. "What's going on?"

"I..." I squeeze my eyes shut and swallow hard, trying to clear the wad of cotton from my throat.

I need to talk to Ewan...

"Heeeey!" Alice calls out, throwing the front door open, her hands full of white, branded, Oh, My Lard! boxes. "I brought pie!"

Good, I'm gonna need it...

2 2

EWAN

I HIT the landing leading to my apartment, my smile growing wider despite the pain radiating up my leg. The grin that I can't stop, no matter what I do. Because about three hours ago, I had the wildest thought of my entire life.

I should have listened to my wife...

My wife.

Yeah, go figure.

Pausing, I lean against the railing, holding my leg out over the stairs to try and stretch it out, rolling my stiff ankle. My first full day out of the boot after nearly two weeks was not the success story I insisted it would be. That stupid plastic torture chamber might have given my foot the chance to rest and do whatever other restorative magic it needed to, but apparently that came with muscle aches and pains I was not anticipating. Maisey, however, knew better, trying to tell me that I should take the boot with me and ease back into regular footwear. But nope, I knew better.

Like I said, I should have listened to my wife.

Errr...girlfriend. Maisey's not my wife.

Yet.

Still, I can't help but smile at how that's where my mind went so automatically. Or that no part of it scares me. The exact opposite actually. It excites me.

The cherry on top of a hell of a good day. One I can't wait to tell her all about. Days like today I understand what my brothers mean when they talk about having it all. Because that's exactly what this feels like.

Exactly what I thought when I hung up the phone this afternoon after getting the call that has the potential to change everything. My business. My life. Our future. To take everything to the next level, just like I told Maisey I've been hoping for.

Now I get to come home to her and share it all with her. I really do have it all.

Pushing forward, I grit my teeth and hide my hobble, not wanting to prove her right. I might be able to admit it in my head, but showing off the evidence is another story altogether.

"Maisey!" I exclaim, throwing the door to the apartment open. "You're never going to guess who called! Auburn University! They—"

I cut myself off, stopping just inside the front door, an intense aroma greeting me. Inhaling deeply, I let the medley of herbs and spices fill my nostrils, my stomach already eager to get in on the action. I'd know that smell anywhere.

That's my mama's country fried streak.

My favorite.

I walk into the apartment, the small entry opening up to the large open concept kitchen, all pretense of hiding my limp gone. I'm too focused on the scene before me.

Maisey's blonde hair is piled on top of her head in the messiest bun I've ever seen, a streak of batter smeared across her left cheek, an intensity in her eyes normally reserved for things like the egg on spoon race on the Fourth of July. She's so fucking adorable it's taking every ounce of strength I have not to rush over to her, scoop her up, and kiss her until we both can't breathe. Followed very promptly by licking the smudge off her cheek.

Then licking the rest of her.

The fully dressed table catches the corner of my eye—complete with placemats that I didn't realize I owned—and tells me I should hold off though. That she's up to something. Something that only makes me smile even harder. Because just when I thought it wasn't possible to love her even more, she manages to surprise me.

"Is that country fried steak?"

Maisey startles, spinning around to face me, her eyes as wide as the cast iron skillet in front of her. Her face flushes, tingeing pink, as if I caught her with her hand in the cookie jar.

"And collards, mashed 'taters, and fried okra." She nods to each one of the sides on the table, simultaneously sounding proud and self-conscious. "And then I've got a cobbler to throw into the oven for dessert."

Holy shit...

"You've been…busy…"

I know it's the wrong thing to say as soon as the words leave my mouth. That my reaction should be appreciation for her efforts, not something suspicious.

"Sorry," I correct myself quickly, stepping into her and hauling her into my side. Pressing a kiss to the top of her head, I linger, letting the sweet scent of her, mixed with the distinct aroma of my favorite meal, swirl around us. "This all looks incredible."

"There's a hitch in your giddyup," she comments, not skipping a beat, leaving my compliment untouched. So much for that worry.

"Just tired, that's all."

Her brow knits and I can't tell if it's concern or she's getting ready to scold me. "This is why I told you to take the boot. Muscle fatigue is a real thing. You could reinjure yourself. And then where would we be?"

"You did such a good job of nursing me back to health this last time," I quip, tugging her into me again, expecting a laugh. Or maybe a smart-ass comeback about how I've met my quota.

Only, I don't get either.

What I do get is a forced, half-hearted smile as she wiggles out of my arms, turning back to the stove. My heart sinks, the overwhelming feeling that I did something wrong taking over. Because something is suddenly…off.

"What about Auburn?" she asks, changing the subject.

Right…

"Remember how I said I had some irons in the fire about expanding the tour part of The Booby Trap?"

She nods, not looking away from the skillet. I hold on for a moment, waiting for more of a response, but get nothing. Not even a glance. To be fair, she's cooking, with hot oil at that, so keeping her focus on that rather than me isn't an indicator of anything.

"One of those things was a potential partnership with some of the local universities. Well, I got a call from Auburn today. Their Wildlife Enterprise Management program is looking for outdoor companies to partner with to give their students real-world experience."

"Oh…wow…"

Wow is right. In fact, it was the exact word I'd used in my head when the call came through this afternoon.

"So…what does all that mean?"

"Details are TBD," I say, leaning back against the island, needing to get my weight off my foot. "But the idea is that as part of an internship or some program like that, they would help provide me with students who are looking to work in the outdoor excursion space. So, tour guides for camping, fishing, hunting trips. Maybe a booking and admin person? There's a lot to figure out, but it's the first, big step."

"Ewan…that's…massive! Congratulations!"

She smiles, everything about her expression looking like it's supposed to, but somehow still wrong. Put on. Like a recording instead of a live performance.

Disappointment washes over me, all of my excitement about coming home and sharing this with her flowing right down the drain. Maybe I built up this moment too much in my head all day, but I expected more out of her reaction. One of her cute little squeaks. A squeal. Hugs, kisses, her jumping into my arms all excited that our future was coming together like we've talked about.

"Maisey…"

I reach for her, my hand grazing her hip, and she flinches. Snapping backward, I freeze, worry starting to replace my disappointment. Maisey has never flinched from my touch. Never.

What is going on?

"Dinner's ready," Maisey says brightly, looking back over her shoulder at me as if nothing happened.

Yeah, something is definitely wrong. Not just off, but *wrong*.

"Country fried steak, mashed potatoes, collards, and fried okra…" I repeat, watching as she pulls the battered steaks from the skillet and places them on a serving platter. Another item I was unaware I owned.

It's an entire feast. A full-on, traditional Southern Sunday dinner feast. One that has every potential to put me into a food coma. Part of me wonders if that's her goal.

"Yeah. I…errr…needed to think…" Beaming even brighter, she swivels, holding up the platter, showing off the beautifully golden-brown battered steaks. My mouth waters, the smell almost too much. "And so I thought, why not try cooking?"

Why not try cooking? Oh boy. This doesn't sound good.

Fuck.

"Maisey, what's going on?"

Maisey swallows, the muscles in her neck contracting slowly, like a snake moving its prey through its body. Trepidation creeps through me, moving faster and faster the longer she's silent, standing in the kitchen, holding a plate of skillet-fried meat.

"Let's go sit down," she whispers. "We need to talk."

We need to talk. The last four words any man ever wants to hear.

I take the platter, gesturing for her to lead the way. I don't care how much of a hitch there is in my giddyup, as she puts it; I can carry our dinner to the table. More than that, concentrating on not dropping the food through the pain is a good distraction from the fact that the woman I called my wife in my head a few hours ago just told me *we need to talk*.

Settling ourselves at the table, we're both silent as we make our plates, nothing but the clinking of utensils filling the air. Every inch of me is screaming to know what is going on. To ask if everything is okay. If we're okay. To reach across this table, haul her into me, and hold her, all while promising her that whatever it is, I'll make it okay.

"I also got a call this afternoon," she says, breaking the silence. Her voice is small, like she doesn't know how to say this. So I simply nod, giving her the space to do what she needs to. "From InterCon MediTrust."

"And you weren't expecting that?"

"Not with a placement offer."

I drop my fork, and the clang of it hitting the plate reverberates through the apartment, bouncing off the walls and seeming to echo off into space, making it almost deafening for a second.

A placement offer...

"Reykjavík."

Reykjavík. Her dream city.

My heart stops. Right along with my breath, all the oxygen sucked out of the room with that one word. The only word that has that power. That could turn our world upside down like this.

"It's a standard twelve-month contract," she continues when I don't say anything. "I wouldn't have to be there until October, but I do have to give them my decision by the twenty-first. And...I..."

Closing her eyes, she sighs, her whole body deflating. I reach across the table, taking her hand and giving it a squeeze, letting her know I'm here. She squeezes back, looking up at me, her eyes filled with tears.

"I don't know what to do."

Her voice cracks as she chokes back a small sob, instantly shattering my heart.

"That's the one you've been waiting for," I comment, still trying to wrap my mind around it.

The northern lights. The glass igloos. The Blue Lagoon. Volcanoes, waterfalls...all the things she rambled on about.

"You're what I've been waiting for," she counters. "What about our future?"

I shrug, because I honestly don't know how to answer that. My gut reaction is that we'd make it work. That we'd figure out a way. It's only a year. But that's what everyone says. That's how all the stories start. And almost none of them end well.

She sobs again, pulling her hand back to swipe at her tears. "Your life is here. The Booby Trap, Hayes, your family. This new partnership with Auburn. You can't leave that."

I nod. My whole life is in this town. By design. Poor design—admittedly—now that I look back on it.

"I could stay. I have my second interview at Tifton Regional tomorrow, and I think I have a really good shot at that position. Actually, I know I do. And even if I don't get it, it's not like Landon and my dad would ever fire me. And—"

"And you'd always regret it. Always wish you'd taken it. It'd be the one that got away."

Tears prick the corner of my eyes and I slam them shut. Now she's gonna be my one that got away. Again.

"I want our future, Ewan. You and me. The sex tent. Family camping trips and Sunday dinners with your brothers and Willa. I want to watch you make The Booby Trap bigger and better than anyone ever imagined."

"I want that too."

"But I…it's just…"

"I get it."

I don't. Not fully. There isn't an equivalent in my life for me to compare this to. That's not what's important though. Not even close.

The important part is that she's in pain and I can't fix it. Because there isn't a good answer here. No matter which option she chooses, it's going to hurt. One a lot more than the other—at least for me. I can't stand in her way though. I won't.

"What did you tell them?" I ask, looking down at the food sitting on the table. For a moment, I think about trying to take a bite, but my appetite seems to have vanished.

"That I needed time to think. That this isn't just my decision anymore."

What?!

"Sure it is."

"Nooo…" She draws out her answer, sitting back in her

seat. Her face morphs into confusion, halting her tears for a moment. "It's not. It's an us decision."

"Maisey, I can't make this choice for you," I bark. It's harsher than I intend, my emotions coming harder and faster than expected. "Like you said, my life is here. Complete with my own big dream come true. Even ignoring that, I am the sole person behind The Booby Trap right now, remember? It's not—"

"Part of Hayes," she finishes for me. "Right…"

She sighs, letting her head fall back. The war inside me continues to rage, the mix of emotions from sadness to anger battling each other for top billing as I watch her, waiting for her to move. To say something. Do something.

Even if it's telling me she's leaving.

I want to leap over this table and shake her. To scream *"Pick me!"* and *"Choose us!"* But I know that's useless. She knows how I feel. And if she's not going to pick our future on her own, then I'm not going to beg.

If she doesn't choose us though, I'm also not sure I can live through losing her a second time.

"Ewan…I want our future…" she repeats. Although this time I don't know who she's trying to convince, me or her.

The walls start to close in on me, the realization that losing her a second time is suddenly a very real possibility. My lungs tense up, making it harder to breathe, and the temperature rises. With each new labored breath, I feel more and more like a giant in a strange land, rather than a man at his own kitchen table.

I need to get out of here. Need to find space to breathe.

"Thank you for dinner," I mutter, pushing back from the table.

"Where are you going?"

Maisey pops to her feet, her gaze following me as I head

for the door. I can feel her eyes burning a hole in my back, but I don't dare turn around.

"Ewan, don't," she pleads. "Talk to me. We promised."

I stop, turning back on my heel. I look at her, hair still piled on top of her head, the smudge still on her cheek, all of her still so kissable it hurts. My perfect, wild, free-spirited girl.

Walking back over to her, I press a quick kiss to her forehead.

"You need to think. So do I. I'll be back."

I kiss her again, then turn to go, letting the door slam behind me. I'm down the stairs in no time, once again ignoring the pain in my foot, making my way to the back alley where I park behind the building. The fresh spring air hits me hard, giving me a moment to catch my breath as I climb into my truck. It's still not enough to solve all the questions in my head though. I don't know what will be.

Because sitting here, one thing is becoming abundantly clear. My life isn't in this town if Maisey isn't.

2 3

EWAN

Sucking in a long, hard breath, I tell myself to just fucking do it. That it's now or never. I'm a grown-ass man and this is no big deal. Just tap the fucking button.

Closing my eyes, I move my thumb quickly, hitting the little spot on my screen, letting the whoosh of the sent text fill the air and sending my anxiety skyrocketing.

> Got time to talk?

At least it's better than *we need to talk*. Although, not by much.

> GUS
>
> Always. At Pour Decisions. Need me to come to you?

My oldest brother's reply is swift and succinct, as if I would expect anything less from him. Looking up from my phone, I scan the parking lot, looking for Gus's very distinct 1971 Glacial Blue Plymouth Barracuda. A car that you could not miss in most crowds if you were blindfolded, but you

225

most certainly don't in Hickory Hills. And you absolutely would not miss it in the all but empty parking lot of your second oldest brother's bar in the middle of the day.

Although it's convenient that he's already here.

My plan had been to go drown my feelings while simultaneously filling myself with liquid courage while I waited for a response, but looks like that's out.

On my way

Piling out of my truck, I make my way into the old, warehouse-like space that now acts as a taproom for Southern Brothers Brewing. The large, open area is filled with tables, with a long roughcut bar on the far end. Two garage-style doors behind it open to a grassy area that is now home to a picnic shelter and tables for their weekly Drafts and Dig In night, before leading to the actual brewery building on the far side of the property. The whole operation has come a long way since Milo and Brandt started it up more than fifteen years ago.

"That was quick," Milo comments from behind the bar as I weave through the tables toward him and Gus.

"What, were you sitting in the parking lot?" Gus quips.

"Actually…" I settle on the stool next to him, letting my non-answer linger. "Speaking of, where's the 'cuda?"

"Spa day with Ken."

Spa day?

I look at my brother incredulously. I know he takes that car seriously—a little too seriously, which is the only way Gus knows how to do anything—but calling your car going in for maintenance a "spa day" is next level. Even for him. I also can't imagine that Ken Noble, the town mechanic, is advertising spa days for vehicles.

Past that, why is he here waiting on his car and not the

office? Pour Decisions is closer to the center of town and A Noble Mechanic than Hayes headquarters where Gus's office is, but it's not walking-distance close. At least, I wouldn't have thought so. So why not get a ride to the office? And where's Margeaux in all this?

Shaking my head, I turn to look at Milo on the other side of the bar, as if he's going to provide some answers. Sassy smile firmly in place, Milo chuckles, tossing his bar towel over his shoulder.

"My advice, baby brother? Don't ask questions you don't want to know the answers to." He nods, and I can't disagree with him. Because I know no matter what I say, Gus will only have an even more ridiculous justification. Not worth it. "Drink?"

"It's eleven a.m."

Milo lifts one shoulder casually. "We don't judge here. But if you don't want a beer, I've got the lemonade we make the shandies with or some bottles of water out back. Or one of Bronwyn's Diet Cokes—just don't tell her."

The fact that our marketing director has her very own stash of her preferred drink behind the bar says a lot. Not that long ago, Milo and his business partner, Brandt, staunchly held to the line about not being a full bar, and therefore only served Southern Brothers beer. He's always kept water on hand too—whether bottles or simply from the tap—but for a long time that was the only other option. Until Brandt came up with the Sobbin' Shandy—mixing their hallmark ale with lemonade—and they started to keep that as well, even if not sold separately. Then we hired Bronwyn, a non-drinker who might as well hook herself up to a Diet Coke IV. So much so there's some in the Southern Brothers mini fridge.

Soda isn't what I need right now, however. This is definitely a beer conversation.

"Actually, a Party Mode sounds good," I tell him, hoping he really meant that not judging thing. Given that I'm not the only brother in here, hours prior to the taproom opening, I think I'm safe.

Milo nods, grabbing a pint glass and tugging on the wooden handle, amber liquid pouring from the spout.

"So, what's up?" Gus asks, closing a manila folder and pushing it to the side. "Everything okay?"

"It's…yeah, it's fine."

Milo slides the pint glass across the bar in my direction, and I take it from him, the glass cold against my hand, sending a shiver through me. I take a long sip, letting the taste of beer settle over my taste buds, distracting me from the wild swirl of thoughts and emotions trying to take over inside my brain.

"That's not terribly convincing," Gus replies, taking a swig of his own beer.

"Sorry, I…" Running my hand down my face, I try to gather my thoughts. "Didn't get much sleep last night. I was up all night…thinking…and…"

I trail off again, still trying to muster up the courage to have this conversation. To ask the fully loaded question. These are my older brothers, and for as much shit as we all give each other, I know they have my back. I know there's no judgment here. Not real judgment anyway. Safe space or not, that doesn't make doing this any easier.

"Ewan, out with it," Gus presses.

It's now or never…

"What would it look like if I signed The Booby Trap over to Hayes?"

Both of my brothers freeze, as if they looked Medusa in the eye and she turned them to stone. I don't even think they blink. The whole warehouse is silent, the proverbial pin drop more than loud enough to be heard. Hell, I think a church mouse could fart and it would echo through here.

"What?" Gus asks, finally spitting something out, quickly followed almost simultaneously by Milo's "Seriously?"

"What would it look like—" I start to repeat, but Gus cuts me off.

"No, I caught what you said. That doesn't make it make sense though."

No, it doesn't. It also doesn't make it hurt any less either. I'm damn proud of the business I've built—*on my own*—over this last decade. The last thing I ever thought I'd do was officially sign it over to the family company. But, if that's what it's going to take to be able to make everything work…then it isn't a question.

"I just need to know what it would look like. What my options are."

"Why?"

Gus's face turns skeptical, his brow furrowing as he searches me for some kind of answer. Like I'm hiding a major secret that will only come to light after he agrees to my demands.

"Does it matter? You've been pestering me about this for years. You brought it up at Sunday dinner a few weeks ago."

"It does if you or the store are in some kind of trouble and it's going to put the company at risk."

Oh, fuck me. Seriously, Gus? That's where your head went?

I roll my eyes, reminding myself that this is who he is, and that deep down, this is his way of showing he cares. He has a funny way of showing it sometimes.

"August," Milo chides, giving him a serious case of side-eye. The only one of us who can get away with calling Gus by his full name, Milo takes advantage of that often, keeping him in check.

"You're not in trouble, are you?" Gus follows up, this time with more concern in his voice.

"No. Exact opposite, actually, from a business standpoint. I've actually got a new partnership in the works to potentially expand my touring operation."

"Fuck, yes!" Milo holds out his fist and I bump it, letting the excitement bubble up in me for a second. But only for a second.

"Then what's really going on here?" Gus pushes. "Because I know you, and you haven't been fighting me on this since day one to suddenly flip the second you're about to level up."

I sigh. Should have known better than to think he wouldn't want all the dirty details.

"Maisey has a contract offer. In Reykjavík."

Silence falls over us again, but this time it's not as harsh. Nor does it last as long.

"I thought she was applying over in Tifton?" Milo asks. "Brenna said something about there being an open position in their ER, and how she apparently made all sorts of friends during your little field trip."

I laugh, shaking my head and handing him a single finger salute for bringing up my accident. Although, he's not wrong. Maisey was the star of the show that day, and every medical professional we encountered made some sort of comment about it. I'm still half surprised the boss lady nurse didn't try to kidnap her right then and there.

The same woman she met with last week. Whose boss she's interviewing with right now. No doubt nailing it too.

"She is, but…" I take another swig of beer, buying myself time. "Reykjavík is her dream city. It's been number one on her request list for forever and a place she's never been assigned. Careful mentioning the city around her though, 'cause you'll get the Maisey ramble."

The Maisey ramble—second only to the tornado tactic in verbal head-spinning maneuvers she has up her sleeve.

"She taking it?" Gus asks.

I shrug. "Not sure. She's…conflicted. And…and I can't be what stands in her way."

"And you think signing over The Booby Trap to Hayes solves that?"

The door to Pour Decisions opens, all three of us immediately looking over at the interruption. Seth Jennings, local plumber and town council member holds up his hand in greeting, awkwardly smiling like he knows he interrupted something.

"Hey, you called about a clogged toilet?" Seth asks in way of greeting.

"Sure did!" Milo responds, working his way out from behind the bar. "I tried the plunger and nothing. Didn't feel like messing with it after that, worried I'd make more of a mess…"

His voice fades as the two of them walk toward the men's room, having about as casual a conversation about a clogged toilet as possible. A problem I'd gladly face right now rather than dealing with this. Seems like that one has a much easier solution.

"Have you talk to Maisey about this?" Gus asks, pulling me back to our conversation.

"No. And don't go saying anything to Margeaux either." I point at him, hoping it comes off as a threat. I know it doesn't work, the eight years between us even as adults too much of a distance for me to ever be anything other than baby brother. "I need to know what the options are. What this would look like. How it could all play out."

Gus nods, his face softening with understanding. "If you move forward with this, I'll have to talk to someone in legal. Margeaux's our IP specialist, but depending on how quiet you want to keep it, she might be the best one to draw up the contract."

"I just need to find a way to make it all work. Let her have her dream of taking this contract, while not losing everything I've worked for here. Somehow still getting this partnership with Auburn off the ground."

"Auburn?"

I grin sheepishly. Guess I left that detail out earlier.

"Yeah. They're looking to expand one of their programs and, in doing so, partner with me. It'd give me the ability to expand, as well as a steady stream of qualified people. Err, well, in theory qualified, if that's what they're getting a degree in."

"Ewan!" Gus is up and off his stool in no time, arms encircling me in a bear hug. I squeeze him back, thankful for his love and enthusiasm. "Proud of you."

"Thanks. But, this stays here. It's not official, and…"

"Everything's confidential, you know that," he assures me, letting go and sitting back down.

Time for real talk though. Because my brother being excited for me isn't solving anything. If nothing else, it's making this tougher.

"But I need to find a way to make it all work, so that—"

"You need to talk to Maisey about it."

I shake my head. No. That's not the answer. Not yet.

"She knows." It's not a lie. She does know about the opportunity. Not all the details, since last night's conversation got derailed with the bomb she had to drop, but still. She does know about it. So what she doesn't know is that I'm here, having this conversation. "It's fine. But if she chooses Reykjavík, am I able to make it all work?"

Gus pauses, watching Milo as he slides back behind the bar. "You know you can't do all that from overseas, right? That you're going to have to be here to get that partnership up and running and off the ground. Maybe if it were more established, you could risk it, but…the first year? No way."

Swallowing hard, I look away, hating hearing those words from him, the reality of it hitting me all over again. I wasn't kidding when I said I didn't get much sleep last night. I was up all night running every possible scenario through my head. Not a single one of them ended with me being able to establish the expansion I want—and that the university would require—if I'm not in Hickory Hills. My hope that Gus would have a suggestion that I couldn't come up with is dwindling by the second.

"Distance isn't an option?" Milo asks, cutting in.

I turn to him, more serious than I've ever been. About anything.

"I chose this town over her once. I can't…*won't* do that again."

My brothers nod, their expressions telling me they get it. That they understand exactly what I'm feeling when it comes to Maisey and my unwillingness to back down on that point. Both of them know what it's like, having experienced their own moments when it came to their partners that they chose not to back down. Milo's resulting in an actual fistfight, while Gus almost walked away from Hayes altogether.

"So, back to my original question, what does it look like if I sign The Booby Trap over to Hayes? How much control do I get to keep?"

"What do you mean?" Gus looks confused.

"I need the store to stay mine. I need to retain control. I don't want someone else coming in and changing everything."

Gus looks to Milo then back to me. "It's never *not* going to be yours, Ewan. All this would do would be to bring the store under the Hayes umbrella. You'd no longer be sole proprietor, but The Booby Trap would still remain fully under you and your control. Just like Southern Brothers belongs to Milo and Brandt, but is under the umbrella."

"You think we don't run this place?" Milo sasses. "We don't listen to this guy just because he thinks he's the boss."

"I am the boss," Gus reminds him. Milo shrugs, not completely convinced. "The Booby Trap would have Hayes Industries backing from a funding, payroll, and insurance perspective, which would change the overall financials, and we'd want to look at the property ownership and potentially create an LLC if that makes more sense, but that's what we have Ernie the tax guy for."

I blink, trying to take it all in. Because this is actually sounding like a decent option. Especially the insurance and payroll part if I have to work on finding someone to run the place in my absence. Another part of this I don't want to think about. But then again, if it's under the umbrella, it doesn't all fall to me to figure that out. I think.

It still means giving up the Auburn partnership though. Gus is right there. No matter what we do, there's no making that work unless I stay put. And the only way I'm staying put is if—

Bang!

The sound of the slamming door reverberates through the room, making me jump, almost knocking over my beer. I catch it in time, avoiding a mess, then turn to see what is going on. Jace's voice gets to us first.

"Gus! Unhire her now."

Jace barrels toward us, madder than a cat dunked in a bathtub. His eyes are trained on Gus as he weaves through the tables seamlessly, clearly on a mission.

"I was unaware you were holding office hours in my bar today, August," Milo jokes.

"Me either," Gus replies.

"I mean it; unhire her right now. You're executive vice

president, so you get final say on every hire. So do it—unhire her. Right now."

He stops just short of the bar, letting out a huff so loud I half expect fire to fly out of his nostrils as his hands land on his hips. Jace is clearly channeling his inner Willa.

"I'd have to know who you were talking about first," Gus responds, leaning back to avoid being collateral damage.

"Presley Callahan. You can't hire her."

"Who even is that?" Gus asks, looking to me and Milo.

"You're kidding, right?" I ask, unsuccessfully trying to hold in my laughter.

Jace glares at me. "Do I look like I'm fucking kidding you?"

"Who are you talking about?" Gus asks again, this time his voice raised and annoyed at not getting his answer.

"The new social media manager. I just heard Bronwyn talking about it."

"Oh, I didn't realize that she decided."

"Apparently on Presley Callahan," Milo snarks, his shit-eating grin taking over.

"Yeah," Jace mutters. "And you can't do that."

"Who is she? And why can't we?"

Jace's eyes bulge and his nostrils flare, and I lose it. There's no holding back my laughter anymore. This is too good.

"Ohh, this is gonna be good…"

"Shut up."

I continue to laugh, loving this way too much. If there's one thing in life that's gotten under his skin, it's Presley Callahan.

"What am I missing?" Gus asks, clearly becoming impatient. "And why do I have to unhire someone that we may or may not have actually hired?"

"She's the one who displaced Jace."

"What do you mean displaced him?"

"Ohhh…" Milo comments, everything suddenly clicking. His smirk grows even bigger and I can tell he's about half a heartbeat away from joining my laughter.

"Ohh, what?" Gus looks between us, his grumpiness becoming more and more solidified on his face. "Someone please fill me in."

"Do you really not remember?" Milo quips.

The bar door opens again, Hux sliding in.

"Hey, is the keg for tomorrow all set…" He stops, halfway to the back room, taking the scene in. "What's going on? What did I miss?"

"Apparently Bronwyn just hired Presley Callahan," I call out.

Hux stares back blankly for a moment, then his face lights up, the light bulb over his head coming to life. "Well, no shit…that chick from high school?"

"Yup!"

"Oh, that's… This is gonna be good."

"Seriously, fuck all of you!" Jace exclaims. "Gus, please."

Throwing up his hands in surrender, Gus turn to face Jace. "Maybe once someone explains who the hell we are talking about!"

"Otis Callahan's daughter," Milo answers, knowing that the fastest way to get Gus there is to connect her to Hayes's compliance officer.

"They moved here when we were in high school, the summer before Jace's senior year. She's the one who made it so he wasn't valedictorian," I continue. "And then continued to beat him at everything after that."

"The reason he was no longer the golden child in town." Hux laughs.

"Ohhhh…" Gus mouths, understanding dawning on him.

We're all so close now that it's sometimes hard to

remember that the number of years between us mattered a lot more when we were younger. There's just under a year separating Jace and me, with a little over two between him and Hux. The three of us were all in school together, while Gus and Milo were all but out of college at that point. Actually, by Jace's senior year, they were both out of college. Hickory Hills is a small town, with a strong rumor mill, but two twenty-something dudes were not paying attention to their younger siblings' high school woes.

Unless that woe is what gets you knocked off the top spot of the honor roll.

"You can't hire her," Jace insists again.

"I can do whatever I want," Gus claps back.

"No."

Gus raises an eyebrow, the bull clearly poked. Nice job, Jace.

"Yes. More importantly, this is Bronwyn's choice. If this Presley is who she wants, then I trust that she's the best fit for the position and I'm not going to stand in her way."

"Are you—"

"C'mon." Hux slaps Jace's chest with the back of his hand. "Come help me with this keg. Put your anger to good use."

Jace follows, still muttering about how he's going to talk sense into Bronwyn, because this *just can't happen*. We wait until they're gone, the swinging door to the back room as shut as it can be, before Gus turns back to me.

"You need to talk to Maisey; you know that, right?"

I heave out a sigh, my mind clicking back to the heaviness weighing on me. Jace's tantrum was a nice distraction, but it doesn't change anything. In fact, it only proves to me that I know what I need to do. Because where Maisey is concerned, there's only one thing that matters.

I made the mistake once. I won't make it again.

I will need to talk to her. It's just not the conversation that Gus thinks we need to have.

"When can you have the paperwork drawn up?" I ask.

"Ewan," Milo chides in the same tone he usually reserves for Gus. It's his warning tone, but I'm not going to heed it. I know what I'm doing.

"Can you have them ready by Munch?"

"You need to talk to Maisey," Gus repeats. "Take it from the guy who tried to make a decision about his professional future without talking to the woman he loves. Talk to Maisey."

I shake my head. "Gus, draw up the paperwork. I need to make sure everything is in place so that no matter what she decides, she can make her dream come true. And there's only one way to do that."

24

MAISEY

"I DON'T WANT to tell anyone about Reykjavík just yet."

I stop short, almost skidding to a halt, loose gravel in the shared parking lot between the church and the library catching under my shoes, my arm tugging on Ewan's as he continues to walk for a step, our hands still joined together. Turning to me, his eyes go wide, asking the question before he does.

"So, you've decided?"

No, not even close. I haven't decided on anything. In fact, I'm so far from a decision it's not even funny.

"No." I shake my head, looking over at the large group already gathering for my grandmother's party in the open field next to the library.

A few hours ago this space was filled with booths and vendors for the weekly Farmers' Market. Now there's a tent with tables, chairs, and a buffet big enough to feed the town. Oh, wait—it is feeding the town.

As the matriarch of Hickory Hills, my grandmother's hundredth birthday is a big deal. To be fair, at this age, every trip around the sun is a big deal, but when you are *the* town elder, it becomes next level. What started out as immediate family only snowballed into something much bigger—with the guest list taking on a life of its own—to the point where we were no longer going to fit in the church hall anymore.

Now, all of my immediate and extended family are here, plus half the town, ready to celebrate. When all I want to do is curl up at home next to Ewan and have a personal existential crisis over my future.

Our future.

"And that's why I don't want to bring it up," I continue, squeezing his hand. Ewan looks down at me, his blue eyes holding mine like they hold all the world's secrets. "Because I don't want to have to answer all the questions that I know are going to come with it."

Like all the questions that are still running through my head. All of the ones that he doesn't seem to want to talk about either.

We'll make it work.

That's all he keeps telling me every time I try and broach the subject, every time I've tried to question how or what we're going to do, tossing out possible scenarios or options. It's the same response every time—those four little words. Said with a confidence that only Ewan Hayes could have. *We'll make it work.*

"You're the only one who knows about the offer, and I…" I sigh, pausing as Dolly's parents walk by, waving at us. "I want to keep it that way. Until we decide."

Ewan gathers me in his arms, kissing me gently. I give in, letting myself relax into him. To surrender. The only moments I haven't felt completely conflicted since I got Cathy's call are when he's holding me. Right now, Ewan Hayes is the only thing that makes sense to me.

This whole situation would be a lot easier if one of the choices sucked. If they were offering me a contract in some mediocre location. Or if my first impression of Allison and the trauma response team at Tifton Regional the day of Ewan's accident had been a fluke. But no.

Reykjavík is the one place I've wanted to go for years. The top of my bucket list. And Allison? We got on even better during the interview than we had during our ER visit. Even her bosses are great. She's exactly the kind of charge nurse I want to work for. I can see myself living both lives, being perfectly happy.

If only there were a way that didn't involve some made-up magic necklace that I don't have access to.

"*You* decide," he corrects, pulling back just enough to rest his forehead against mine. "I can't make this decision for you, Mais."

"I'm not trying to start a fight in a parking lot, Ewan, but…this is *our* future that we're talking about here. I appreciate you respecting me and my independence, but this is something we should kinda decide together. Because one of the options requires you to give up—"

He cuts me off with a kiss. This one not nearly as gentle as the first. Not even close. His hands cradle my face, fingers weaving into my hair as he deepens it, and I whimper. *Fuuu-uck*…this isn't fair. When he kisses me like this, the world stops. Nothing else matters.

We aren't standing in the middle of a public parking lot, surrounded by every one of my aunts, uncles, cousins, and half this town. We don't have big, life-altering choices looming ahead of us. And we most certainly don't have to behave ourselves.

Except…we do.

We have all those things.

"We'll make it work, beautiful. Whatever you choose."

There's that confidence again. I'm glad he's so sure. One

of us has to be, and it's certainly not me. I'm not sure of anything at the moment.

Except him.

Wrapping an arm around me, Ewan places another kiss on the top of my head before we head into the tent. The large, open-air space looks much like it did for Dolly and Hux's wedding last month, only with a few more tables in place of the dance floor, giving everyone more room to spread out. I can already smell Dolly's famous honey butter biscuits, the scent of freshly baked bread lingering in the air.

Standing right by the buffet, peering into an open chafing dish, is the birthday girl herself. Pointing to her, I direct us that way, wanting to see what kind of trouble she's causing.

"Checking to make sure it's up to your standards?" I ask, gently nudging her with my shoulder.

"I was checking to make sure that the specific items I requested made the list."

"Because you thought Dolly wouldn't follow your request?" I ask.

"It wasn't Dolly I was worried about," she snarks, giving me a knowing look.

Oh, got it...

I nod, letting her know I understand. "So, what is it that you requested that's so special?"

"Chicken 'n dumplings, red beans and dirty rice, and cheddar hush puppies."

Now that's a combination. Then again, at one hundred years old, I suppose no one gets to comment on your food choice.

"Sounds fab."

"It will be, since our Dolly is cooking."

I laugh. Can't argue with that.

"Now, Ewan Hayes, I hope you don't mind, but I'm going to steal this beauty from you for a little bit," Grandma continues, looping her arm through mine. "I haven't gotten near enough time with her since she's been home."

Guilt rips through me. I did promise her that we'd have plenty of girl time when I arrived back in town. A promise I have not lived up to, since most of my spare time has been spent with Ewan. Whooops...

"No problem, ma'am. She's all yours." He winks at us. "Although, do y'all want me to get you something to drink before I leave you to talk about me? Or are you all set?"

Ewan Porter Hayes!

"Oh, that would be lovely. There's a lot to catch up on, so I'm sure we will be quite parched."

Thanks, Grandma...

Ewan nods, turning to leave us and head off in search of drinks. I shake my head, looping my arm through my grandmother's and leading her over to a table where we can sit.

"Happy Birthday," I say, making sure she's securely seated before I grab the chair next to her. "How does it feel to hit this milestone?"

"Psssh." She waves me off. "When you get to be my age, one birthday is like the next. You're just happy to see it. I care more about how *you* are. Haven't seen you much since Dolly's wedding. Priorities shifted a bit once you got back into town, huh?"

Ooof, way to call me out...

Then again, I deserve that.

"I didn't mean to ditch you," I tell her. "I'm sorry. Things moved fast and—"

"Maisey Margaret Phillips, stop right there. I do not blame you one bit. I'd also pass on hanging out with an old lady like me in favor of some rather respectable wienering."

Rather respectable wienering? Well, that's a new one...

I press my lips together, biting down as I try to hold it together and not burst into laughter. Rather respectable wienering. But I'm not sure I can. I need to though. Which means I need to think of something. Anything.

Anything other than Ewan. And his very respectable wienering.

"It is respectable, right?" she follows up. "Based on the way Dolly lit up like a pinball machine once she finally ditched that Jeff guy and upgraded herself to Huxley, I know she is properly taken care of. I assume based on your newfound glow, you are too."

Heat races up the back of my neck. That's not a glow; that is straight up fluster. Grandma has always been a straight shooter, but phew…I was not expecting her to come right at me about my sex life.

I won't lie though. I kind of love it.

"Perfectly respectable," I inform her with a firm nod. Then, I think better of my answer, leaning in to whisper. "And sometimes not so respectful…"

"As it should be. Every girl needs a rip in her jeans."

I laugh, unable to hold it in any longer. It's a phrase I've heard her mutter many times before and never thought anything about, usually attributing it to my need to follow my own path. But now that I hear it in this context, I'm starting to think it might be a bit too much information about my grandfather.

Although, good for Grandma…

"I'm happy to see you so happy, Maisey," she continues, her voice turning serious. "There was a part of me that was worried when your mama told us about everything that happened with your job in Central America and that you were going to come spend some time back here to regroup. That's never been who you are, my little free spirit. You always had your own drum to dance to. But you found your way."

A single, wry chuckle escapes before I can stop it. If only

she knew that I'm in even more of a pickle now than I was a last month when I arrived back in town. That this happiness that she's so happy about is not a facade, per se, but may be a little bit in jeopardy right now. My heart not far behind.

I look up at her, wishing I had a way to tell her everything. Other than outright telling her everything. That is an option, other than the fact that I literally told Ewan not fifteen minutes ago that I wanted to keep it between him and me. Doesn't mean I can't change my mind.

"Something on your mind?" Grandma asks.

You could say that...

Executive decision—Grandmas don't count.

That, and it's better to ask for forgiveness than permission. Right? Right. Ewan will understand. Especially since my seeking forgiveness will involve whatever the female equivalent of *rather respectable wienering* is.

"I am happy," I tell her, not bothering to hide my smile. "I did find my way, because what I didn't realize was that drum was leading me back here. That…"

I sigh, sitting back in the chair and slouching down. I wait for her to correct me—tell me that's not how a lady sits—but she doesn't. Simply lets me loaf here with bad posture.

"That its matching beat was here the whole time, waiting for me."

"But…"

"How do you know there's a but?" I challenge.

"Maisey, you're not sitting in that cheap folding chair like a discarded sock without there being a *but*."

Fair point.

I sit up, straightening myself out, not liking the discarded sock comparison one bit. That was a little too vivid.

"Have you ever had to make an impossible choice? One that you somehow know that no matter which option you choose, you're always going to wonder *what if?*"

The corner of my grandmother's mouth lifts, her expression softening as she thinks. "At the time I thought so. Although looking back…"

She shrugs, her contentment still clear.

"What happened? How did you choose?"

"Life kind of chose for me. Made it clear which path I was supposed to take. Turns out, there wasn't as much wondering as I expected. Almost none, actually. Looking back on it now, I can't even imagine having chosen the other option."

I nod, letting her answer settle inside me as more people pour into the tent, the noise level kicking up a notch. Pretty soon we'll be interrupted, people wanting an audience with the guest of honor.

"I'd really like some of that kind of clarity right about now," I tell her.

"You'll find it. When and where you least expect it. The universe has a weird way of gifting those kinds of things to us." Reaching over, she takes my hands, squeezing them. "Know what I would like?"

"What?"

"That drink we were promised. I wasn't kidding about being parched."

I sputter out a laugh. Totally fair. We did lose Ewan somewhere along the way. Yes, the tent has filled up exponentially since we arrived—and it's not like we were even close to the first ones here—but that doesn't mean it should have taken him this long to have grabbed a couple of sweet teas. I've got ten bucks that says one of his brothers roped him into some stupid conversation and he needs rescuing. Or worse, he's at the mercy of Aunt Hattie who put him to work.

"Let me go figure out where Ewan got to."

"Thank you, dear."

Pushing to my feet, I lean down, kissing her cheek. I'm no closer to an answer, but somehow, I am more at ease. At least a little bit. There's still a chance I'll choose wrong—but there's more of a chance that I'll make a choice that simply shapes the way my life goes. Or so I hope.

Then again, I thought that the last time. My decision then had shaped how my life was going. All my years traveling and seeing the world. Missing out on what was happening here. Missing Ewan.

Who is just as much of a consideration. Because it's not just my life I'm shaping. It's his. It's ours. I don't care how much he says *we'll make it work,* this is an us decision. And just how does he think we're going to make it all work?

Okay, I take it back. I'm not at all at ease. I am still very wound up. And not in a good way.

Bam!

I slam into something solid, the sudden stop sending me backward, trying to catch my balance. Shit, I should have been watching where I was going. A pair of hands grabs my shoulders, steadying me, and I blink, still trying to regain my composure.

"Oh, shit, Maisey, are you okay?"

I nod, my wits back about me, my eyes settling on Seth Jennings, the town plumber. Average height, sandy-colored hair, and brown eyes, he's the kind of guy that would probably get lost in the crowd if you weren't looking for him, but always nice enough, going out of his way to help me whenever I needed it back in high school. Including driving all the way to Tifton to get supplies the night before our physics group project was due because I accidentally knocked it over and we had to start from scratch. Ewan used to tease me that Seth was only that nice to me because he had a crush on me, despite my protests that he was wrong. At least up until Seth asked me to prom, and then I didn't hear the end of it.

I bet the second Ewan sees Seth talking to me, he brings it up again...

"Hi, Seth. I'm fine. I didn't mean to plow into you like that."

"Don't worry about me." He laughs, dismissing my apology. He doesn't let go of me but instead gives me a long once-over, dragging his eyes up and down my body, checking to make sure I'm steady. "I'm more worried about you."

Stepping back, I remove myself from his hold. "No need. Just stuck in my own head. Should have watched where I was going."

"I'm glad I ran into you. Literally." He laughs at his own pun. I force a smile, not wanting to be rude. "Your father mentioned you'd moved back and were working as an EMT for the town—"

"When did you talk to my dad?"

The question fires out of me like a bullet from a gun. There's no stopping it. Nor is there any stopping the creeped-out shiver that runs down my spine at the thought of Seth Jennings—a guy I haven't seen or spoken to since high school—talking to my dad about me. Not that I blame Dad—I can promise he didn't think twice about it. Especially if he was talking about me joining his team at the fire department as an EMT. I know how excited and proud he's been. If the text I get at the start of every shift telling me so wasn't enough of a giveaway, the way Mama gushes about how he "talks about it nonstop" is.

None of that explains why the town plumber was asking though.

"He mentioned it at one of the council meetings."

Council meetings? As in the town council? I take a moment to rack my brain. I know that both my parents mentioned that Ellen Potter, the longtime at-large member passed away a couple of years ago, but they didn't tell me that Seth replaced her. And really, Seth?

"I didn't realize you were on the town council now," I verbally tap dance, trying to keep my face in check. Which is becoming harder and harder the longer this conversation goes on.

"I am." He beams, prouder than a peacock. *Oh boy...* "Anyway, I realized I don't have your number, so I dropped by the station a couple of times and you've either been out on a call or not on shift..."

I shift my weight awkwardly from foot to foot, pulse kicking up a notch and my skin starting to prickle as my nerves take over. I already know where this is heading. He has the same sheepish look on his face from senior year, hand anxiously rubbing the back of his neck, as he talks in circles. At least this time he's able to make eye contact with me.

"I saw you briefly at Reel Madness, and was gonna come say hi, but then you disappeared..."

"Well, we did have a medical emergency that we had to tend to," I say, trying to shift the conversation. "And it was a busy day all around."

"Absolutely." He nods, rubbing his neck again. "But, now that I've got you, I was wondering..."

Please, Seth, no...

Not at my grandmother's birthday party. Actually, not at all. I didn't say yes to you then, and my answer isn't going to be different now. Past that, there is no way that the news of Ewan and me hasn't reached him. Especially if he's been talking to my father. Pretty sure Daddy's not been shy with that factoid either.

Sometimes I think Aunt Hattie rubbed off on him more than he realized.

"...grab dinner with me?"

Well, sir...I'll give you this, you're shooting your shot. Good for you. Here's hoping you accept rejection gracefully.

I muster up my best nurse smile, the one I use when I know that I am going to have to use all my defense. "Thank you, Seth, but I'm with Ewan. He's actually why I came back to Hickory Hills."

There, nice and easy. Plus, it's the truth. Hard to argue with that.

Seth's face morphs into something unreadable. In a split second he went from average, everyday affable, rural, small-town, blue-collar guy to something harder. Grittier. Like someone ripped off a piece of him and left the rough edge.

"Even though he's leaving?"

Leaving? Excuse you?

"Leaving?" I laugh nervously "Ewan's not leaving."

Seth nods, his face still hard as stone. "Yeah, he is. Selling the store and going…somewhere. Which pisses me off since he bought it off my grandfather and gave it that obnoxious name, to now just turn around and do this."

My jaw goes slack, my brain trying to catch up with what Seth is saying. I don't bother correcting him—letting him in on the fact The Booby Trap was my idea and that obnoxious name, as he put it, was a nod to a joke I made. That's a different conversation. Right now I'm too focused on why he would think Ewan was selling the store.

That's the last thing Ewan would do. His sole proprietorship of The Booby Trap is one of the things he's most proud of. Something he's fought with Gus over for years. There's no way he would simply up and sell.

"Seth, I think you're mistaken."

"No. I overheard him talking to Gus yesterday about selling the store. I was at Pour Decisions fixing a toilet and they were holding a secret little meeting over there so no one would know about it."

And yet here you are talkin' about it… Fucking small towns…

"He was adamant too. Told Gus to draw up the paperwork."

The earth shifts underneath me. Suddenly, I feel even more unsteady than when I tried to steamroll Seth a moment ago. Although, right now I'm starting to wish I had knocked him on his ass and kept moving.

This doesn't make sense. He had to have misheard them. Of all the things on this earth that the oldest and youngest Hayes brothers were not discussing secretly in a bar on a Friday morning, it was *that*.

Unless…

We'll make it work.

Those four words echo in my brain, ricocheting off every corner like a wild cue ball on the billiards table. With each new bounce they get louder, more piercing, until they are so sharp that everything else ceases to exist. I'm no longer standing under this tent surrounded by more than a hundred people on a bright, sunshiny, spring afternoon. Instead, I'm completely surrounded by a weird multicolored palette of four words that suddenly make even less sense than before.

He can't do this.

I can't let him do this.

25

MAISEY

"No…"

"No?" Seth questions.

I look at him, realizing I said it out loud. Shit.

My chest tightens, my lungs constricting, and I know that no matter how many deep breaths I try to remind myself to take, it's not going to help. All the breathing techniques in the world aren't going to make a damn bit of difference. Not now that I'm doing that math.

We'll make it work.

No. No…no, no, no…

"Maisey?" Seth steps forward, placing his hand on my arm again.

The touch shocks me back into the moment and I flinch, pulling away instantly. I don't need his comfort—which is anything but comforting in this moment. I need air. Space. Room to think.

I don't say anything. Simply turn on my heel and go, weaving my way through the crowd that formed around us. I don't know where I'm heading, but it's somewhere that doesn't involve Seth Jennings.

Back to Grandma—that's where I need to go. I need to sit back down and wait for Ewan to come find us with those drinks. Let myself take a moment to wrap my head around this.

Ewan is going to give up his dream so that I can have mine.

No, not give up. Destroy. He's about to take everything he's worked for and built and light it on fire. All so that we can be together and I can move to a country that I randomly fell in love with.

So that we can hike the volcanoes and waterfalls. Visit the Blue Lagoon. Fall asleep under the northern lights in a glass igloo. And all the other things that have held a special place inside me for so long.

Only now, the thought of all that leaves me feeling hollow.

SLIPPING around the outside of the tent, I rush back toward the table where I left my grandmother. Anxiety builds inside with each step, still not finding Ewan along the way. Where the hell did he disappear to?

Oh...

I stop dead in my tracks, my grandmother's laugh cutting me off. She's leaning forward, clutching her chest, her smile as big as I've ever seen it, with Ewan on one side and Hux on the other, the two of them cutting it up, keeping her laughing.

In any other moment, this scene would be perfect. I'd pull out my phone to secretly snap a photo and send it to everyone we know. Possibly consider printing it and framing it. I'd for sure text Dolly to get her ass over here so we could stand here, watching our men and swooning over how absolutely adorable they are—and then giggle about all the dirty things we were going to do to them later.

Instead, all I can think to do is cry.

Because this moment really is this perfect. Our future could continue to be this perfect.

And I'm the one who is about to ruin it.

I can't let him do this.

I also can't walk over there right now and demand an answer. This isn't the time or place, for a number of reasons. Still, I have to figure out a way to stop this.

"Maisey."

The deep, jovial southern drawl treats my name like it's the chalice that Indiana Jones went looking for. It sends a rush of warmth through me, feeling like a hug, making me realize just how much I need one of those right now. Turning toward the voice, I exhale harshly, letting my tears escape.

"Oh, darlin'…" Auggie coos, wrapping me in a massive dad hug like only he can. I let myself fall into him, knowing that this is about as safe a place as any to break down. The only safer place would be in Ewan's arms. "What's going on?"

"Is he really doing this?" I look up at Auggie, hoping to find some answers. His familiar features are older now, but somehow still exactly the same as my childhood. Ewan favors Miss Belle with his lighter hair and blue eyes, instead of Auggie's slightly darker features, but there's still no denying they're father and son. "Please tell me no."

Furrowing his brow, Auggie takes a half step back, careful not to fully let me go. Just as I did him, he silently searches me for answers, although I don't have any more than he does.

"If you're askin' if he spiked your grandmother's sweet tea, I think we can honestly believe that of all my children, Ewan would not be the culprit there." Looking over at the group of them at the table still laughing, he smiles, then turns back to me. "Huxley, however, could go either way."

I sputter out a laugh, wiping away my tears. Leave it to Auggie to be able to cheer me up in my moment of panic.

"There we go." He wipes away one last tear, nodding succinctly. "I'm not great with tears. Luckily, Willa was never a crier. Her tongue can be sharper than a razor blade, but I didn't have to deal with tears."

"I'm a crier," I admit. "Happy, sad, stressed…all tears."

"So, which ones are these? Happy, sad, stressed?"

Good question...

"Confusion. Panic. Guilt."

"That's quite the trio. Especially for a birthday party."

No kidding.

"Auggie, I'm going to ask you something, and I need for you to please be honest with me. No matter what you might have promised Ewan or whatever business paperwork is signed, or whatever. Please."

Auggie turns serious, once again looking over at his sons, then back at me. "I promise."

"Is Ewan really selling The Booby Trap?"

Shock flashes in Auggie's eyes, and he blinks quickly, maintaining his composure. But I see it.

"I must admit, this is the first I'm hearing of it. Are you sure?"

I shake my head. "No, but…I…" I heave out a sigh, trying to put my jumbled mess of emotions into coherent thoughts. "But I also don't want to go ask him. Which I know sounds counterintuitive, but if he really is doing it, then I think I know why, and it's for a reason I can't ask of him, but he's not going to listen and…"

Auggie hold up his hands, signaling me to stop. He's got me. Twisting, he looks over his shoulder, his expression turning even more serious. A serious that I didn't realize that Auggie could have.

"August!"

Oh, shit…

Gus's head whips up, as Auggie reaches out, grabbing his arm and yanking him over to us. The oldest brother's eyes are wide, clearly familiar with this face.

"There something you want to tell me?" Auggie asks.

Looking between his father and me, Gus swallows hard, the muscles in his neck contracting as if in slow motion. I watch the trepidation flit across his features, as he tries to figure out the right answer to the question.

"Is *want* the verb we're going with?" Gus asks, careful to hold back his sass.

"Out with it."

"I take it he didn't talk to you then," Gus says, looking directly at me.

My heart plummets, stomach lurching with that response. Because no, he didn't. I didn't even realize that he'd talked to Gus. I'd gone to my interview on Friday and assumed Ewan had gone to the store like every other day. Things had been weird enough after how our dinner had gone Thursday night. When he'd come home late that night to silently slip into bed, I'd been happy that he seemed back to his normal self.

I should have asked more questions. I should have pushed more. Should have used the tornado tactic.

Shaking my head, I fight back more tears. Ones for an emotion I can't name. All I know is that it's all I can think to do. Because I can't ask him to do this.

"I told him to talk to you first," Gus continues. "But he was adamant that this was the way he wanted to handle it."

"So, he's really selling it." My voice cracks, but I manage to keep my emotions in check.

"What? No. Well, not outright. It's a transfer of ownership, technically. Making The Booby Trap officially a part of Hayes Industries, rather than his sole proprietorship."

My insides loosen, unraveling enough for me to be able to breathe again, while still holding tight. That's better news than I thought. But it's still not the answer.

Click…

Like a puzzle piece snapping into place, in an instant, I know what *is* the answer. The one I've been searching for so hard these last few days. The decision that Ewan has been so insistent that only I can make.

Well, sir, I'm making it.

"Gus, I need you to do something for me."

"Okay…"

"And I need you to keep it a secret."

"For fuck's sake," Gus mutters, throwing his hands up. "Are you two incapable of talking?"

"Gus…" Auggie warns.

"Please," I beg.

I turn to look over at Ewan, who is still at the table with my grandmother, but facing my dad, the two of them deep in conversation about who knows what. My heart squeezes, ready to burst as I watch them, my two favorite men, sitting back having a drink. The sight solidifies my answers, making what was already clear even more so. Leaving no room for wondering. Just like grandma said.

"It's my turn to make the move. But I'm gonna need your help to pull it off."

Gus is quiet for a second, his permanently stoic expression cracking ever so slightly.

"Okay. But you gotta move quick. He wants to sign the papers Monday before Munch."

Munch? Damn, that is quick. But I think I can do it. Just depends on…

"You know, if we're talking grand gestures, we do happen

to have a self-proclaimed 'expert' with a whole library full of them in the family," Auggie tosses out, finger quotes and all.

Gus and I look at each other, our devious grins matching each other, mind clearly going to the exact same place.

This just became a family affair.

26

EWAN

THE SMALL, decorative clock that sits on Gus's desk ticks, audibly counting out each passing second and getting louder with each one. Fuck, that's annoying.

And taunting. Leaving me feeling like Captain Hook, listening to the tick-tock, tick-tock fill the silence, driving me straight to the point of being willing to launch myself into the crocodile's mouth. If Gus doesn't get here soon, that is going to sound like a better option.

I lean back in the leather guest chair across from his stupidly pretentious dark wood desk, stacked neatly with piles of folders and papers, his computer monitors off to one side, the whole thing looking like a stock photo used for a website somewhere. Not someone's actual desk where work is done. I can pretend as much as I want that it's his office that is making me this anxious or his taking his sweet time even though he insisted I be here at eleven sharp, but that would be a lie.

Because I wasn't sitting in this office last night when I couldn't sleep. Or this morning in the shower when my chest was so tight that I had to lean against the wall to hold myself up and catch my breath.

Still, it's the right move. One I've been resisting for years. Said I'd never do. I also said I would never drink flavored coffee creamer or have sex in my place of business during work hours, so my word in that department means nothing. Either that or pigs are flying somewhere out there. Either way, we're here now.

Flying pork or not, this is about Maisey. About making her happy and showing her that I support her following her dream no matter what that is or where it takes us. About doing what I should have done the first time she told me she had a job offer.

The universe not only gave me a second chance with her, but another go at making this right. At making the right choice here. So that's what I'm going to do. No matter how tough it is.

"Sorry," Gus says, rushing into his office. "The morning took a weird turn, and things took longer in legal than I thought."

He crashes down into his chair, the papers on top of the neatly stacked piles waving a little from the breeze he caused. The normally stoic look on his face is firmly in place, mixed in with some extra concern. Like he's still not sure about all this.

Oh, how the tables have turned...

"There a problem?"

He shakes his head, flipping open a folder. "No, not a *problem.* Just a..."

A what?!

I sit up, leaning in, waiting for him to finish that sentence. To give me some kind of clue as to what the fuck is going on.

"...a situation."

"A situation?"

What, had he been hiding out in the hallway, looking up synonyms for the word "problem" in the thesaurus, trying to church it up? Or was that the term legal gave him to use so that I didn't freak out? Maybe someone down in Public Relations got ahold of this and is trying to put a spin on things. Whatever it is, that has corporate speak all over it.

"Nothing to worry about. It's not bad," he tries to explain. Only I can tell he isn't so sure. That something isn't right. "I have all the paperwork to bring The Booby Trap under the umbrella of Hayes Industries and make it part of the network of companies. But…"

For fuck's sake. I've wanted to lunge across a table to strangle my oldest brother more times than I can count over our lifetimes, over who knows how many different things, big and small, but this might take that cake. It's like he's doing this on purpose. Dragging this out, just to be a jackass.

"But what, Gus," I snap, the gnawing inside taking over. I want to threaten that if he doesn't just say it, I'm going to take that *but* and shove it up *his*…however that would be juvenile and not get us anywhere.

"There's someone else interested."

Errrr…what?!

There's someone else interested. Interested in what? That statement doesn't even make sense.

"In the store?" I clarify, because I'm still not sure I follow.

Gus nods, as stoic and solemn as always.

"How does anyone else even know about this? I asked you to keep it to yourself. You even said you'd ask Margeaux to be the one to do the paperwork so that it was kept in the family. How the fuck does it get out to someone who would be interested in outright buying it between Friday and now?"

What the actual fuck. This isn't happening. How…

"This is Hickory Hills; things have a way. You know," Gus

starts, his voice fading, my own train of thought plowing straight through his attempted explanation.

I sit back, running through our conversation at Pour Decisions. It was just the three of us. Until Jace barged in. Then Hux. But they weren't even there for the conversation about the store. Jace turned everything on its head with his demands about Presley Callahan.

The bar wasn't even open. That was why I was even willing to have the conversation there. It was safe. The last thing I wanted was for this to get out, get around town, the same way my interest in the store had made its way around when I made an offer to old man Jennings ten years ago.

Old man Jennings.

"Seth Jennings," I mutter, not bothering to hide my disdain.

He was there. He was fixing a toilet and must have somehow overheard us talking. That jackass never liked that I bought the store from his grandfather and changed the name—a fact he's never bothered to hide. On top of that, he's always had a thing for Maisey. How that would play into this, who the fuck knows. But I got ten bucks that says it's Seth Jennings who thinks he can try and take the store from me.

And he can fucking think again. He's going to have to pry it out of my cold, dead, and lifeless hands. In fact, even then, he's not going to get it, because I'm going to make sure The Booby Trap is so solidly tied to Hayes in every way possible that he couldn't dream of making an offer. Hell, I'll burn it down and donate the land to the town first.

"What about him?"

"He can't fucking have it."

Gus throws his hands up. "I don't know when everyone in this family decided they could just say someone's name and then a very definitive statement and expect everyone else to follow along, but between you and Jace… Christ on a bike. Explanation is necessary, you know."

I glare at him. He's not wrong, but that doesn't mean I want to concede his point. I'm too angry. My anxiety morphed into indignation pretty quick, but I don't care. It's nice to be feeling something else right now.

"It's him, isn't it? He's the one making the offer. He overheard us while fixing the toilet at Pour Decisions. He's always hated that I changed the name, and now he thinks that since he's on the town council he's got some power and can try and get it back," I grumble. "And after what he did to Hux last year, this is just his next power move."

Now that I think it through, it all tracks. He tried to veto Hux's request to revamp the town's playground last summer as a gift to Dolly, stating it wasn't a good use of town funds. Coincidentally, it took Dolly threatening his pastry habit to get him to change his vote.

Somehow I don't think that would work here. Her cinnamon rolls are good. They aren't *that* good.

"Next he'll put a move on Maisey," I tack on under my breath, then push to my feet. I need to move, get some of this energy out of me.

"What?"

"He had a thing for Maisey in high school."

"Oh. Right, well…" Gus pushes to his feet, rounding his desk and walking over to me. He stands directly in front of me, stopping my ability to pace. "Will you just come to the conference room so that you can talk to them?"

"I don't have anything to say to the plumber."

Gus lets out an exasperated sigh, clearly done with me and my shit. To be fair, I would be too. There is already a part of me that is thinking that this is a sign that I need to reconsider. That this isn't actually the way to go.

Reykjavík…

Maisey's sweet voice flows through my head, the lightness in her tone as she says the name of the city she's always wanted to go to. The pain in her eyes the last few days as she's agonized over her choices, so afraid of making the wrong one. My heart cracks, splintering into tiny pieces that are barely holding on, knowing that I have a way to take that pain away.

A way to choose her over this town. To tell her that she means more than our hometown. More than anything else in this world.

"Ewan, please. I promised them you'd at least hear them out," Gus pleads. "If you hate what they have to say, fine. We come back in here, we sign the original paperwork, and we go have Munch. Deal?"

I nod. That I can do.

"Good."

Turning to go, I follow Gus out of his office, making a left to walk down the long executive hallway. I pause, letting him get a few steps ahead, not sure why we're going this way. There's only one conference room in this direction—the executive conference room—which is generally reserved for internal, senior staff level meetings, and on Mondays, is always reserved for Munch. It's incredibly rare that a meeting with a non-Hayes employee would be held in that room—Monday or not. The last non-employee I remember even being allowed in there at all is when Nash crashed Munch two years ago to profess his love for Willa.

"We taking the long way?" I ask, still keeping enough distance between us for Gus to do an about-face if he realizes he's on autopilot and has gone the wrong direction.

"Nope, I've got everything set up in here."

He stops just outside the executive conference room, and now I'm really stumped.

"Everything else booked?"

"Ewan, you're killing me."

What'd I do?

He opens one of the double doors, holding it open and gesturing for me to enter. I lift a shoulder, trying to tell him I don't understand his confusion, when I'm the one who has no idca what is going on here. None of this is making any sense.

Walking into the room, I stop. Right along with my heart.

It all makes even less sense now.

Sitting at the head of the table, the spot usually reserved for Auggie—or maybe Gus if he's trying to get all bossy—is the very last person I expected to see. Jesus himself would be less of a surprise.

"Ewan, may I introduce you to your prospective buyer," Gus whispers from behind me. "In fact, I think you might know each other."

I nod, unable to breathe. Especially when that smile hits me.

"Maisey."

27

EWAN

THE DOOR CLICKS BEHIND ME, but I barely hear it. All of the blood rushes through my veins, punctuated by the thrum of my pulse filling my ears, erasing my brain of everything. Except one thing.

Maisey.

Maisey is here. And she wants to buy The Booby Trap?

"You're not Seth Jennings…"

Maisey's brow furrows, a giggle escaping her pretty pink lips. "Not the reaction I was expecting. Although, I'm going to choose to accept it as a compliment."

Pushing out of her chair, she walks over to me, so light and smooth she might as well be floating on air. The concrete blocks my feet have turned into won't move for all the world, keeping me solidly in this spot.

Maisey…

I continue to blink rapidly, convinced that my eyes and brain are deceiving me. That I have entered the upside down or the inside out or opposite land…or something. Some place where everything isn't as it seems.

"Hi."

She presses her lips to mine, gently, softly. Almost as soft as her greeting. My heart wants to burst, my hands gingerly resting on her hips, afraid that if I make any kind of move that I'm going to end up like Lennie in *Of Mice and Men*, my strength taking over when I don't mean it to.

"Hi."

I try to mirror her softness, but it comes out gruff and suspicious. Like I don't trust why she's here. There's no denying that I'm curious. That my mind is running wild. But no part of me hates it.

"Would you like to hear my proposition?"

Oh, would I ever...

"You're propositioning me?" I quip, not bothering to hide my meaning. Winking at her, I smirk, moving my hands to the small of her back. If this is going to be that kind of conversation, then I more than trust myself to touch her.

"Business proposal!" she corrects, smacking my chest. Giggling, she tries to wiggle out of my arms, but I hold tight for a second before letting her go. "It's a business proposal."

I laugh. "Yes, I would love to hear your business proposal."

"Well then, right this way, Mr. Hayes."

She gestures for me to come sit down by where she was seated before, in the chair to the right, the one Gus usually sits in during Munch. It feels weird to be taking his spot, even though he's not here, but I sit, watching as she returns to the head of the table, looking absolutely adorable in her sundress.

"As I believe the elder Mr. Hayes informed you, I have expressed interest in procuring The Booby Trap. I—"

"Maisey—" I start to cut her off.

"No, Ewan. Please, let me finish."

Her beautiful blue eyes plead with me, making my heart squeeze. They are so full of love and tenderness that I know I need to hear her out. Holding up my hands in surrender, I nod, signaling her to continue.

"Thank you." She tips her head to me. "As I said, I have an interest in procuring The Booby Trap. Since its inception, it has always been locally owned and operated. The current owner has single-handedly grown the business exceptionally, and I feel that should continue. This operation is not one that should be corporate owned, but should continue to be run by someone who loves it."

"And you think that someone is you?"

"Sorta. Mostly, I know a guy."

I nod. Okay, I'll play along.

"You know a guy…"

"I do. Hunting, fishing, camping…he loves it all."

"And what if I were to say that the deal is already done with Hayes?" I lift an eyebrow, trying to feel her out. Maisey doesn't react, her poker face perfectly intact. "That there isn't an offer you could make me."

"I'd tell you the God's honest truth. My offer is better than anything Hayes Industries could muster, I promise."

I sit back, her words hitting me like a hurricane wind. Better than anything Hayes could offer? Those are some big words. I have no idea what Gus told her, but my family's legacy is a Fortune 500 company. We have a lot to muster up if we really wanted to. So Maisey really must think she has something. Or she's bluffing.

Knowing Maisey, it's the latter.

"And what's that?" I ask, ready to see what she has.

"Ketchup."

My heart stops. *Ketchup.*

There's so much confidence in her voice. But even more love in her eyes and wild in her smile.

I all but come undone.

Reaching down, she pulls out three ketchup packets from

underneath the table, lining them up and laying them out in front of me.

"One for our past, one for our present, and one for our future."

Not just ketchup. Ketchup pacts.

My heart gets caught in my throat, tears starting to burn my eyes as I continue to stare at them. Maisey is offering up ketchup pacts for The Booby Trap.

Holy shit.

"Ewan…" she whispers. Her voice is so strong, even as quiet as it is, weaving its way into my soul. I can't take my eyes off the damn condiment in front of me out of fear of the dam breaking, but I nod, almost imperceptibly so she knows I hear her. "Please don't sign the store over to your brother. I know it's not what you want. It's not what I want either."

I whip my head to look at her. Tears be damned. She smiles back at me, the most beautiful sight I've ever seen.

"What?"

"I called InterCon MediTrust this morning and turned down Reykjavík. So, fingers crossed I actually get the job at Tifton Regional or I'm gonna be working for my father and Landon for a little while longer."

"What, no," I exclaim. "That's your dream—"

"It's not." She shakes her head. "It was, don't get me wrong. But dreams change. What I want is to stay here, with you."

"Maisey, take the job; we can make it work."

Reaching across the table, she takes my hand. "Are you listening? I don't want to *make it work*. I want the sex tent. And a matching pair of children. And our blue heeler. Family camping trips. I want to try and weird Willa out with our sex noises!"

Errrr…what?!

"Where did that last one come from?"

"Dolly told me about how you knew about Willa and Nash before anyone because you could hear them through the walls," she answers sheepishly.

Oh, yeah, that.

"Gotcha. Okay, we can add that to the list..." I make a mental note to *try and out sex my little sister*. Although I'm not exactly sure how one does that.

"That can't be done from an island nation in the middle of the north Atlantic."

No. No, it can't.

"You are what I want, Ewan. And *our* future is here. We can go visit Iceland. Take a vacation sometime, maybe to celebrate you getting the partnership with Auburn up and running. Because the only person I want to be hanging out with in the Blue Lagoon is you. And it's you that I want to be curled up with in a glass igloo watching the northern lights. But more than that, I want to wake up next to you every morning, living our life. On whatever adventure it takes us on."

Her soft sigh and the tip of her smile lets me in on her thoughts—her mind going to more than just *curling up* under those northern lights—and my pulse skips a beat. I shift in my chair, trying to accommodate for all the blood now rushing to my dick as I sit here and think about that new fantasy.

"So, what do you say? Do you accept my proposition?"

She must be out of her mind if she thinks I could ever say no to her. Then again, I did once. Time to right that wrong once and for all.

Pushing up from my seat, I kneel down in front of Maisey, taking her hands in mine. I drink her in, letting this moment settle around us.

"You are my life, Maisey, with or without this town. So if

here is where you choose, then here is where we will stay. I love you."

"I love you."

I reach up, cupping her face in my hands, and kiss her hard. The taste of forever is on her lips and I want to capture every drop. Maisey whimpers, leaning into me, trying to deepen the kiss, and I know I have to be careful. I am still at work after all.

Although there is a very large part of me that wants to lock those doors and have my way with her on this conference table. Ten bucks says I would not be the first Hayes man to do so with his woman either.

A knock on the door interrupts us, and we break apart quickly, like two teenagers getting caught in the act. Miss Harriett pokes her head in, ready to set up for Munch, letting me know that we should vacate the room. For now.

"So, now that I've invested in the business," Maisey says, continuing her bit, "does this mean I get to attend Munch?"

"I got a better idea," I tell her, pulling her into the hallway and pressing her up against the wall. "How about I take you home and make *you* my lunch?"

Maisey pretends to think for a moment, pursing her lips to the side. "I feel like that is an acceptable counteroffer."

"Then you have yourself a deal."

MAISEY

Christmas Eve

"So we have to be where? And when?"

The tired in Ewan's voice is so deep that a part of me thinks it might never leave, despite the fact that he hasn't moved from that couch since he flopped down on it immediately after emerging from the bedroom this morning. His plan to spend the day "couch rotting"—as he put it—isn't a bad one. Necessary even. The hours he's been putting in these last few months have been crazy.

But this last week before Christmas? Forget crazy. It's been unreal. At one point this week, I actually thought he might just use the camping display and spend the night. Retail during the holiday season is no joke—especially when your own family's rifle division comes out with a new product right in time for the gift-giving season.

He peers over the back of the couch at me like I'm a walking, talking calendar, ready to spout off the answer. Which, of course, I am.

"We have to be over at my parents' house at six for dinner and gifts with them and Grandma tonight. But then tomorrow we don't have to be over at Magnolia Manor until noon."

"So we have the morning to celebrate, just us?"

I round the couch and park myself next to him, lifting his legs and slipping under them so I can scoot in closer. He's not the only one who has been working long hours, making our downtime limited. Although as much as I want to couch rot with him, these gifts aren't going to finish wrapping themselves.

"We do. Although my shift starts at four tomorrow, so I do have to duck out of the Hayes family celebration early."

Ewan shifts, pushing himself up. His muscles flex under his old T-shirt, stealing my attention as he moves, pushing the priority of wrapping those presents even further down the list. That's what gift bags are for, after all, right?

Cupping my face, he runs a thumb over my cheek, the callous on the side of his knuckle rough against my skin, sending a shiver through me. One that is dirty, delicious, and comforting all at the same time. Because in the hands of this man, I know I am loved and safe.

"Then maybe we need to start our celebration now."

A shiver zings down my spine, anticipation starting to fill my veins. Yeah, gift bags it is.

"Just what did you have in mind?" I say, running my hand up and down his thigh.

Ewan's eyes light up like the tree in the town square, his smile following just as quickly. Which means he's got a plan.

Swinging his legs off the couch, Ewan pushes up and walks over to the fireplace, grabbing my stocking and slipping it off the hook. Silently, he walks back to the couch, just the one stocking in hand, still beaming like he sunk the winning putt at the Masters.

"Here."

He holds out the cross-stitched Christmas decoration with my name proudly displayed over a teddy bear wearing a Santa hat. I take it from him, confusion taking over. What is he doing?

"Santa isn't filling these until tonight," I say, trying to keep my voice playful.

Peering around him, I look at his stocking, a semi-matching design, his with a snowman complete with corncob pipe and top hat, still limply hanging from the mantel. I have a bunch of goodies to secretly slip in there later tonight—or first thing in the morning—when he's not looking. Including the chocolate orange I know he's looking forward to.

"He dropped something off early."

He remains standing in front of me, watching me intently. My pulse kicks up a notch, the anticipation from earlier morphing into a weird set of nerves to match my confusion.

"This isn't a trick, Maisey. Promise." Ewan laughs, kneeling down. Placing a hand on either side of me, he looks me squarely in the eye, leveling me with that Hayes smirk. "Open your stocking, baby."

I slip my hand inside and pull out an envelope. An envelope? Really?

Then it hits me.

Ewan is kneeling in front of me. It's Christmas.

OMFG...

Internally I squeal, trying to keep as much outward composure as I can. I don't want to give away that I've figured this out. That inside this envelope is the biggest question I've ever been asked. The one I've been waiting for. Whose answer is already on the tip of my tongue.

Slowly, I flip the envelope over, running my finger under

the flap and opening it. I want to take my time. Want to remember this. Commit it all to memory—every single second of it—so that when I get to tell the story over and over again, I get it all right.

Inside is a piece of paper. A regular, eight by eleven piece of printer paper. Okay—that's fine. Doesn't have to be fancy. In fact, I don't want it to be. Ewan isn't fancy. Nothing about our life together is. This part shouldn't be either.

I unfold the paper, holding my breath, ready to read the words. The four big words. Even more ready to shout my answer. My even bigger answer.

Only—those four words aren't what is staring back at me.

It's a reservation. For the Aurora Igloos in Hella, Iceland.

Ohhh...

My adrenaline rush comes to a crashing halt, my excitement instantly deflating. I feel numb for a split second, torn inside on how to react. On one hand, this is a place that I've talked about visiting for years. An experience that I've dreamed about. That Ewan paid attention to—listened to— and then acted on. He's literally gifting me the bucket-list item I walked away from earlier this year when I chose him.

A choice I haven't regretted for a single second.

Which is why I'm left feeling like this. Because it's not what I thought was coming. And I know I should be excited. I am excited. We're going to Iceland and we're going to sleep under the northern lights.

"I did a bunch of research," Ewan says, filling the silence. "Turns out Iceland doesn't have the glass igloos quite like Finland and Norway, but they do have transparent domes, and then what one place called glass tiny lodges. I went with the transparent dome over the tiny lodge because it's a little more remote for viewing the lights, but also there is a day tour of caves that I figured would be fun."

I smile, tears filling my eyes as I scan over the printed confirmation in my hand. Of course Ewan did a bunch of research on the best option before booking. He's an outdoor guide himself, so he wouldn't settle for anything but the best experience for us.

"There's just one problem."

What?!

I whip my head up, the tears in my eyes wobbling slightly but staying put. Problem? How could there possibly be a problem? Unless he thinks that I'm unhappy. Oh, shit. No. I can't have him thinking that.

Because this gift is perfect.

"What problem?" I ask, choking back my emotion. "Ewan, this is amazing. There are zero problems here."

"Well, you see, the timing is just a little off."

What is he talking about?

I look back down at the paper, scanning to find the dates. March. He booked the trip for mid-March. Okay, so what? Gives me enough time to request PTO at the hospital, so that's not an issue. And spring hunting season usually doesn't start until late March, I think. Unless it starts earlier next year…

"Well, all the research says that the best time to see the lights is around the equinoxes. Some argue January/February because the nights are longer, but there is more geomagnetic activity around the equinox, making them more active and vibrant."

I nod along, trying to follow where he's going with all this environmental science speak. There is a point, surely.

"But, March is only three months away, which I have learned, thanks to all these new women in my family, is not enough time to plan a wedding, upending my thought process of spending our honeymoon visiting your dream country. So, I guess I have to settle for taking my fiancée to Iceland, instead of my wife."

Fiancée...? Did he just say fiancée?

"Meaning I'm going to have to find some brand-new dream location to sweep you off your feet with when we're husband and wife."

Husband and wife...

I can't breathe. My lungs constrict, tears returning with a vengeance as Ewan leans forward, digging in between the couch cushions and pulling out a little velvet box.

He wobbles a bit as he straightens out and I grab ahold of him, ready to throw my arms around him and kiss the fuck out of him. And then fuck him.

But that would be getting ahead of myself.

"Maisey, there is a part of me that feels like this bit is just a technicality. Because I've been calling you my wife in my head for longer than you know. That's how sure I am that you are my everything, baby. My life, my future. All of it. But I do know that I have to actually ask the question."

Ewan takes my hands, interlacing our fingers and pressing a kiss to them. A soft sob tumbles over my lips, happiness overtaking me.

"I can't wait to build our life together. Whether it ends up looking exactly like your plan with our matching pair, or something else entirely, as long as we're together, I know it's going to be perfect. All that said, Maisey Phillips, will you marry me?"

YES!

I shout my answer—or at least I intend to—nothing but a squeak coming out. The tears running down my cheeks make it hard to concentrate, so I swipe at them, swallowing hard, trying to regain my composure. But it's no use. I'm a mess.

A great big, happy mess.

So I nod. Furiously. Not wanting to waste a single second, or leave Ewan thinking that this is anything but an overjoyed reaction.

Popping the box open, Ewan holds it up, showing off the contents. And the waterworks start all over again.

Inside, staring back at me, is a little white ketchup packet, except instead of the normal label, this one has been custom printed. Still in the traditional red and black—because of course—but in place of nutritional information or even a company are two words that steal my heart completely.

SAY YES

"Of course…" I choke out. "Fuck, yes. Whatever you need to hear. Ewan Hayes, I will marry the fuck out of you."

"Glad to hear it."

Reaching into his pocket, Ewan pulls out the simple platinum band embedded with peridots and rubies—our birthstones—slipping it on my finger.

"I know it's not the traditional solitaire, but I also remember you saying that you were worried about such a thing snagging gloves and getting caught on things while working, so I went with this. We'll have to pick out something to go with it for the wedding band, but I figured we could do that together."

I launch myself at him, throwing my arms around Ewan's neck and burying my face against him. He chuckles as he catches me, pressing a kiss to the top of my head. I don't bother to hide my tears, letting them flow out of me right along with all of the joy that I can't contain.

"I need you to stop being so perfect, please," I mutter into his chest.

"Only when you do."

Tightening his embrace, Ewan sighs and I melt into him even more. My fiancé. My future.

I lift my head, just enough to look at him, the love in his eyes shining back at me.

"What if we did get married in March?"

"Excuse you?"

"Or sooner." I shrug. "You, me, Judge Robinson. That's all that's really required. Then we can have a wedding later. But we could technically elope, get married, and then go on a honeymoon to Iceland. Maybe even a secret one that no one knows about."

"Our mamas would lose their minds," Ewan says. But I can see the wheels turning in his head.

"They expect this kind of thing from me at this point. So, whaddya say?"

Ewan pushes to his feet, taking me with him, and kisses me hard. I whimper, giving in to him, his taste and power moving through me like a drug in my veins, making me want more. Good thing I get to keep him for forever.

"I think that a phone call to Judge Robinson is in order the day after Christmas."

Fuck, yes...

"But first,"—he thrusts up into me, his groin making contact with my core, sending me reeling—"I've got other ideas for you."

"Let's get forever started now then."

Maisey reveals on their camping trip that she hopes for a "matching pair". But, does she get her wish? Download the bonus scene and find out!

Presley Callahan turned Jace's world upside down once. It's been seventeen years since high school, but she's about to do it all over again. This time, she's not alone. Grab Already Callin' You Mine now!

ACKNOWLEDGMENTS

Shout out to Captain FloridaMan (and your nurse!) for all the stories, inspiration, and mostly, the laughter.

Kate - thank you for not firing me as a friend or a client.

Amy - for being my right hand, my Girl Friday, and the better half of my brain.

KKSB - S is for sisters…and salty bitches. And you four are the best of the best.

Linda - for the tough love, the moral support, and *alllllllll* the pep talks

As always, Drew, for your unending, unwavering, unequivocal support in *everything*. Thank you for loving my particular brand of crazy. *Ik hou van jou*

Good Directions
More Than My Hometown
Already Callin' You Mine

Adlers of Hickory Hills

Son of a Peach

All Snowed Gin

<u>World of True North</u>

Cakewalk

<u>Stand Alone Novellas</u>

A Novel Seduction

Hot Mess Christmas Express

ABOUT THE AUTHOR

USA TODAY Best Selling Author Claire Hastings is a walking, talking awkward moment. She loves Diet Coke, gummi bears, the beach, and books (obvs). When not reading she can usually be found hanging with friends at a soccer match or grabbing food (although she probably still has a book in her purse). She and her husband live in Atlanta.

She can be found here:

Instagram | Facebook | GoodReads | BookBub

www.ingramcontent.com/pod-product-compliance
Lightning Source LLC
Chambersburg PA
CBHW020131310726
48970CB00006B/1819